The Color of Ice

Gordon Mathieson

SinoAmerican Books
www.sinoamericanbooks.com

Other books by Gordon Mathieson:

Quissett
The Hyannis House
The Greater Boston Challenge

[For more information about the author, visit
www.gordonmathieson.com]

ISBN: 978-0-9769259-6-5
Library of Congress Control Number: 2009939606

Published by SinoAmerican Books [www.sinoamericanbooks.com]
South Glastonbury, CT

Printed in the United States of America.

Cover by Kathy Crowley.

Acknowledgements: I would like to thank editor and publisher, James
Counsilman, PhD, who, with his background in Asian culture and biological sciences, was a great match and mentor for this project. I would also
like to thank those scientists from the Woods Hole Oceanographic Institute who wondered why I asked so many questions of them but who
always accommodated me. Chuck Woringer's meticulous review and
encouragement came at just the right time. And, lastly, I want to pay
tribute to Miriam (Mim) McLeod, who inspired me to undertake this
project. I miss our brainstorming sessions during the embryonic stage of
this story. I know she still continues with her own entertaining prose in
another place.

Prologue

In 1942, the precursor to the Central Intelligence Agency (CIA), the Office of Strategic Services (OSS), was created by the United States government. Its purpose was to clandestinely address projects that could potentially bring an abrupt end to World War II.

A group of twenty four distinguished anthropologists was recruited by the OSS to investigate ways of destroying the Japanese people. Only recently has top secret information about this program become declassified within the United States.

The project team was charged with identifying dietary, cultural, hygienic, and physical characteristics unique to the Japanese people. Using this information, the group intended to develop a biological contagion that matched the chosen ethnic criteria. That biological agent would become the first ethnically targeted disease. Because of the disease's planned contagious attribute, the victims would infect other Japanese on contact. To test new biological agents, the OSS scientists were to have access to thousands of subjects, that is, residents of Japanese ancestry incarcerated in prison camps scattered throughout the United States.

About the time that the project starting receiving attention from the military, the atomic bombs dropped on Hiroshima and Nagasaki proved to be sufficiently effective in ending the war with Japan.[1] The hidden group of scientists was disbanded on the assumption that a racially or ethnically specific weapon was neither needed nor its development achievable.

The current leaders of several Western and Asian countries no longer accepted this assumption. The knowledge of DNA sequences from the Human Genome Project and vastly improved genetic technologies make the development of such a weapon far more feasible today than it was during World War II. The problem now is one of will rather than way.

---

1 David H Price. *Anthropological Intelligence: The Deployment and Neglect of American Anthropology in the Second World War*. Duke University Press. 2008.

ONE

A swig of the cold beer chased down the spicy chili con carne. Setting her mug back down on the bar, she glanced out through the tavern's large, front window. For a brief moment, Dr Carrie Bock let herself become mesmerized with the aimless, drifting snowflakes that reflected the green neon sign of the Shamrock Tavern.

A well-dressed man sitting several bar stools away finished off his third martini. After laying a few bills on the bar, he swiveled off the seat. Without any eye contact, he ceremoniously twirled a Burberry scarf around his camel-hair overcoat. Grasping his leather briefcase, he stepped outside into the wintry cold and left Carrie as the only patron.

"Hey Doc, how was my famous chili tonight?" The baritone question came from the far end of the mahogany and brass trimmed bar.

Carrie smiled at the tall, barrel-chested bartender and gave him a wink. "It's still one of the best, Kevin! I always look forward to my Thursday night suppers at the Shamrock Tavern."

Pushing her empty bowl away, she tilted her head to look up at the flat screen TV. The station's cameras focused on a young, handsome newscaster. He stood in front of Boston's historic State House for dramatic effect. A tiny microphone hugged the lapel of his trench coat.

> And so earlier today, on this cold, snowy Inauguration Tuesday, January 20th 2009, we all watched history made with the first black American sworn in as President of the United States. Supreme Court Justice Deborah Katz listened as the articulate Senator from Illinois, and now President, Bartholomew Bowa, parroted the oath with the famous words "...to preserve, protect, and defend the Constitution of the United States."
>
> Many dignitaries, including past Presidents, sat in the West Capitol patio for the ceremony. Perhaps the guest with the most solemn face belonged to his Party's former political adversary, Zachary Hinton. But now, Hinton has been tapped

as the Secretary of State on Bowa's recently assembled cabinet. His confirmation is assured.

Today, with the precarious US economy, the wars in Iraq and Afghanistan still unresolved, unemployment at its highest level, and the world's perception of this country at its lowest ebb, the new President has a full plate. There will be no honeymoon for this young, and what most people consider, inexperienced Senator from Illinois. But the American people are expecting him to hit the ground running tomorrow, after tonight's scheduled dinners and festive balls.

And now for Channel 5 News, this is Vince Bevacqua reporting from the State House on Beacon Hill.

Back to you, Kayla!

Kevin Reilly, the amiable tavern owner, flipped a dish towel over his shoulder and walked towards the end of the bar where Carrie sat.

"What do you think, Doc? Do you think this guy can do it? He sure as hell has an uphill battle. The poor bastard inherited problems that began long before he ever thought about running for President. Man, I hope he does well. Not because he's a minority, but because I think he's a good guy and means what he told us during his campaign."

Carrie listened to the melodic, Celtic brogue while she drained her glass of beer. Keeping with her routine, she playfully pointed her index finger towards the Bunn coffee maker.

The bartender, picking up her cue, pivoted and grabbed a clean, ceramic coffee mug. He filled it up with steaming coffee for one of his favorite customers.

"Yeah, Kev, he is a good guy! And I can tell you that from personal experience."

Kevin, wearing a full white-linen apron over his plaid shirt, placed a small pitcher of milk on the bar in front of Carrie. Familiar with her tastes, he pulled two sugar packets out of his apron pocket.

As she poured the milk, the oversized man with a shock of thick, wavy red-brown hair leaned forward and spoke to her almost in a whisper.

"Have you ever personally met the man, Doc?"

Carrie's left hand shook a paper sugar packet vigorously, ripped it open, and dumped the contents into the steaming mug. She sucked in a deep breath and exhaled slowly while her hand noisily swirled a spoon in the milky coffee.

"Yes, my good friend. I have met the man," she smiled. "In fact, I was with the man many, many times in the past."

The barkeep's eyebrows arched over his sparkling blue eyes.

"Many times, Carrie? You're a college professor. I never read where President Bowa was ever involved with test-tubes, lab rats, and all that stuff. How the hell did you ever get to meet the Senator from Illinois? Were you one of those political campaign workers?"

Carrie took a gulp of the sweetened coffee and deliberated whether she should disclose some personal history to the friendly pub owner.

Hell, it's been over twenty years. Fuck it! Telling my good friend here about some secrets I've kept for a long time can't be consequential now. It's funny; very few people know what took place over two decades ago. Now it seems surreal to me. As of today, Bartholomew Bowa is the most powerful man in the world. And me? I'm sitting in this Irish pub in Boston and drinking a cup of coffee with the owner who is lonelier than I am.

"Let me tell you something, Kevin Reilly. Something most people don't know. Bart and I once were a well-kept secret. We were what you might call an item back in our days at Harvard."

"Oh?"

She sipped her coffee before continuing.

"He was a third year law student, and I was working on a PhD in microbiology. We met at a political rally one night and continued to see each other afterwards."

A smile broadened the bartender's fleshy face.

"Isn't that something! So you know quite a bit about our new President, since the two of you were students over in Cambridge."

Carrie's fingertips lightly traced the coffee mug handle.

"That's right, Kev. I know quite a bit about him and…and he knows quite a bit about me."

3

"Yeah, Carrie, but college romances are always fleeting. Young kids are always exploring and finding out who they are before they get serious with someone else."

Carrie gulped the last of the coffee down while it was still hot. She swirled off the bar stool and buttoned her full length herring-bone winter coat. Reaching over to the stool next to hers, she grabbed her black wool beret. She peered into the bar's mirror and tilted the cap to one side to expose most of her trimmed and highlighted auburn hair.

"Put this on my tab, Kev. I'll settle up next week. I've got to get going."

"Sure, Doc, but tell me, did you two just, you know, just go out on a few dates?" Kevin asked in a fatherly brogue.

She grinned back at the inquisitive tavern owner.

"No. We lived together for a year in a little apartment over in Somerville."

TWO

"Mr President. That was an excellent meeting this morning. I think the Cabinet members have become more comfortable with you and each other. It takes a while."

The tall, handsome black man stood behind the Oval Office desk and slipped out of his cordovan leather loafers before sitting down. Now in his stocking feet, he seemed prepared to take on the challenges of the Presidency.

"Charlie, for God's sake, it's April. They should be comfortable. And busy! We've got lots to do. We should be further along on the economic stimulus programs, and I have to deliver on my Iraq withdrawal promises. The cabinet members knew me and my agenda when they signed on months ago."

"Before I forget, your Secretary of State needs half an hour this morning. He says that it's top-secret and needs your attention."

President Bowa's habitually beaming expression turned into a frown.

"Tell Zachary he can have fifteen minutes. I need to spend some time with Parker Wilson on the Treasury Department's status. We need to fine-tune our plans so we don't hang ourselves by the balls on these home mortgage revival programs. Call Parker and tell him to get over within the hour. I'll see Hinton now."

Chief of Staff, Charlie Hurst, placed a folder of briefings for the President in the far left corner of his desk. The stocky, energetic man with thinning blonde hair pivoted and swiftly left the office.

When the newly confirmed Secretary of State stepped into the Oval Office, he walked towards the President while exuding an air of confidence. He had spent many hours inside the hallowed office in the past. His right hand clutched a thin manila folder. The light gray suit nearly matched the color of his thick, wavy hair. It was no secret that the popular sixty-two year old man preferred to be sitting in the younger man's chair and not opposite him on the far side of the hand-carved oak desk.

5

"Mr President, we have something developing that I think could be of great importance."

"Zachary, everything in this office is of great importance. What do you have?"

The head of the State Department shot a "pissed off" glance after the gratuitous remark.

"My Under Secretary, Warren Lee, informed me last night of a rather bizarre incident. He received a brief note at his home requesting that he call a certain phone number to receive further instructions. It didn't appear to be official in any way. At first, Warren thought it was a way to get his attention or perhaps might even be some creative fund raising tactic."

"And did he call the number?"

"He did last night, about ten thirty. The number he reached only instructed him to call a second number. Thinking it might be some prank from friends, he made that call as well. However, this time he was told that he was speaking with an operative from Beijing's Ministry of State Security [MSS] on an untraceable cellphone number."

President Bowa's head shot up at the mention of China's MSS. He knew the organization functioned as the counterpart to the United States' Federal Bureau of Investigation (FBI), Central Intelligence Agency (CIA), and Department of Homeland Security combined. It also resembled the Russian government's infamous Komitet Gosudarstvennoy Bezopasnosti (KGB) with its reputation for ruthless tactics. The Ministry, which was involved in clandestine affairs both nationally and abroad, had existed for several decades. Most nations considered the organization to be an elite intelligence gathering group.

"And what did our Mr Warren Lee learn from this individual?"

"The operative told Warren that the MSS had discovered some highly sensitive information. They had learned that the Pakistani terrorist organization, Sipah-al-Nahijdeen, better known as SAN, has developed a highly effective lethal virus, a virus capable of wiping out entire races within weeks."

"Entire races? You mean entire countries, right?"

"No, I meant exactly what I said, *entire races*. According to this MSS operative, the Pakistani's lethal bioagent has genetic specificity so it can selectively target Caucasoid, Negroid, or Mongoloid races."

The President reclined slowly in his leather chair.

"Zachary, I'm no scientist, but I'm not sure identifying a race gene is possible. I had read somewhere, years back, that there was a theory that a single race gene could be identified, but the article stated emphatically that the thesis was never proven…and has since been discarded."

"Warren told me the same thing. Seems my talented Under Secretary was a life science major in his undergraduate days before entering public service. Warren learned that the Pakistani scientists have a way of targeting racial characteristics. The virus can be manufactured in such a way that it becomes lethal only for a specific race. There was no further discussion concerning how the terrorists have managed this. If SAN does have such a weapon of mass destruction, we have to move immediately!"

President Bart Bowa looked angrily at his former political party opponent.

"Zachary, we'll move on this when we must. And mentioning WMDs is something that I've asked you and other members of my administration to avoid, if you recall. Those words caused the American people, dedicated servicemen and women, and Congress to be tragically sucked in by the Bush administration. Such irresponsible claims will never intimidate them under my watch. Now, where is this note that Under Secretary Lee received?"

With a show of annoyance, Hinton opened up the manila folder. He handed over the note and envelope that had been addressed to Lee at his home in Bethesda.

The brief message, scripted in handwritten Chinese characters, meant nothing to the President. He scrutinized the envelope. It was postmarked from Portland, Oregon. There was unlikely to be a trail to the original source.

"Have this note verified with another person who is trained in the Chinese language. Then have it stamped TOP-SECRET—JINGAR. And keep me in the loop."

The Head of the State Department nodded in tacit agreement. With his top security clearance, he was aware of the protocol. Anything identified with the label, TOP-SECRET, and its corresponding code name, JINGAR, held the highest degree of security and sensitivity. The code name kept it out of the hands of anyone who did not have that security clearance or anyone who simply did not have the "need to know."

"There's more, Bart, ah… Mr President," Hinton said, painfully saying the title to the man who had narrowly defeated him in a close primary campaign.

"The contact in Beijing requested a meeting soon with Warren, who is a Chinese American. He wants to discuss an alliance so we can jointly combat such a biological weapon. According to the phone conversation, the premise is that if China and the United States worked together, we could come up with an antidote or perhaps a prophylactic serum to prevent the effects of such a lethal bioagent."

"You mean they're proposing that the United States and China jointly develop a vaccine to protect people against the racial virus? Is this for real?"

"It seems that Beijing is scared shitless of its ungovernable neighbor, Pakistan, having a lethal bioweapon. They're convinced it will supersede nuclear warfare. And their anxiety begs a quick answer from us. Warren obviously didn't offer an answer to the Beijing informant, but asked for my and of course *your* direction on the matter."

The President stood up and paced slowly around the office in his stocking feet without speaking. This habit was well known to those in his inner circle. He routinely did this whenever he wrestled with an issue needing his decision. The protocol for anyone in the room was to remain silent while awaiting the world's most powerful leader to provide further directions.

The President stopped pacing. He turned to the Secretary of State, who was still sitting and watching him.

"Let's have that meeting, Zachary, but we must be cautious about any leaks. If the media inquires, the story goes that we're simply improving our relationship with Beijing. I don't want to give any premature signals based on a questionable phone conversation. Have the meeting take place on our turf on, say, one of the Hawaiian islands. And let's get Burke and Janet involved. Burke can send someone from Homeland Security. And Janet, as Director of the Central Intelligence Agency, can either attend the meeting or send someone. Have this...this Warren Lee go as well, since he's the original contact. They will probably feel better with him being a Chinese American. I want the meeting to take place soon. But we must determine if it's a hoax or decoy, or if there is any plausibility to this new bioweapon. The PRC [People's Republic of China] will have to open up to us if they really want to have an allied project."

"I'll get on it," Zachary replied, not looking at the President as he turned to leave the Oval Office.

As he opened the door, the Chief of Staff, Charlie Hurst, slipped inside and closed the door behind him.

"Mr President, Parker Wilson is ready to brief you on the Economic Recovery Program."

The President, now sitting back in his desk chair, waved for Charlie to bring the Secretary of the Treasury in.

THREE

On a warm May afternoon, Professor Carrie Bock had just delivered her last lecture and lab session of the spring semester at Tufts University's School of Medicine. She walked briskly along the crowded corridor towards her air conditioned office.

She closed her office door behind her and put away her lecture materials from the cell biology class. As she approached her desk, she shrugged off her white lab coat with the blue university logo embroidered on the front pocket. She stood near the window stuffed with an old, laboring air conditioner and ran her fingers through her hair. She picked up her mail and reviewed her phone messages after plopping down into her upholstered desk chair. A light knocking sound came from her office door.

Damn! It's probably another student worried about the final exam coming up. The pattern never changes year after year. Give the semester's last lab lecture and get a parade of anxious undergraduates flowing through your office door.

"Come in!" Carrie yelled out.

It wasn't a student, but Dr Clancy Roche, the Department's Chairman. The tall, hulking man's shock of white hair and bushy eyebrows contrasted with his pink Irish complexion. After he closed the door, he approached his younger colleague with his perennial smile.

"Clancy! Pull up a chair. I haven't seen you around here in weeks."

"Yes, it's been awhile. I was in Geneva delivering a paper. I decided to take some time off and become a tourist and visit friends. I actually found that I enjoyed myself and didn't miss my work at all."

The imposing man, over six and a half feet tall, sat opposite her. His light blue seer-sucker suit complemented his buttoned down white shirt and trademark bow-tie, which today was a deep maroon color.

"I'm sure you enjoyed Europe. I haven't been there in years. I should get back again soon to see friends, too. As you know, Clancy,

I've spent most of my travel time in the Far East working and touring. They always seem to go together."

"With your background and training, Asia does make more sense. I stopped by to talk to you about two things, and both are equally important."

Dr Bock sat back in her chair with attention to her beloved boss.

"Carrie, you're scheduled to take a sabbatical soon. And I'm here not only to remind you of that but also to encourage you to take it this time. You're overdue. You've been working non-stop teaching classes and working in the lab on your research."

Carrie smiled at the man whom she had known for over two decades. Once her advisor during her PhD program, he had gracefully morphed into a father image for her, especially after her own father was diagnosed with the dreadful Alzheimer's disease. It was the same time she was going through her divorce.

She reflected how the globally renowned microbiologist had always been there for her, both when she was a student and now as a colleague. It was his sensitive, genuine support and advice that had always been comforting when her father's disease prevailed.

"I don't know, Clancy. Dad still needs me to see him at the home. And to be honest, I do enjoy those visits, especially for those brief moments when he still recognizes who I am. The pattern is so typical. He doesn't know who I am when I enter the room, but every so often his memory works and he calls me by my name during my visit. In fact, I'm driving over there tonight. It's his birthday, though of course he has no idea."

The big man sat back in his chair facing the professor's desk.

"I certainly don't know exactly what you're feeling. I can only imagine how difficult it is for you."

His gentle blue eyes looked deeply into his younger colleague's sadness. He defused the silent tension. "How old is your father now?"

Carrie smiled. "He's seventy five today. Mom and I used to celebrate his birthday at our place on Cape Cod. It was always our first celebration of each summer after we opened up the cottage for the season."

Carrie let herself privately reminisce. It was strangely comforting to remember the good times when struggling with the bad. She caught herself and politely returned to the conversation.

"But Clancy, you told me you had two things to discuss with me. Now that you told me to take a sabbatical, what's the second thing?"

The older man squirmed in his seat and looked sheepishly down into his lap. He was obviously uncomfortable with the next topic.

"I'm going to be stepping down from the Chairmanship of the Department and very soon. And...and I'll have to recommend my choice for someone to step into the job. I immediately thought of you. I know you're focused on your father's care and your research work, but I wanted to know how you felt about this before I submitted your name to the Dean."

"Clancy, you're such a great Chairman! Why are you stepping down? Are they forcing you to vacate the position?"

The older professor looked down into his lap again.

"I made a decision to retire because I enjoyed Europe and traveling so much that I want to do more. And I have some health issues that I need to watch. So I've tendered my resignation effective at the end of the next semester. I want to travel and also spend time with my daughter and her family. I thought what better person to pass the Chairman's baton to than you."

Carrie felt like she had been thumped on the heart. But the pain was purely emotional. As she sat in her chair, numbed with the news, she felt alone, with her failing dad and now her surrogate father both drifting away. With no lover in her life, she needed family more than ever.

"Carrie, I didn't know how to spring this on you. I... "

The office door swung open after a few quick, loud taps. The Department's administrative assistant filled the doorway with a surprised look on her face.

"I'm sorry to interrupt, Dr Bock, but you have an important phone call on line two. It's someone from Washington who wants to know if you can speak right now."

"Who is it, Brianna?"

Carrie and Clancy could see that the woman was unusually nervous.

"The man said that he was calling for the President of the United States. I wasn't sure if it was a joke or not."

Carrie chuckled at the assistant's anxiety. "It's okay, Brianna. I'll take the call."

Clancy stood up. "Carrie, I'll see you later." The Professor and assistant left.

Minutes after the door closed, her desk phone rang. Before she picked up the handset, her heart beat so forcefully that she thought she could hear it.

"Hello. This is Dr Carrie Bock."

"Hello, Carbo! This is Barbo."

FOUR

It was his voice. It was him. And he spoke the private nicknames that they had always used for one another.

After hearing the nickname, she had an immediate flashback, back to their student days at Harvard. At the time, most colleges still used the Social Security number as the student ID, the same ID number printed on every school document, including class schedules, grade lists, academic transcripts, and tuition bills. The students insisted the school not use Social Security numbers. They wanted to protect their privacy and confidentiality from an ID number assigned by the US Government.

The university complied. Working with the student body, they adopted an alternative system that used the first three letters of the first name followed by the first two letters of the last name. The students' four-digit month and day of birth followed the cryptic pseudonym. Carrie Bock was Carbo0613, and Bartholomew Bowa was Barbo1218.

As Carrie Bock and Bartholomew Bowa became friends and later lovers, they adopted their university mnemonics as their personal nicknames. They called each other "Carbo" and "Barbo." But they carried it out secretly, as they did with their romance. The aliases were used privately in their phone calls, emails, and especially inside their one bedroom apartment in Somerville.

"Barbo! Or should I say, *Mr President*? Congratulations!"

"Thank you. It's been what, about twenty years, Carbo?"

"Yeah, but now in your new job, you can find me pretty easily."

His easy chuckle was still the same. She envisioned seeing his beautiful smile and hearing his laugh.

"Carrie, I'm sure you're busy these days, but I need to see you."

The statement struck her without warning. It was the last thing she expected to hear. She was still shocked by Clancy's news. Now the President of the United States has asked to see her.

"What is it, Barbo?" Her voice became serious.

"I can't discuss it over the phone. If you're willing, I can have a limo at your house first thing tomorrow morning to take you to the airport. We can meet, have lunch, and I promise I'll have you back in Boston before early evening. I'm sorry this is the way for us to see each other again after all these years. But, Carrie, it's very important…for our country's security."

The message was clear. And somehow it let her breathe a little easier. He wanted to see her on official business and not for anything personal, despite their intimate relationship so many years ago.

"Sure, Barbo. It's the weekend, and I've got nothing else going on. I must be back up here as soon as possible to check up on my father."

"How's Jimmy these days? Is he still playing golf? I remember him trying to teach me, but I never got the hang of it."

"He's doing okay," she lied. "I look forward to seeing you tomorrow, Barbo."

"Same here, Carbo!"

On Saturday morning, a second limo driven by a Secret Service agent whisked her away from Ronald Reagan Washington National Airport. It was soon speeding past the sparse weekend traffic to 1600 Pennsylvania Avenue.

When she was escorted into the spacious reception area known as the "Blue Room," Carrie felt her anxiety escalate. It wasn't the invitation into the White House that gave her anxiety but the thrill and uneasiness of seeing Bart Bowa for the first time in twenty years. The thrill was from the memory of the man she once loved and who had once loved her enough to want to marry her. The uneasiness was from the memory of her rejecting that love and marriage proposal after their graduation.

The door opened and she looked directly at the man with whom she had shared laughs, love, and dreams so many years ago.

Naturally, and without hesitation, they rushed towards each other. They embraced warmly and kissed each other on the cheek.

When they separated, he looked into her eyes.

"My God! Carbo, you haven't changed a bit. You look the same as you did when we first met. You're still twenty two years old."

The flattering comment made her smile and shed a joyous tear. She reached inside her suit jacket pocket for a tissue. Wiping away the tear, she laughed.

"You still look the same, except for those few gray hairs I first noticed on TV while you were campaigning."

"Come, follow me. I have a private meeting room for us on the next floor. We don't need the formality of the Oval Office, and we can have lunch sent up later."

The oversized den had walls lined with oak shelves that were filled with a wide variety of books. Some shelves held American law books, and others held hardbound novels and nonfiction books.

"This is a mini-library. I come here often to think without any interruptions. There's a fresh pot of coffee and some hot water for tea over there."

Carrie couldn't take her eyes off the man with whom she had lived for a year during her young and ambitious life. He hadn't changed. He still had the same relaxed personality and was comfortable to be with.

"Carbo, if it's okay with you, I want to get right to the reason I asked you here. As I said on the phone, it's important that we meet."

"That's why I'm here," she replied.

The President provided Carrie with detailed background to the Pakistani terrorist group, SAN. He explained how Beijing's spies had gathered intelligence about the little known terrorist group. He outlined how the SAN had possibly acquired or developed a racially selective bioweapon. His briefing included the initial contact between an agent of China's Ministry of State Security and Under Secretary of State Warren Lee and several follow-up meetings with staff from Homeland Security and the CIA.

"We first thought that such a weapon was improbable. However, after some convincing arguments, we decided that we needed to explore the feasibility of such a specialized virus. If a virus with genetic discriminating capabilities has already been created in the laboratory, we must do the same and test its effectiveness. The assumption is that our scientists can identify the three major racial groups of humans: Mongoloid, Negroid, and Caucasoid. And we've speculated this might be done, not precisely, but by searching and identifying genetic markers of skin melanin, hair type, and other ethnic or racial traits.

"If we can develop a synthetic-organic viral agent that is racially discriminating, we'll shift our goal. The next phase of the mission becomes simple and focused. We must create an antidote, or preferably, a prophylactic serum, a vaccine, to inoculate and protect people from such a racial bioagent. It's the only way to prevent any attempt now or in the future at any biological genocide."

Carrie listened intently to her former lover tell the story. When the President stopped speaking, she sipped her coffee before commenting.

"First of all, Barbo, I'm not a geneticist. I agree that no single race gene has been discovered yet, and it's doubtful that one will ever be found. You mentioned clusters of genes representing characteristics of a race. On the surface, I believe that this is scientifically possible, though, as you alluded, not without a margin of error."

"We realize that. We have also been told through Intelligence sources that the virus is designed to be incredibly contagious. After a person is infected, he spreads the disease to others of his own race with similar genetic clusters. And as with extremely contagious epidemics, the number of victims would increase exponentially. Can you imagine hundreds of millions of people dying, whether Whites, Black, or Asians? The potential pollution and spread of other diseases from rotting corpses could kill millions more. The thought sickens me deeply."

Both the President and Carrie were silent as they considered the almost unfathomable consequences.

President Bowa took a sip of coffee, more to break the tension than to quench any thirst.

"And despite the questionable accuracy of Chinese intelligence about such a weapon, we have no choice but to be prepared to counter it. As I said, if it is feasible, we need to develop a way to prevent it from infecting the people of the world. I personally feel an antidote isn't the solution."

"Why?" Carrie asked with a furled brow.

"As is usual with infectious and contagious diseases, the antidote is administered much too late for some victims, and possibly in this case for very many."

"All of what you have told me is horrifying," Carrie answered. "You don't need me to tell you that, or about the difficulties in creating a solution. You have access to some of the best scientists, including specialized bio-geneticists, in the country."

"That's true."

Carrie leaned back into her chair. "So, Mr President, why did you really ask to see me?"

FIVE

Professor Carrie Bock watched as the man with whom she spent a whirlwind year of her young life stood up. He casually walked over to the thermal decanter of coffee. Again in stocking feet after slipping out of his loafers, he stepped to the table without facing her. He stood there, deep in thought, holding a steaming cup in his right hand.

He snapped out of his cerebral journey and looked directly into her eyes.

"Carrie, I know you don't have top-secret clearance, but nonetheless what I've already told you, and what I will tell you, is considered classified information. I have to ask officially that you keep this information to yourself. It is highly sensitive, and things are still developing as we speak. In fact, your coming here to visit me today is known by only a few people."

She looked over at the man who once made her knees quiver. She knew him. His face told her he was now deadly serious and wasn't taking the topic lightly.

"You know me, Barbo; sealed lips."

"Why I wanted you here today—no, why I needed you here today—isn't just because of the work you do and your professional background. The scientific challenge is daunting enough, but the human factor has some mysteries. And they need to be solved secretly, without notice and without disruption."

Carrie's brow furled again after hearing his cryptic statement.

"I don't understand. It seems straight forward. Get a group of scientists together with lab facilities; probably in some remote location. Then have the team work around the clock to determine the bioagent's feasibility. If such a bizarre bioweapon in virus form is possible, move into the next phase and develop the vaccine. Barbo, I'm not minimizing the task at hand, but provided you select the right people, you should be successful."

The President looked across at her and gave her one of his trademark warm and contagious smiles.

"I always loved your ability to break things down so matter-of-factly. But this is more complex."

President Bowa revisited the background by describing the unusual Chinese involvement in the project, including the unrelenting persuasion by the Chinese to ally with US scientists on the project.

"Has anything materialized from these top-secret meetings with the MSS?"

"Lots! And I mean lots! We've already formed a team of scientists, or I should say, Warren has formed a team. He has become the de facto project manager representing the United States. He has recruited top-notch biologists, geneticists, and even an anthropologist to plan how to move forward. Warren's counterparts from Beijing have also volunteered some of their ace researchers to see if we can catch up with the SAN terrorists on this terrible weapon."

"Has this project team started working yet?"

"Yes, but very preliminarily. Warren spends a good deal of time at the top-secret lab. We've made a virtual fortress of the site, and he shuttles back and forth between there and Washington."

"He's not a research scientist, is he?"

"No. But he's incredibly bright and had significant biology education as an undergraduate at Stanford. His primary role is essentially a liaison between Washington and Beijing. So far, it has gone well, and I haven't had to stop anything that has been initiated."

It was Carrie's turn to stand up and walk around as she digested the information so foreign to her as an academic researcher and professor. She paced around the den, peered out through the window, and skimmed some of the book titles on the bookshelves. She raised her hand and ran the tips of her fingernails over the book spines.

"There are a couple of things that immediately strike me. It sounds like the Under Secretary of State is now reporting directly to the President of the United States and not the Secretary of State. Was this done on purpose because you and Zachary Hinton can't play in the same sandbox?"

Carrie followed up with a teasing smile. It was a shot at the public, often vitriolic, relationship between the two candidates during the primary political campaign. As soon as she asked the question, she realized how easy it was to fall back into the comfort zone the two of them had once shared. Despite twenty years of separation, the same chemistry and rhythm they had as graduate students and lovers had easily returned.

"It's no secret that Zachary Hinton as Secretary of State wasn't my first choice. He had put a lot of pressure on the Party to become my running mate, but I would have nothing of it. We compromised, and I offered him a Cabinet post. Between you and me, if I keep sending him on good-will trips around the world, he'll soon get tired and pissed off."

"Pissed off? Why? Doesn't he like being away from his wife?" Carrie chuckled again.

"No, that's not it. But sending him to Europe, the Middle East, and Russia keeps him out of the country and out of touch with what's going in Washington. And it's no secret he loves getting photographed for his next run at the Presidency."

"How does he feel about Warren Lee reporting to you on this top-secret project?"

"To be honest, Zachary Hinton and I haven't addressed this chain-of-command situation. Obviously, he knows I'm the boss. And he realizes that I need Warren to ramp up the project, which by the way has a code name. It's known as Project V—the 'V' stands for vaccine. With all that's going on, I may need to retain Under Secretary Lee in this role permanently. And Zachary has no idea about that option. Besides, I've kept him busy traveling to Israel and Syria. He's got his plate full with problems brewing over there."

Carrie nodded. She understood that politics never go away in public service.

"This Warren Lee. He's a Chinese American?"

"Yes. And lately, I've learned more about him. He has an impeccable record. After graduating Stanford, he went on to the John F. Kennedy School of Government at Harvard. He later served as a major in the United States Air Force and was a decorated F-16 fighter pilot. After being discharged from the military, he started his own computer network company. It was financially successful, and he sold it for a huge profit. Then he ran for Congress from northern California and won, hands down. He could have run again but evidently wanted to know more about the inner workings of the Executive Branch. Zachary Hinton drafted him as his Under Secretary."

Carrie was quiet. She stood behind a chair and stared intensely at the man sitting opposite her before she spoke.

"I'll ask you again, Mr President, what the hell does this top-secret project, Project V, have to do with me, a professor of microbiology?"

Bart Bowa paused before answering and stared directly into her bright blue eyes.

"Carrie, do you remember our first date?"

She felt some warmth spread over her face. She knew her cheeks were turning a bright pink as they always did when she became the slightest bit embarrassed. Her hands grabbed the back of one of the high-backed chairs in an attempt at casual diversion. She leaned in with a flirting stare.

"Of course, I do, Barbo. I took you to a restaurant on Tyler Street in Boston. It was right smack in the middle of Chinatown."

His smile broadened.

"Yes. And I knew on that first date, I was going to fall for you. I was impressed with the confident way you spoke Chinese to our waiter. You explained to me that although the young man was Cantonese, he would still understand your Mandarin. I was in awe all evening as you casually spoke to the restaurant staff in their own language."

"Barbo, I had told you before we went on that date that I had minored in Chinese Studies at Yale. And you knew I had lived in China for a year and half while working on my undergraduate degree."

"I know, but it still intrigued and impressed me."

Carrie gave him an appreciative smile.

"Aha! I see the acts of this little play. The Beijing researchers are working with Mr Warren Lee in shrouded secrecy. Now, enter Carrie Bock, a microbiologist trained in the Chinese language and culture. Why you sneaky son of a bitch!" she said with a chuckle.

"And I thought you missed me and wanted to see me again," she said with a flirtatious wink.

The President leaned back in his chair and grinned at the humor.

"If I wasn't happily married to Nicole and with two beautiful daughters, I might have considered that. But I confess, your credentials were part of my motive. Now, let me be direct."

"What is it?"

"I had thought if you could spring away from the university for a while, you would be a nice fit on the research project team."

"Hell, Barbo, I'm sure you have talented scientists already on board. Adding me to the team wouldn't make that much of a difference. Remember, I know you well. There's something else here besides me putting on my lab coat and working some centrifuges to find this perhaps nonexistent biological weapon and vaccine. Again I ask, what is the real reason you want me on this top-secret team?"

The President nodded in acknowledgment of her demand.

"It's our Under Secretary of State, Mr Warren Lee."

SIX

Carrie walked over to the sideboard and refilled her cup of coffee without saying a word. When she returned, she sat down at the table opposite the President.

"You told me about all the accolades associated with this guy. He seems like a model citizen, a successful leader, and a good public servant. Now you tell me he's someone with whom you're not comfortable. Do you trust Warren or not?"

"It isn't that I don't trust him. It's that I don't know what's really going on. I don't know why the MSS contacted him directly rather than going to a high official in the CIA or Homeland Security. The original note, the launch of this whole project, was directed to Lee in handwritten Chinese. It was clear the connection was intended to be between him personally and the Beijing operatives."

"At the major bilateral conference with Beijing recently, you emphasized in your speech that China and the United States need to engage in intelligence sharing. The internationally televised speech underscored how both countries could prevail over terrorism if we protect each other with intelligence."

"I realize that, but…"

"But the method of contact could be simply circumstances. Perhaps the MSS operatives didn't really know who to contact with their sensitive findings about the SAN terrorists. Does Warren have any background with the government in Islamabad?"

"There's none of that on his curriculum vitae or State Department dossier. He spent his military tours in the Middle East."

Carrie sipped her coffee. "What is it, Barbo? You see me joining this research team to bird dog your man from the State Department?"

"I don't know for sure, to be honest. What's really bothering me is not that mysterious initial connection, but that now he meets privately with the Beijing people and reports only a summary to me. Those meetings are top-secret of course, and all of the conversations are in Chinese. There's some English, when necessary I suppose, but the substantive plans are communicated in Mandarin."

"That doesn't seem like an alliance. If the US and Beijing are in this together, there should be more monitoring of what is said at the project meetings between the two countries."

"This project took shape so quickly, and with Warren spearheading the whole thing, it has taken on an aggressive and independent life of its own. I have had to give him broad latitude in meeting Beijing's request for a bilateral research team. I did insist that the top-secret laboratory be located here in the United States. I felt that if we're going to participate and provide some of our talented research scientists, they should not be stationed in China. Warren got them to agree to that."

"How many are on the team?"

"I don't know. I would guess about eight or ten by now, with additional support staff. You may have heard of some of them. They've been recruited from some of the best universities and research labs in the world. Some are still waiting for top-secret clearances. There are two project team co-leaders. One is from China and is supposedly a top-notch researcher. Her name is Dr Lan Ying. Our guy comes from the National Institutes of Health. He is a Clinical Research Director there. We hope he'll be on board soon after his top-secret clearance."

"Who is this NIH guy?"

"His name is Josef Marotsky."

"I've read several of his articles on microbial genetics that have appeared in prestigious journals, such as *Nature* and *Science*. But I haven't met him."

"Warren seems pleased with the two leaders selected, and so far everyone seems to be getting along. My Secretary of State, and Warren's official boss, has no idea of the everyday details of the project, and, the truth is, neither do I. It makes me feel extremely uncomfortable for someone in my administration who I hardly know to be in such a critical position."

"Barbo, I think it'll be all right. When Marotsky comes on board, you can get him to attend the meetings with Warren and perhaps use him as your mole to find out what's going on."

"Marotsky doesn't understand the Chinese language or culture. And the Chinese don't want any outside interpreters. They only want key people on the project. My concern is not knowing what the Beijing people discuss with Lee; and not just at the official meetings but also outside of those meetings."

"And perhaps what Lee is telling the Beijing people?"

The President looked at her without replying to the comment.

The unsettling silence was interrupted with a tapping on the den's door.

"Come in," said the President.

A slight man dressed in a white chef's jacket and toque wheeled in a cart with food covered by sterling silver covers. After he set up two place settings at the table, he left.

Carrie looked at the lobster salad sandwich on a croissant and green salad set before her.

"Barbo! You remembered. That is so sweet."

"Of course I remembered your favorite lunch. You always loved lobster. Besides, if you're going to work for me I need to get on your good side."

She smiled at him and took a bite of the appetizing sandwich. Her face turned serious after she swallowed a bite of the succulent, fresh lobster.

"Look, Barbo. There's something I have to tell you. When you asked on the phone about my father, Jimmy, I kinda lied. I told you he was okay. But the truth is, he's not okay. A few years ago, he was diagnosed with Alzheimer's disease. I had to put him in a special nursing home south of Boston. It's a top notch place located in Quincy. He has become progressively worse, but I do see him almost every day and that seems to help. I mean... I know it helps me, and I hope it helps him."

"Carrie. I'm sorry to hear that. I had always liked your dad."

"I know. And he liked you as well. The truth is, he had more interest in your political ambitions than I did. Anyway, I'm telling you this because I can't possibly take on the role you have for me. Barbo, I can't leave the Boston area. I need to be with him. I can't possibly spend time in some remote laboratory. It wouldn't work."

The President took a sip of his iced tea.

"I haven't told you where this top-secret laboratory is located, and you haven't asked."

"I figured the location is especially sensitive. And since I won't be going along with your top-secret plan, I let it go."

"Yes, the lab is hidden in a remote wooded area far away from here. It's a former retreat and conference center once owned by the Massachusetts Institute of Technology. It's called the Elliot House, and it's located in the town of Dedham about fifteen minutes from Quincy."

Carrie nearly choked on her salad.

"My God! I figured it was hidden somewhere in New Mexico or Wyoming. You know out west in some remote desert. But it's in my backyard."

A broad smile returned to the Presidents face.

"I also wanted to tell you that the retreat center is a four story facility. The newly constructed research laboratory is hidden deep in the bowels of the existing building. The top floor has several apartments replete with kitchens, bedrooms, and living rooms. Carbo, I thought you might consider moving into one of those top floor suites."

"Move in? What for? I mean if I did agree to take on the job, I live not that far away. My condo is in South Boston. I'm only about forty minutes from Dedham."

"Yeah, but Carbo, I want to know what goes on inside that retreat center at all times. When Warren goes there, he stays over-night in one of the hotel-type rooms on the third floor. I don't know who he sees socially or what he does with his free time when he stays there on these trips."

Carrie raised an eyebrow. "And?"

"And, I want to know. I have to know everything about this guy. Carbo, he makes me too damn nervous. Although I could take him off the project, the Beijing team would protest and we would learn nothing. The Beijing boys are very comfortable with Warren…perhaps too comfortable."

Carrie stared at the man who had once loved her so much. She knew him well enough to sense when he was upset or nervous about something. She had seen it when he was in his last year of Harvard Law School. Back then he always confided in her. She listened and somehow made things better for him.

"Carbo, twenty years ago, I was in love with you. We shared our dreams and lived in our secret little apartment in Somerville. I had fervently hoped we would continue together forever. We both knew I was destined for politics. But I was never sure how you felt about that, and with hindsight, I know now I should have been sensitive to that. I can remember those final days together like it was yesterday. I had just received my JD degree. It should have been a time for joyous celebrating. But when you told me it was over between us, I was devastated. You knew it, and even offered to accompany me to the train station to see me off to Chicago."

"I remember, Barbo." Carrie looked away.

"*And* I remember the words you spoke when we last embraced. You told me, 'Whenever you need me, call. No matter what it is, I'll come.' I never forgot that."

"That's true," Carrie responded softly.

The President stood up and began to pace again.

"When this unusual situation surfaced, I immediately thought of you. I haven't told anyone about you or about us. But I personally felt you were someone who could help me get through this challenge. I called you yesterday to take you up on the offer you made many years ago."

She paused before commenting. She stood and looked up at the man who towered over her.

"My promise was like those that all parting lovers make. You can't really expect me to honor it? You thought of me because you need a research scientist who happens to speak Mandarin fluently."

The President reached out and grasped Carrie's hands with his. His fingers gently massaged hers with his thumbs.

"Yes, I do expect you to honor it. There's the promise *and* the fact that you're a brilliant researcher *and* speak Mandarin. *And* more."

"More?"

She recognized the personal sincerity in his eyes. "I trust you above almost everyone else I know."

SEVEN

Carrie used the flight home from the Capitol to digest the substance of the meeting and to consider the offer from the President.

He was right. She was the perfect person for the job. Professionally she understood the protocols of biological research, still retained her fluency in Mandarin, and would be loyal to President Bowa for personal and not political reasons.

As the aircraft approached its landing at Logan International Airport, she thought about the coincidences that had led to the President's request. The series of events were uncanny. Her combination of language and science credentials was critical. But the location of the top-secret laboratory was also propitious. It was minutes from her father's nursing home. And all of these "coincidences" came just after the discussion with her beloved chairman, Clancy Roche, who encouraged her to take a sabbatical before he officially retired.

The more she thought about it, the less coincidental recent events appeared. She heard her deceased mother's distant voice echo from her childhood. "Things in life always happen for a reason."

After landing in Boston, she drove directly to the Holly Home, a facility in Quincy used exclusively for Alzheimer patients. She spent some time with her father in his quiet but pleasant room.

Her fingers grasped his age-spotted hand while he stared blankly at the TV. Her memories returned of how he had always been the person with whom she would first bounce new ideas or challenges off of. He had been a great listener and sounding board for her during most of her life.

Her mother had passed away from a bout with cancer soon after her high school graduation from the prestigious Fontbonne Academy. Her father stepped in and soon became her best friend. He visited her often in New Haven while she majored in Microbiology and minored in Chinese Studies at Yale. He visited and spent time with her when she lived abroad in Beijing, and he later invited her closest girlfriend from China, Lu Wei Xing, to their home in Boston.

And he had been a rock for her when she struggled with her divorce over ten years ago.

While driving home that evening, she pulled out her cellphone to call Clancy at his home. She expected to hear his deep, melodious voice but instead got a message. It would be nice to tell him about her offer of a new job for the government without disclosing the details. She would love to be able to tell her father too; but that wouldn't happen. With cellphone to her ear, she heard the recorded message, "Hello, this is Clancy. I'm not home now but on my way to Sweden. I should be back in about two weeks."

Carrie was surprised that the man had already taken off again to tour the world.

That night she had trouble sleeping. There was too much anxiety with the sudden winds of change blowing into her life.

She had agreed to let Barbo know her decision before Monday morning. His last minute instructions were to text message him on his private cellphone with just one word, "Yes" or "No."

She tossed and turned under her bed sheets for hours. Finally she sat up and swung her legs over the side of the bed. Reaching for her cellphone, she pulled out the mini-keypad and scrolled down to Barbo's private cellphone number. She texted the single word, "Yes."

She fell back down in her bed and immediately drifted into a deep and satisfying sleep.

* * *

The next morning she received a text message back from the President thanking her for her decision and support. He also provided a special White House email address to which she was to forward her professional resume. She sent her curriculum vitae along with her most recently published articles on infectious diseases.

Later that morning, she received an email back with her curriculum vitae attached. The succinct message was from an unnamed member of the White House staff.

> This is a copy of your revised CV. The Registrar's office at Yale University has already changed its transcript files in case anyone privately investigates. An identical copy of this modified CV will

be sent to Mr Warren Lee. Please bring it to a breakfast meeting with Mr Lee on Tuesday at the Fenway Hotel. He has already been briefed on the President's recommendation that you join the project because of your professional credentials. Your meeting is scheduled for nine o'clock. From there, you'll be introduced to the new facility and will be driven home in the afternoon.

Carrie looked at the copy of the revised CV. Most of it was identical to her original copy except for a few critical lines. Where she had previously listed her minor at Yale as Chinese Studies, now her minor was Political Science. Her studying abroad in Beijing had been struck from the resume.

Her first reaction was that the changes should not have been made without her prior knowledge. But gradually she understood. She was now entering a new and completely different world. It was a world she hadn't known during her academic and research career. She had known espionage and subversive activity only through spy novels and over-the-top Hollywood movies. Carrie Bock was a scientist, not an actor, and certainly not a spy. As her new role became clearer, there was a sexy, intriguing fire that ignited deep within her. The rush of excitement took her mind away from her ailing father, her lonely celibate existence, and her beloved colleague's imminent retirement. The new assignment and its uncertainty displaced the painful thorns that had previously pierced her personal life.

She had a cunning smile as she printed a copy of the fraudulent CV on her desktop printer.

* * *

The Fenway Hotel was a historical and revered landmark in Boston. Located near Copley Square, it faced the oldest public library in the country. Carrie stepped from her taxi and walked onto the carpeted entrance. The restaurant was on the second level. When she approached the hostess, she was asked if she was Dr Carrie Bock.

"Yes. I'm meeting another party here this morning."

The hostess escorted her to a booth situated in the back of the restaurant, away from earshot of any other patrons.

Moments after Carrie sat down, Under Secretary of State Warren Lee approached her confidently and greeted her with a broad smile. He was impeccably dressed in a navy blue suit with a tangerine-colored silk handkerchief neatly stuffed into his jacket pocket. The handkerchief matched the color and material of his necktie.

The handsome Asian man spoke clearly while keeping his eyes riveted on hers. His charming smile was merely the welcome mat into his charismatic personality.

"Dr Bock, it is my pleasure to meet you. I understand you've been friends with President Bowa for over twenty years, and you come highly recommended to work on this project. The President has told me how happy he is with your decision to join our research team. After we have breakfast, my limo will take us to the Elliot House where you can tour the facility."

"Great, Warren, I'm looking forward to that," Carrie said with a confidence that equaled his.

"I understand that you might consider temporarily moving into the top floor apartment. That would be convenient. I know how often you scientists work late into the evening."

The waitress came to take their breakfast order.

"I'll have coffee and an English muffin," Carrie responded.

Warren studied the menu, folded it, and handed it back to the waitress.

"I'll have one egg over easy with a side order of smoked salmon and capers. And I would like a glass of tomato juice at room temperature, not chilled, with a slice of lemon. My toast will be wheat. And I would like a small pot of Oolong tea."

The Fenway Hotel waitress wrote down the detailed request, turned, and left.

This guy sure is meticulous in his wardrobe and as fussy with his food. What strikes me as odd are his eyes. Although he's Chinese, he has the double fold in his eyelids like a Westerner.

They ate quietly with intermittent talk about her research work at Tufts and of her cell biology grant work on communicable flu diseases. She told him how she also had experience studying other infectious diseases with several biotechnology companies in Boston and Cambridge.

Under Secretary Lee seemed keenly interested in her latest scientific work.

Later, inside the limo with the privacy glass separating them from the driver, Warren talked about specifics.

"I'm convinced that the Pakistani SAN terrorists already have the bioweapon, Carrie. We need to move on this as soon as possible. I have brought together some of the brightest minds with outstanding credentials to work on the project team. Today you'll meet Dr Ying Lan from Beijing and Dr Chen Jiang Hong, who has a high level position at the Centers for Disease Control and Prevention [CDC] in Atlanta."

In her role as someone ignorant of Chinese culture, Carrie asked, "I am confused. I thought their names were Lan Ying and James Chen?"

"Carrie, you are a sheltered academic," Warren replied. "In Mandarin and all the dialects as well, surnames are given before given names. Many but not all Chinese who come to the West reverse that order to avoid confusing Westerners and adopt a Western given name, as has Dr Chen."

The Under Secretary obviously enjoyed lecturing people, Carrie observed.

The limo driver took an exit from the Southeast Expressway and drove along country roads. Only a few houses interspersed stretches of thickly settled woods. The car pulled into a hidden driveway. At the entrance, a small sign read: The Elliot House, United States Government Educational Retreat Center. The car traveled along a forest lined, unpaved road that led up to a wrought-iron gate and fenced property.

At the gate, two US Marines, with automatic weapons hung from their shoulders, stood at the parade rest position. At the sight of the limo with its special license plate and official barcoded windshield sticker, they jumped to attention and saluted. One Marine waved the vehicle onto the Elliot House property.

Just inside the former retreat house was a security post set up in the expansive foyer. It looked like an airport security checkpoint. A conveyor belt was capable of moving packages, briefcases, and luggage under a scanner while two guards, one male and one female, wearing US Homeland Security uniforms, stood ready to conduct outer body searches. Each guard also had a sidearm pistol.

"Homeland Security guards are here 24/7. You'll have to go through this checkpoint every time you enter or leave the building," Warren told Carrie as they passed through the detector.

Warren led her down a staircase to the lower level. At the base of the stairs, they faced a steel door without windows. Warren looked up at a device that appeared to be an electronic scanner or camera.

"We have retinal scanners throughout the lab for access to sensitive or secure areas. Later, we'll scan your retinas, and get your personal pattern into our database."

Carrie was already familiar with that established access control technology. The infrared beam scanned the unique blood vessel pattern behind an individual's eyeball. If the vessel pattern matched those in the stored database, a computer program signaled the electronic solenoid in the door to open the lock. The access control technology had been around for years and now was also used for authority to log into computer systems in place of passwords.

Warren gave Carrie a brief tour of the lab. Her eyes panned everywhere as they strode along a well lit corridor lined with glass partitioned mini-labs on each side. About a dozen scientists dressed in knee length lab coats were working. Some were peering through microscopes; some monitoring electronic balances, bench top incubators, centrifuges, or mixers; and others working under ventilated chambers. Each lab section was immaculate, brightly lit, and equipped with state-of-the-art tools.

They arrived at a small alcove. Within this area, they faced another solid black metal door. The universal biohazard symbol was affixed to the door under the name, Dr Lan Ying.

Warren again cocked his head slightly to face a small camera, and the door opened.

They entered a large room that was set up like a laboratory office, with a few short workbenches equipped with computer monitors, keyboards, and desktop printers.

"Is this the brain center of the project?" she asked Warren.

"It is." He turned towards her. "And this is where you'll be spending most of your time."

A young Chinese man wearing a light blue lab coat approached them.

Warren spoke first.

"Carrie, I would like you to meet Dr James Chen. He's a Senior Associate on the bioagent development team and a very good friend of mine."

Carrie saw a warm smile light up the man's expression when she faced him. As he took her in with his eyes, she couldn't stop staring at the drop-dead, gorgeous man with bronzed complexion and wavy black hair. His pure white teeth seemed to glisten when he smiled.

While shaking her hand firmly, he maintained eye contact. His directness warmed her and simultaneously sent a lovely little shiver up her spine. It had been a long time since she had had an immediate physical reaction to something as simple as a smile and a handshake from a good-looking stranger.

"Carrie, I'm happy to meet you." He spoke in a soft voice without losing his smile. "And I'm delighted you've decided to work with us. I've already received a copy of your curriculum vitae. I'm impressed with your background at Tufts, Harvard, and Yale, three outstanding schools. I welcome you here and, please, call me Jim."

The man seemed to speak honestly to her, which made her feel as though he truly wanted her on the project team.

Maybe he's excited to have the additional help. If everyone here is like Dr Chen, my time could be professionally gratifying. Maybe even personally gratifying.

"Thank you, Jim. It's an honor to work with you and your esteemed team. My background is quite limited in the real world, but I'm proud of my academic work."

Warren looked nervously around the office. He became agitated.

"Where is Lan? Isn't she here today?" he asked.

"She left for New York to train staff for the initial field tests. She'll be back before noon."

A gradual smile softened Warren's expression.

"Field testing?"

"It's very preliminary. She's addressing the staff and their testing protocols," Jim added.

Warren seemed to ignore what Jim had told him. Instead, he arrogantly turned his attention back to Carrie.

"Listen, I've got to fly back to the Capitol tonight. I know you have to get settled in over the next few days. I'm sure Jim will get you acclimated and busy. You know that we must move speedily on this project."

Jim didn't comment.

"Carrie," Warren continued. "There'll be a car ready for you outside whenever you choose to return home. I'll call you soon to find out how you're getting along. At the gate, we have security personnel who will protect you and everyone else here at the Elliot House. And they'll use a wand to inspect you, and everyone else, each time you leave the grounds. They'll also request to look inside your pocketbook, briefcase, or any bags you carry with you."

"Warren, before you leave, is there any word on when Dr Marotsky will be coming on board?" Jim asked.

"Not yet. But continue with your work, and I'll worry about Marotsky."

Warren's condescending attitude was becoming evident. Jim's slightly sour expression suggested that there was no tight bond between the two men.

In the few hours Carrie had spent with the Under Secretary of State, she sensed there was a lot more to this complex man than appeared on the surface. She could now understand why Barbo felt uneasy with the "Asian wonder boy" spearheading this project.

Warren turned again towards her. A smile lit up his face, but it was an obligatory grin and not without his characteristic egotism.

"Carrie, I wish you the best with your assignment, and we expect good outcomes from your research."

Okay, Mr Lee. I have my assignment here for the research, all right. I'm researching you.

"Thanks, Warren," she replied with her own obligatory smile.

EIGHT

As soon as Warren left the office, Jim's warm smile returned.

"Come with me. Let me introduce you to the project team."

Jim did his best to make her feel at home by showing her where all the essential equipment was located and introducing her to the other scientists. They all had the title of Research Associate. The staff included researchers from university medical schools and commercial research laboratories.

Each researcher had agreed to the unusual but short-termed working conditions, for which they were paid extremely well. Except for Carrie, Jim, and Lan, each was given a piecemeal assignment to insure that they didn't see the whole project. They were told only that they were working on a super vaccine.

As she met with each, shook their hands, and heard their names, she immediately knew she was in the company of elite scientists. She had previously read some of their articles in professional journals. Their backgrounds and credentials in scientific research were impressive.

As Carrie followed Jim back into the main office, she noticed a room with the label "Cold Room" on the door.

"What's in the Cold Room? Is it for storing frozen specimens?"

"Yes. Let's go in, but I warn you, it's chilly."

He stepped by the door to face the eye scanner, and the door opened.

Inside the room, the temperature was forty degrees colder. There were several freezers, some vertical and some horizontal. The stainless steel units had large colored labels adhered to them. They were yellow, black, or white in color. There was a large, industrial ice-making machine at the focal point of the room. The model was similar to those found in hotels and restaurants.

"Carrie, we'll set up your retinal scan so you can come in here from time to time. There are only a few people who will have access to this room. That's you, Lan, Josef Marotsky, when he comes on board, and yours truly. You'll meet Lan later this afternoon."

"And when will I need to come in here?"

"You'll come in here for only two reasons. When the research assistants require human tissue samples to perform local tests, you'll collect the samples for them. We control the distribution of samples from the Caucasoid, Negroid, and Mongoloid freezers so they won't know which is which. Only the three of us will know which race they're testing. You'll log the data into this book. It will include the section of the human body the sample was from, the date, time, and from which freezer the specimen was taken."

"The yellow labeled freezer is for Mongoloid samples, black is for Negroid, and white for Caucasoid, right?" Carrie asked.

Jim grinned at her.

She grinned back. "I'm glad all my years of advanced academic study have paid off," she replied, continuing with the implied levity.

Carrie liked that he had a sense of humor. Working with him might be fun as well as rewarding. She already felt comfortable with her new boss.

"The second reason you'll be here is to assist when we produce the samples for testing. Right now our plan is to make the test samples in the form of ice cubes."

"Ice cubes?"

"Yes. One of the requirements is that the virus must sustain its deadly potency in water. If the virus must be water insoluble, it makes sense to use it in ice cube form. We have strict procedures set up to make the test batches. Ice cubes also make transporting easier, since we'll be doing our final testing in upstate New York. You'll witness this process later on."

Carrie asked a few technical questions before the two finally left the Cold Room to the warm air of the office.

Carrie caught herself staring at the striking man as he sat down at a workbench.

Jim's thick wavy hair made him appear even taller than his actual height of about five feet ten inches. His face was his most alluring feature. Everything changed when he smiled. He exuded warmth. His expression transformed into what any woman would call seductively handsome. His jaw line was strong with high, well defined cheekbones. His smile lit up his dark, bedroom eyes. She stopped staring when he turned to speak to her.

"I want to give you an overview of what we're doing and how we go about it. You may have already heard some of it, so bear with me."

She listened closely while he described their goal of discovering a vaccine to prevent any virus specifically targeted at one or all of the three major racial groups. He detailed how most of the preliminary research work would be performed on the computer by running simulation software. He told her how her job would be to fine tune the simulation algorithms based on a variety of synthetic and organic compounds.

Jim further explained how each workstation was equipped with knowledge based software, what once was commonly called "artificial intelligence." These programs with state-of-the-art graphics packages supported all DNA attributes and were linked dynamically to the Genome Database. He told her that most of the current software logic had come through the CDC.

"The good news is, I think that we've already identified a Mongoloid race profile," Jim announced.

"Really? Wait. You mean there really is a specific race gene?" she asked.

"Actually, no, there is no single race gene. What we did find were gene clusters specific to Mongoloid people. We were supposed to identify Caucasoid, Negroid, and Mongoloid racial traits in that specific order. But last week I decided to change the order. I did so because the Mongoloid race has more unique and frankly easier to identify traits. We converted those attributes to a software model, and it's loaded onto all of our workstations. Now we're exploring whether we can find a viral agent that will affect only Mongoloids while not affecting Caucasoids or Negroids."

"It sounds to me that using gene clusters to determine race puts a new meaning to racial profiling."

Jim chuckled. "You're right. It is racial profiling and perhaps is only about ninety percent accurate. But if those terrorists now hold a race specific bioagent, this seems to be the only way it can be done."

"What have you discovered about the Caucasoid and Negroid profiles?"

"Little so far. We believe that by isolating the unique Mongoloid profile, or rather a model of gene clusters for that race, models of the other two will follow closely behind. Then we can begin our real work, that of finding whether there is such a biological agent that's lethal to only the one race and not to the others."

"I was skeptical at first that racial genocide was possible, even though it has been bandied about for decades."

"Yes, in historical, darker times. Now ethnic cleansing using an engineered disease has surfaced again. Keep in mind that we want to ultimately create a shield, a vaccine, so that racial genocide can never become a reality."

Carrie's body shuddered at the thought, though as a scientist, it was exciting to be a part of a project to determine if such biological weaponry was feasible. If it was, she wanted to be on the team that discovered the vaccine.

"Are there other requirements of the agent?"

"Yes. Not only does the virus have to identify and infect people of a specific genetic profile, it must also be water insoluble, as I mentioned, and highly contagious."

"Why is that so necessary?"

"Warren has made that a basic requirement. His Beijing informants have told him that it is likely the terrorists will initiate an attack by delivering the agent to sparsely populated sections of a country. If, for example, vegetable or animal food sources were the delivery systems, they would simply be avoided after being discovered. Therefore, the virus has to be viable in water and contagious. After it's ingested by a critical mass in some location, it will become a highly transmittable and airborne pathogenic virus; infectious through physical contact, or coughing, or sneezing. Like any typical virus."

"Like the plague."

"Like the plague, which we know can easily infect and kill many people under the right conditions," Jim commented.

"Any guess as to how long it will take from initial onset to obliterating a race?"

"The PRC intelligence sources speculate the terrorists' bio-weapon could kill most people of the targeted race in multiple geographic areas within weeks. We speculate that water sources, like drinking reservoirs, lakes, and ponds, might be their targets for starting the epidemic."

"And the other races, immune to the virus, will remain alive and healthy," Carrie added.

As they both considered each other's comments, the office door opened.

A tall and slender Chinese woman walked into the office. The leather heels of her dress boots clicked in quick cadence with her confident stride. She appeared to be in her mid-thirties. She wore no makeup; nor did she need it. Her smooth golden skin was flawless. A clinging white scoop-necked jersey revealed full breasts, and tight, straight blue jeans revealed well shaped buttocks.

She smiled fleetingly as she walked towards Carrie with her hand extended.

"You must be Carrie. I'm Lan. Lan Ying. I'm happy to hear you'll be joining us on Project V."

Lan's handshake was firm, and the woman's dark, intrepid eyes seemed to pierce straight through to the back of Carrie's head. Like Warren, Lan's smile was forced. Carrie sensed that this woman was a driven, self-confident, and independent woman.

"Nice to meet you, Lan. I'm looking forward to working with you. And, I'm eager to get started."

Lan forced another smile.

Carrie continued to observe the Asian woman and was struck by her beauty. Lan's long, black hair was pulled back from her face and secured with tiny silver barrettes. Her face had a smooth, yet angular contour. Long lashes accented coal-black intriguing eyes. She wore no earrings, necklace, or bracelets. Her only accessory was a large multi-functional watch with a thick black leather band strapped to her delicate wrist.

"I'll catch up with you later, Carrie, but for now, I'm sure Jim will make you familiar with our work area."

Her spoken English, like Jim's, was articulate with a distinctly Asian accent. Her diction was enunciated as if she had been specially coached in an elocutionary class. Carrie sensed Lan's disinterest with social chit chat.

Maybe she's one of those techno-geek scientists. Or, perhaps she wasn't really happy to learn that a friend of the President had joined her on the top-secret project. In any event, I can see Lan Ying will be a personal challenge.

Lan glided over to the far lab bench. On her way, she pulled a lab smock from a coat hook and threw it around her, though she buttoned only the lower portion, apparently to continue showing her figure. She sat straight, with her chest out, in front of a workstation.

Carrie simply stared at the woman. Her moves and physical posture were intentional. It seemed she wanted Jim's attention.

Jim's smile again warmed Carrie.

"Okay, let's get you started. I want you to have that workstation over there," he said, nodding towards the desktop computer behind her. "There's a tutorial for the simulation program loaded onto the file server. After you take the tutorial, you'll be able to develop your own DNA models to modify and run preliminary tests. If something looks like it might become a race-specific agent, you'll test it out on the same programs with your data. If the results look promising, we'll have a prototype organism developed in the labs by our research associates. The research associates will then infect a tissue sample. If that looks promising in the incubator, we'll follow up by producing ice cube samples. That is the point in time when Lan will take the ice cubes for field testing."

"So Lan is always waiting on us for her testing?"

As soon as she asked the question, the Asian woman's head swiveled to face them.

"That's right, Carrie," Lan said with a raised voice. "I'm waiting to perform field testing. I'm also researching generalized vaccine programs to prevent the effectiveness of any race-specific germ. My part of the project is what we're all after, the vaccine. I'm leading the ultimate phase of the project." She turned back around to resume tapping on her keyboard.

Carrie felt Lan's tone was clearly defensive and sophomoric. She checked Jim's reaction. He looked mildly disturbed. He slowly inhaled and exhaled deeply before he spoke.

"Lan. Of course, thank you for sharing that."

Jim glanced over and smiled at Carrie. He gave her a sly wink aimed at the awkward situation.

There's definitely more to this Lan Ying chick. In the short time I've been here, I can already feel the polarized personalities and chilly politics that hang inside the Elliot House research lab.

NINE

Over the next few days, Carrie moved into an apartment on the top floor of the Elliot House. It certainly was smaller than her condominium, though adequate. A comfortable bedroom, a small living room, and kitchenette were all she would need for the duration.

She learned that there were several auxiliary staff who worked at the Elliot House. Most of them worked in the central dining facility while others worked in administrative offices. Breakfast and lunch were available every day, and upon request a chef would stay on to prepare dinner.

After Carrie had moved into her apartment, she discovered that the drive to the Holly Home, her father's Alzheimer facility, was closer to the Elliot House than was her home. She tried as usual to keep busy at night. She wound down her semester work at Tufts. She emailed her former chairman, Clancy Roche, to inform him she was now officially on sabbatical.

She routinely woke early for a morning run. As she jogged along, she marveled at the Elliot House grounds. It was obvious why the former retreat house was a perfect location for a top-secret research lab. The facility, located deep in the New England woods, hadn't been used by MIT for years. They sold it to the government to escape the costly maintenance for the infrequently used building and grounds. As she ran, she could see the beautiful tree-lined paths and walkways. There were over ten acres of property encircled by a high metal, obviously electrified, fence. A three-level parking garage adjacent to the main house had been built for attendees to the seminars and conferences in the past.

Completing her morning run, she walked into the Elliot House and was met by James Fontana, who served as the retreat center's manager.

"Dr Bock, this was hand delivered for you late last night."

The older gentleman handed her a plainly wrapped package. There was no writing on the outside.

"Thank you, James."

She jogged up the stairs rather than take the elevator. Inside her apartment, she opened the package after locking the door.

Inside the cardboard box were a purple-colored cellphone and a set of keys. She wondered if that was by coincidence or if he remembered; purple was her favorite color.

She unfolded a piece of paper and recognized the handwriting.

> Carbo,
>
> I wanted to give this to you personally, but couldn't find the time. I'm pleased and grateful you took on the assignment. The keys are to a little bonus for you signing on with me and the project. You will find the bonus in the Elliot House parking garage. I hope you like it. Also enclosed is a special cellphone. You should use it only to contact me. Any voice or texting gets scrambled on this phone and can't be intercepted.
>
> Please be careful on your assignment. I learned today from our own Intelligence mavens that there may be a covert connection from Project V directly to the Chinese PRC government. There might be a subversive agent working not only for the alliance but also for the PRC. And you know who I am concerned about. But I'm leaving it up to you to find out.
> Best of Luck and Thanks,
> Barbo
> P.S. Please destroy this note after reading.

She brought the handwritten note into the kitchenette and after reading it again, burned it—as ordered by the man she once would have done anything for and now apparently would again.

After showering and dressing, she ran outside and up the cement staircase to the parking garage. When she opened the metal door on the first level her eyes expanded on seeing her "sign-on bonus," a gift with a huge, purple flower taped onto it. Before her was a brand new Harley Davidson.

Barbo had remembered how she liked bikes. He didn't share her excitement at speeding along as he held onto her waist from the rear seat. But when they were young lovers, he always rode with her whenever she asked.

Back in those days, she often went for rides while he studied. After they broke off the relationship, she kept riding. But as the years wore on, through a broken marriage and a busy career, bike riding became neglected. In a way, she thought, it wasn't too different from her personal life. She made a mental note to change that while she lived at the Elliot House with her new job.

Unable to wait, she tore off the flower, jumped onto the vehicle, and was soon riding it around the grounds of the Elliot House. Unable to go at a high speed, she still enjoyed the comfort and feel of the new cycle. She planned to take it out on the road later in the day, perhaps when she visited her father at Holly Home.

The next few days flew by. Carrie spent most of her time and cerebral energy learning about the Genome Database, the computer application programs, and the routines of the research lab.

She made it a point to meet and socialize with the other research staff at lunch. They often took their meals on a large patio outside the first floor cafeteria. Some of the conversation was on topics relevant to molecular biophysics and biochemistry, viral diseases, and methods of testing organic specimens. When not sharing scholarly information, they chatted about the weather, the promises of the new Presidential administration, the Red Sox, and other social topics. The details of Project V's mission were never discussed. It was as if nobody knew what the others knew and didn't want to cross any lines. Carrie had learned long ago that scientists are often more interested in the process than the purpose of their research.

Jim joined her at lunch when he could. She soon learned he was a quiet man, though she had the distinct feeling that he had a lot to say.

On one sunny afternoon, they both happened to take a late lunch break and found themselves alone at a table on the patio. Carrie had a large salad in front of her, and Jim had a cheeseburger.

"I got some sad news from Warren, Carrie. Josef Marotsky won't be joining us. He didn't get the required security clearance to become Project Leader. Turns out his extended family still has some remote ties to the Moscow authorities. And the Feds feel that that isn't acceptable for a key position in Project V. So he's been redlined."

"That sucks. I was hoping to work with Marotsky."

"Warren has appointed me as the new Project Leader. There'll be an announcement."

"That's good for you! How do you feel about that?"

He shrugged his shoulder. After wiping his mouth with a napkin, he answered her question.

"The only thing I want is for this project to come to a quick end so I can return to the CDC. And I miss Atlanta."

"How long have you been with the CDC?"

"Ten years."

"Are your wife and family back there; back in Atlanta?" Carrie asked before forking a slice of cucumber into her mouth.

Jim now had a new smile, a different smile, in reaction to her personal question.

"No, Carrie, I have no children. I'm still officially married under Chinese law. However, my wife, who is still in China, has finally agreed to a divorce. Our marriage had been prearranged by our fathers, and because of our respect for them, we went ahead with the marriage. It's an old and outdated tradition, but we both went through with it. In effect, we have a non-marriage and divorce is imminent."

Oops! I stepped into it. Time to change subjects.

"So you're buried in your work at CDC as was I at Tufts. I guess when you're alone, that's the natural thing to do."

"But I really love my work there. At least at the CDC, I'm doing something I believe in. I can make things happen down there. It's much different than being recruited for a mission based on dubious intelligence, though I understand that we have no choice but to pursue a vaccine. And Warren is not exactly my dream boss."

That is the sort of thing I need to hear. These two men have some personal history.

"I met Warren. He seems intense, but I really don't know him yet. He said during our introduction that you two were good friends."

Jim pushed his plate away and reached for his iced tea. He took a swig before answering.

"That isn't really true. We were friends many years ago, but that's changed over time. Or should I say, Warren has changed."

The handsome Chinese American scientist stood up, which marked the end of the conversation.

But it was a good start. She would find out more about Warren as time went on. This was the opening that she had hoped would happen.

TEN

The next morning Lan was already at her workstation when Carrie walked into the office. Carrie noticed that Jim hadn't arrived yet, which was unusual.

They exchanged brief pleasantries as Carrie walked over to the counter to make a pot of coffee. She felt especially good after jogging around the Elliot House grounds for four miles in the warm June morning.

As she positioned the chromed coffee carafe under the percolating machine, she realized that the wide chrome band served as a mirror that reflected everything behind her. She could clearly see Lan sitting at her workbench. Her colleague wasn't facing her computer screen, but rather was staring directly at Carrie with a strange grin on her face and her eyes fixed on Carrie's every move.

When Carrie turned to say something, Lan swiftly turned to face the computer. She acted as though she had been riveted there. It was obvious that she didn't want Carrie to know that she had been staring.

Why was this woman staring at me? What's up with her? I wonder if she's suspicious of my joining the research team? She may suspect I'm here on a different mission than the rest of the scientists; or she may be pissed off because the President of the United States recommended that I come on board and that makes her nervous.

Just as Carrie carried her coffee to her workbench, Jim came into the office. His face had a disturbed expression.

He greeted both of them with little enthusiasm. Without a word, he shrugged out of his jacket and grabbed a lab coat. He walked directly toward his workstation and quietly focused on the computer screen.

Something was bothering him, but now was not the time to probe. Carrie returned to her job of developing and running software tests.

Later that morning, she saw Warren walk into the office with his arms outstretched as though he were on stage. He was singing in a melodious baritone voice.

The Under Secretary of State was singing a piece that seemed like an Italian opera. He outstretched his arms in theatrical fashion while bellowing out a beautiful aria.

Carrie glanced over to Lan. Her colleague now had a sparkling smile that showed she was enjoying the surprising intrusion. She panned over to Jim, who held only a stoic stare toward Warren.

When Warren finished singing, Lan applauded. She stood up and shouted "Bravo! Bravo!"

"Good morning, my friends, good morning! I feel great today and wanted to share with you an aria from Rossini's *La Cenerentola.*"

Carrie said, "Warren, I had no idea you had such a great operatic voice."

Absorbing the flattery, Warren simply grinned.

"There are many things you and your sponsor don't know about me. Singing opera is only one of them."

Carrie's smile faded.

It's funny he used the phrase "you and your sponsor" to allude to me and the President. Aren't we all working for the same boss here? Warren, maybe we don't know everything about you, but that's why I'm working in this lab, my friend. I intend to find out more about you than you could ever imagine.

"I don't have much time," Warren said. "Let's go into the conference room and discuss your progress."

As they took their seats around the small conference table, Carrie wondered about the protocol to these project status meetings. As the "newbie," she decided to sit back, listen, and observe.

Jim was the first to speak.

"We've made some excellent progress in the past two weeks, Warren. We've identified several genetic characteristics that are unique to the Mongoloid race. Although some are linked to physical attributes, such as hair texture and skin melanin, some are associated with the immune system. We're now running hemoglobin tests on

Mongoloid tissue samples this week. We should know more in a few days."

Warren's complexion seemed to change instantly from a soft bronze to an inflamed red. He breathed in and out deeply, which caused his nostrils to flare widely.

"The Mongoloid race? Jim, we agreed that the Mongoloid test would be the *last race* tested. You know the sequence of tests, first white, then black…. What…why the hell are you initially testing for agent yellow?" he demanded.

Warren's intense reaction filled the small room. His anger caught Carrie and Lan by surprise, and made them sit quietly like young school girls.

Jim didn't waver. He only stared coolly at the Under Secretary and paused before replying.

"Because Warren, along with my associates, I believed that it would be easier and faster to identify DNA attributes unique to the Mongoloids. And this will become our model to emulate when testing the Negroid and Caucasoid agents. When we successfully isolate genetic clusters for Mongoloids, we can mimic the procedures for the other races. In the end, it will expedite the whole project."

Carrie watched Warren stare at Jim without speaking. The dynamic exchange was intense.

Without an apology for the outburst, Warren turned to Lan. "If Jim's hypothesis is correct, you'll be doing field testing soon. Have you identified your subjects?"

"Yes. We have a test group already screened. They're being transported to upstate New York as we speak. I'm ready to test at a moment's notice. We have also finished constructing the special testing ward inside the Saratoga Prison Hospital."

Lan's response sounded much like that of a teacher's pet in her overly patronizing, syrupy tone.

"That's all positive news. I hope to meet with the three of you again next week." He turned to face Carrie.

"I trust that Carrie is getting used to the routines around here?"

She offered him a confident smile, though she mentally flinched at his juvenile use of the third person while sitting in front of him.

"I'm beginning to feel like I've been here for a year already. Jim is an excellent teacher."

Warren showed no reaction. It was as though she hadn't even spoken. He stood up to leave but Jim stopped him with a direct request. "I need to have a moment with you alone before you leave," he said in a low, serious tone.

Warren arched one eyebrow in surprise at Jim's request. "Sure, Jim. Let's stay while the ladies return to work."

Carrie sat in front of her computer running her software routines, though wondering what was taking place in the conference room. She assumed it had to do with Jim's new position as project leader.

Ten minutes later, the two men came out of the small room. Warren stormed out of the office without saying a word. Jim walked directly to his sport jacket hanging on the hook. He grabbed his cellphone from the pocket of the linen jacket. With phone in hand, he left the office.

Minutes later Carrie left for her lunch break. When she walked out to the patio, she found Jim sitting alone at a table. The tray on the table in front of him held only a bowl of chowder. Next to the tray was his cellphone.

Taking a deep breath, she slowly walked over to him. "Is it okay if I join you or would you rather be alone?"

"Please join me." His face softened.

"I didn't know if you were busy. You seemed preoccupied earlier."

Jim smiled. "You should try the clam chowder today. It's especially good."

She could see through the veiled façade.

Had he and Warren been discussing her? Is there a problem with the President's friend working on the Project V team? Or maybe some suspicions have surfaced about my real purpose. I had better tease that out sooner rather than later.

"I know that this is an intensive and important project. If I'm not up to your standards, I hope you will let me know. Is there anything you want to tell me?"

"No, no. You're doing very well. In fact, you're a tremendous help now that you're up to speed on how the system works. I'm happy you're working with us."

When his smiled deepened, she felt the surge of relief.

"Carrie, I apologize for my unsociable conduct earlier. It's that I got some disturbing news from China last night, and I had to let Warren know about it this morning. It's a bit complicated and this really isn't the place to discuss it."

"No, not if it's personal business. No need to explain."

"Yes and no. If you and others notice my behavior, it's a problem. Something is on my mind. And between you and me, I might have to leave the project temporarily and visit China for a while, unless Warren can intervene."

As Carrie picked at her dish of chilled pasta and pesto, she guessed it might have something to do with his getting a divorce. It wasn't a good subject to breach, even if part of her wanted to offer support. It wouldn't be appropriate, culturally or professionally. She searched for something to change topics. She noticed the owner's manual for her new Harley motorcycle sticking out through the top of her bag. She picked it up and waved the cover in front of Jim.

"Hey, Jim, here's my new toy. What do you think of it?"

He looked at the glossy photo of the Harley and chuckled. "I can't believe it! A fellow biker?"

"You too? Do you have a bike?"

"I have a Harley Fat Boy. It's my recreational therapy. I've been riding for years. What's your bike?"

"It's a Harley Springer, the new Softail model. I haven't even broken it in yet; just riding around the grounds a little. Where do you ride?"

"Everywhere. So you want to fire it up and see what it can do?" His voice bubbled for the first time with enthusiasm.

Who would have thought it? Two research scientists with a Harley connection? Maybe that's what attracted me to Jim. Even though most of the time he has been ultra-professional, I sensed there was something else at the core of this guy.

"Let's ride tonight," he suggested. "I'll show you a spot where you can open it up and the local cops don't patrol."

"I'm on. Just tell me where we can meet."

She shivered with a rush of joy at the idea of taking the bike out for a real ride.

"There's a Little League ball field about three miles straight down the main road. I'll meet you there by the chain linked backstop. Say, five thirty?"

"It's a date."

The words came out more quickly and a bit louder than she had planned.

Jim looked at her with his usual boyish grin curling up his lips. Carrie blushed as soon as she spoke. She had meant a bike-riding date, but Jim might have misconstrued it. Then she thought how silly she was reacting.

Hell, he knows what I meant. It's an agreement to go riding together. I'm overreacting. Forget it!

She wanted to say something to defuse the awkward moment. Before she could, another researcher approached their table wearing an extra large lab coat, snugly buttoned at his bulging waistline.

"Can I join you two for lunch on this beautiful first day of summer?" His deep guttural voice lightened the lingering tension.

She was looking at the world renowned geneticist, Dr Hans Hartmann, balancing a full tray of food.

"Yes, please join us, Hans. I forgot today is the summer solstice," she said. She pulled the empty chair away from the table to enable the wide-bodied Hans to slide into it.

"This is always a special night, according to myth and legend. You know what they say: anything can happen on the night of summer solstice!"

The scientist with the thick German accent let out one his infectious belly laughs.

* * *

Carrie rode her new bike out of the compound at five twenty that afternoon. She wore straight blue jeans tucked into calf-high leather boots and, because the afternoon was still hot, a snug navy blue cotton top.

She easily found the baseball field and spotted Jim sitting on his Harley Fat Boy. He too wore blue jeans, but with a black muscle shirt that showed off his well defined torso and arms.

He smiled at her when she pulled up next to him.

"We'll ride around the neighborhood for about ten minutes until we get to an abandoned airfield I discovered."

Jim slid on his electric blue helmet. Pulling the visor down, he waved for her to follow him.

Within ten minutes, they stopped at a wide abandoned airfield. Ahead of them was a narrow and neglected runway. Tall weeds poked through the cracked asphalt randomly, but most of the runway was still clear.

"This airfield hasn't been active since it was used to train pilots for the Korean War," he explained. "So, you've got a nice straight place to open up your new bike."

It was perfect. Her heart was already pounding with anticipation. Without a word, she turned her Harley Softail and sped away from him. Within seconds, she had opened up her bike to maximum speed. She loved the thrill of speeding along without concern for pedestrians or other traffic as the warm breeze flowed by her.

Deteriorating asphalt and taller weeds marked the end of the runway. She slowed down, turned the bike around, and sped back towards Jim. She repeated the routine twice with growing comfort in the bike's capability.

She finally pulled up in front of Jim still sitting on his bike. She took off her helmet and shook her hair from side to side.

"That was a treat. Thanks for showing me this place!"

He extended his arm and pointed to the west. "Look over there. Those woods lead up to the Blue Hills. The tallest peak is called Big Blue. Let's drive up there."

Soon they were speeding along the winding tree-lined road that would bring them to the apex of the Blue Hills.

They stopped at the pinnacle near a guardrail.

With helmets off, they both stared out over the terrain. The hills were densely populated with pines, hemlocks, and spruce trees that provided a variety of verdant colors. The view was breath taking. They stayed at the summit and appreciated the view of nature for some minutes without speaking a word.

Jim broke the silence. "I come up here often to unwind and clear my head. It's a great spot to do that."

"Yes. Peaceful," Carried added.

"I don't know about you, but I could go for a cold beer and a bite to eat. Follow me."

She followed his bike down the steep hill. Within minutes, he pulled up to a small tavern that was standing alone on the side of the country road. The blue neon sign, Dew Drop Inn, could barely be seen with the summer twilight approaching.

Jim led her inside to a small table in the far corner of the dimly lit bar. A few customers sat at the bar with their eyes glued to the overhead TV.

Over chilled draft beers, they talked about their bikes, places they had ridden, and where they dreamed to ride in the future. They also shared some personal topics on where their careers had taken them.

Jim made her feel comfortable—or perhaps it was the harmony of having much in common, including bikes. He was an intellectual equal, without the academic snobbery that often goes with it. Despite his aversion to secret research projects, he was the best person to lead Project V.

She liked the balance within the man. He was a bright, methodical, and patient scientist but still enjoyed the thrill of a speeding Harley between his legs.

She now wanted to get to know him more personally, a lot more personally.

ELEVEN

"Carrie, I wanted to come here so we could talk. I really meant what I told you at lunch today. You should know what's going on with me. And you should know what's going on with Warren and me. Especially if my mood shows any sign of change. It affects others, and I apologize for that. "

The purple cellphone rang inside of her hand bag. Carrie opened it up.

"Carbo, can you talk?"

She looked over at Jim. "Do you mind if I take this outside?"

Jim waved his hand in approval.

She paced around the gravel parking lot while the President spoke.

"Carbo, first I want to know how you're doing and then let you know, I just got some Intel you should know about."

"I'm doing fine. What is it?"

"Sources tell us that the SAN, the Pakistani terrorists, are getting anxious to take action. The word is that they're going to either test their bioweapon soon in some small remote place or deploy it widely. Some of our foreign intelligence analysts believe it will be aimed at India or China. Others speculate it could be the United States. I've talked with Homeland Security, and they won't raise the warning level until there's more concrete evidence. It would be a generalized warning of course; not one about a biological agent. That would cause a panic beyond imagination.

"I also wanted to know if Warren has shown any signs of dissention or disloyalty. I can have him taken off the project if you become suspicious of his motives."

"No, there's been none at all. Barbo, it's still too early. I'll work on that as fast as I can."

"Okay. I understand. Stay posted. Any questions?"

"Just one. What the hell are you doing using your Blackberry? I thought the Secret Service took it away from you!"

Her question was a playful tease.

"They'll have to pry this baby away from me. You know how stubborn I can be, Carbo! I have a new model. The Secret Service tells me it's supposed to be spy proof, so nobody can hack into it."

After she reentered the tavern, Carrie apologized for taking the call. When she saw that Jim looked okay with that, she resumed their conversation.

"I sensed the tension this morning. Warren had told me you two had known each other for many years. I thought you two were the best of friends."

Jim held her gaze.

"We've known each other for many years, yes. Best of friends, no. Let me give you some background. Warren and I met when we were undergraduate roommates at Stanford. We were both eighteen at the time, and I had come from Jinan in Shandong Province. Warren was from Baltimore. I needed to improve my English and learn American customs. So sharing a dorm room with him made a lot of sense. But during those four years, he changed from a warm, fun-loving person into a domineering jerk."

"He couldn't take the academic pressure?"

"No, that wasn't it at all. We both majored in microbiology during our early undergraduate days. For a time, we both intended becoming medical doctors. But he switched to international finance in his sophomore year."

"He went from microbiology to international finance?" Carrie chuckled. "That's one helluva switch. What happened? Did he hit the wall at organic chemistry, like so many students?"

"No. It wasn't the subject matter. It was Allison Wellington. She was a business major, and he wanted to be with her as much as he could. And as time went on, it was pretty little Allison and her family who changed him from the amiable, good friend into a driven, egotistical son-of-a bitch."

"Geez. How the hell did that happen?"

"He met Allison at a faculty-student party. After that, he couldn't get Ally out of his mind. They began dating, and by that summer the two spent every minute together."

Carrie shrugged. "Sounds like a nice love story."

"Yes, and it was. For the next few years, Ally and Warren were inseparable. They secretly rented an apartment in a Palo Alto suburb. That was unknown to her parents, because the Wellingtons would never have approved."

"They wanted their daughter's virginity to last through their tuition payments?" Her attempt at wit, with the hope of lightening things up a little, brought a sweet grin to Jim's face.

"No, it wasn't that. The Wellingtons apparently couldn't accept the thought of their daughter in bed with a Chinese man. It was too distasteful to them, according to what Warren later told me. They were the old school WASPs."

"And what happened?"

"One day, Warren came rushing into my dorm room. He wanted to show me the beautiful diamond engagement ring he had bought. He was going to give it to her on her birthday, on August first. Ally and I shared the same birthday, which is why I remember it."

"Did he give her the ring?"

He nodded. "And Ally loved it. But during that same summer, Ally left for an impromptu vacation to Europe with her parents. They toured the Mediterranean and Greek islands. While she was away, Warren didn't hear from her. Some weeks later, a messenger knocked on my dorm room door and delivered an envelope and a small box wrapped in plain, brown paper. The package was intended for Warren, so I contacted him. He came over and opened it in front of me."

"What was in it?"

"The letter from Ally told him how she had to break off their engagement. She planned to live in Europe for a few years. The box contained the engagement ring. He couldn't contact her because he didn't know where she was living."

"I'm guessing the parents either kept her in captivity against her will or they bought her off."

"I'm sure it was the latter. Warren hoped she would reconnect with him, and they would run away together. That never happened. Six months later, Ally's photo was in the New York Times Society page with the announcement that she was marrying a Scandinavian business tycoon."

"Wow, she couldn't have ever loved Warren if she fell in love so soon after the break-up."

"And that triggered the change in Warren. He went into a deep depression. His heartbreak was excruciating for others to watch. He had been used to always getting what he wanted. Now the woman he loved, that blond-haired, blue-eyed Allison Wellington, would never become his wife. When he finally came out of his depression, he had transformed into an intellectual bully. He was condescending to friends, had little social interaction, and became an outright racist."

The word resonated through Carrie's brain. "A racist?"

"He was outwardly anti-white and anti-black. All he talked about was the strength and wisdom of the Chinese people. He had become a bigot like the Wellingtons. For a while, he had nothing to do with white people or any person of color. On top of that, he would boast of how he was a pure descendent of the Tang Dynasty. He was extremely proud of his lineage and became quite boorish about it. Most of all, I lost respect for him because of the way he treated others. Warren was taking out his anger and heartbreak over Ally on any and all non-Chinese people. He had a fierce vengeance for the Wellington bigotry but adopted the same values for himself."

"I don't know the man, but it is hard to believe Warren was like that."

"Carrie, this happened many years ago. Later, I attended Johns Hopkins Medical School. He too was in a graduate school, but at the Kennedy School of Government at Harvard. When I later learned Warren interned for a US Senator in Washington, I truly believed he had changed. And he did. When we met again, he appeared to have changed for the better with no more of his hostility and racial anger. He had transformed again, this time into a polished politician, and he seemed to enjoy it. It also appeared that he had extinguished Ally from his mind. He later married Feng Lu, and they have two gorgeous children."

"That's quite a story. Thanks for sharing it."

"I wanted to let you know about the relationship I had with Warren and how it is now. I later left Baltimore and worked my way up to a senior position at the CDC. And truthfully, as I told you before, I can't wait to get back."

"Why did you come here? Why did you volunteer for Project V?"

Jim drained his mug of beer. "I'll get into that, but what do you say we split a small pizza? They're pretty good here."

"Sure. I'll have pepperoni."

Jim gave the bartender his order at the bar and returned with two more draft beers. He took a long draw from his glass and waited a few moments as though he were gathering his thoughts.

"I didn't volunteer to be on this project, Carrie."

She looked at him while trying to hide her confused expression.

"Warren recruited me. He knew I had a good reputation. He had read some of my published articles on vaccines and airborne pathogens. He contacted me a few months ago. He offered me more money than I would make in the next five years to come here and also the opportunity to do some top-secret microbiology research. I wasn't interested in the money, and, as I've mentioned, I was skeptical that *anyone* could develop such a weapon."

"But you came on board anyway."

"Because he offered me something I couldn't refuse."

"Which was?" She almost whispered her question as their heads dipped closer together.

"Warren knew that my younger brother, Jiang Ming, was in a detention prison in China. Jiang Ming is a journalism professor. He was always getting into trouble for his human rights articles and lectures. The government kept a tight leash on him and watched his every move. He had been one of only a few college professors who had the balls to stand up for human rights every chance he got. One day, Chinese secret agents audited his classes. After they heard the liberal philosophy that he espoused directly to students, he was arrested and sentenced to a labor camp. He's been in there for almost two years now. I can only contact him infrequently and only in covert ways. Given this situation, Warren made me a deal."

"What kind of deal?"

"Warren told me that he had close ties to several high-level Chinese authorities and could arrange to get Jiang Ming released. First I had to sign on with this project and successfully create a racially targeted virus in Phase I. Even though I usually create vaccines, I need to understand how these manufactured viruses behave to come up with the antidote or prophylaxis. He told me I needn't stay around for the development of the vaccine in Phase II. Lan and other colleagues would be responsible for that challenge. His thinking was that the creation of the racially specific virus was the more difficult part of the project, and he wanted me involved in that phase."

"And you agreed."

He nodded. "If I could develop the virus that attacked all three major races, he would convince the Beijing leaders to release my brother and let him come to America."

"Now you believe in the project and are confident that you can develop a racially selective set of viruses?"

"What I now believe is that we have no choice but to try with the greatest effort with which we are capable."

"I understand."

"So Warren and I agreed to the salary and the conditions, including a small house nearby. Once my phase of the project is completed, I am free to leave and my brother will be released immediately."

Carrie sipped her beer while taking in all that Jim had told her.

"You mentioned earlier something about a disturbing phone call last night," she prompted. "Is your brother all right?"

"Jiang Ming got access to a cellphone and called me last night. The officials told him he would be transferred to a facility in Wuhan. That prison is quite distant from Beijing. It's also much more violent, with many hardened and psychotic criminals; something that he's certainly not accustomed to. This morning I asked Warren to pull his political strings in Beijing. I want to keep Jiang Ming where he is until his release."

"And was Warren confident he could do that?"

"This time I have the leverage. He has to get them to agree. If not, I leave him hanging with this SinoAmerican allied bioweapon project. He knows I'm the best person to do this job. In fact, I think he's happy that Marotsky didn't get security clearance. He feels comfortable with me as Project Leader. He doesn't want to lose me as much as I don't want my brother transferred and possibly harmed."

"I appreciate you telling me all of this. Now I know a little more of what's going on, not only here, but also back in Beijing."

The bartender brought their steaming pizza. They didn't speak again until he left.

"This is one thing the northerners do right: pizza. I like it up here, but I still miss some southern dishes," he said.

Carrie pulled her own piece of pizza from the tray, stretching out the mozzarella cheese high into the air. "I like pizza, but I actually miss eating other things more. It's difficult when you're alone."

"Really? What do you miss eating because you live alone?"

"I miss most eating steamed clams and boiled lobster. But that's not something you order when you're alone, whether at a seafood restaurant or at home by yourself."

Jim had spoken candidly to her, without shifting his eyes as he talked. There was exceptional warmth in his low, soft voice and deep, ebony eyes.

"God, I hope things work out," she said, keeping her voice low. "I wouldn't want your younger brother to be sent to that awful prison."

"I couldn't really leave; the project is far too serious. It's probably one the highest priorities our country has now. And Warren has undoubtedly guessed that. But I made sure that he understood that I would go to his boss, or yours, to get action on this. That would not help his career, and he knows it. I gave him an ultimatum this morning." Jim's eyes were riveted to hers.

"Warren could bite that bullet and replace you."

He nodded, but then his expression softened a little.

"I wouldn't like that for many reasons," Jim said with a boyish grin.

"Such as?"

"You and I wouldn't have our next date."

He caught her off guard with his remark, and she felt a heat surge in her cheeks. She found his eyes, matched his grin, and then looked away.

She liked the way things were developing, but there certainly were complications. He was married, even though the relationship was a sham. And she was supposed to be concentrating on her assignment to secure intelligence on Warren, as well as performing her own work in the lab. Did she really have time to get involved with an affair? Her heart whispered the answer, but she tucked it away.

The bar became quiet.

"What about you? I know that the President recommended you, but why did you want to join the project? I bet you were content teaching and working on your own research grants. Who twisted your arm?"

The sports fans were starting to leave the tavern. The Red Sox game had ended, and the ten o'clock news was on the TV.

She began to formulate a response to his question. One that would certainly be a lie, but the volume increased on a TV news story that caught their attention. The news reporter had a distinctly Australian accent.

> ...and the residents of this tiny Pakistan island, Astola, are in shock with today's deaths. The German zoologists, eighteen in all, aboard the vessel *Stuttgart*, were found dead before they could begin research on the island's famous Hawksbill Turtles. Initial reports indicate that the European scientists may have died from a highly contagious virus. Except for the ship's docking crew, who were all Pakistanis, the only survivors were the cook and lab assistant. The Pakistan government has ordered an immediate quarantine and an investigation into what might be a widespread medical threat.

Jim looked at Carrie. They both became quiet after hearing the surprising news from Pakistan.

Carrie reflected on her earlier call with the President. His sources may have been right. This event could have been the first test of the genocidal virus.

"We had better get going," she said.

* * *

She and Jim parted on the highway close to the hidden driveway that led into Elliot House property. After parking her bike, she ran up the stairs to her apartment.

In her bedroom, she stripped off her clothes to prepare for bed, washed up, and put on a pair of boxer shorts and a T-shirt. A quick glance at her laptop told her that she had email.

Sitting at her computer, she opened the message from her friend living in Beijing, Wei Xing.

It was an upbeat message covering trips Wei Xing had taken. She hoped to visit Carrie again in the United States in the following spring. She still enjoyed her career within the Ministry of Education. Wei Xing was leading a project to develop educational software for Chinese citizens to learn English and other foreign languages more easily.

It was obvious from the email that Wei Xing was happy. Perhaps it was a similar happiness that Carrie was feeling that night.

She replied to the email and included a description of Jim, how they worked together, his love for motorcycles, and his sense of humor. As she continued tapping on the keys, she realized that she hadn't told her best friend that Jim was also her boss. She also failed to tell her that he was married. She sighed loudly and sat back in her desk chair to think.

What the hell am I doing? I'm fantasizing about Jim actually being the new man in my life. This is foolish thinking. With any luck, the two of us could be friends, bike buddies and that's all.

She deleted all of the text that she had entered and replaced it with an upbeat response to Wei Xing's news.

After closing down her computer and putting out the desk lamp, she looked out through the window at the moonlit night. Silvery clouds gracefully drifted in front of the brightly lit, late June moon. As she stared up at the celestial body, she reflected how good she felt being with her new friend. Although Jim was married, she wouldn't, or couldn't, deny her own natural feelings.

As she turned her bedcover down, she smiled at the recollection of what the jolly Dr Hans Hartmann had said to her earlier in the day with his infectious belly laugh. "Anything can happen on the night of summer solstice!"

TWELVE

Early the next morning, her purple cellphone vibrated with a text message.

She opened it.

Call me at 3:00 pm today. Barbo.

She stopped at the dining hall for a quick bowl of cereal. While eating, she picked up a copy of the Boston Globe. Her eyes focused on the Associated Press article describing the mysterious and fatal illness on the island of Astola. The tiny island population was now quarantined by the Pakistani government. The article emphasized how Islamabad officials want to be sure that there was no chance of a virus epidemic. They were still frightened by the earlier threats of the mysterious influenza A virus subtype H1N1, the so-called "swine flu."

In between spoonfuls of shredded wheat, she learned that the island, only a mile and a half long, is notable for its exotic flora and fauna. It had essentially been left uncontaminated by human intrusions for centuries. The island boasted the largest population of Hawksbill Turtles, which were extinct in most other parts of the world. The reporter underscored how the deaths of the German zoological researchers had drawn worldwide attention to both the mysterious tragedy and the island.

After reading the article, she headed downstairs to the lab office and settled into her work.

Despite her best intentions to remain cool, her heartbeat increased when Dr Jim Chen walked through the doorway. His quiet smile made her blush slightly. Still alone, there was an opportunity to exchange pleasantries a little longer than usual that morning.

"I guess Lan is coming in late today." She glanced over at the woman's empty workstation. "She's usually in by now."

"Actually, she won't be in today. In fact, she'll be out for a couple of days. I had a voice mail from her when I got home. She's gone to Saratoga again to train her staff on more testing procedures."

Carrie's mind shifted into high gear. With Lan gone, she would have an opportunity to learn more about the mysterious ice woman and the field tests.

"Jim, I need to ask you a few things," she said.

"Sure, but let me first get a cup of tea. It makes me much more civil in the mornings." He spoke while sifting through notes left for him from the other research staff.

After preparing his hot tea, he pulled his bench seat up very close to her chair.

"What's on your mind? Do you have questions about the software?"

"No. Actually, I'm really curious about Lan Ying, and I want your opinion. I appreciate focused concentration, but this woman hardly speaks a freakin' word when we're working together. She can go all day without saying a thing. I've tried some small talk with her, but she simply replies with curt comments. And she never shows any side to her personality. Is she always like that or is it since I joined Project V?"

Jim smiled and then sipped his tea. "The short answer is no. It's not you. She's always like that. She's very distant and cool with everyone. She came here from China soon after I arrived. I assumed Lan was also handpicked by Warren, like everyone else. I didn't ask any questions. All I can tell you is, she's a very quiet person. Even when she joins people for lunch, she rarely makes small talk."

"Is she married?"

"No."

"Where doe she live?"

"She lives in Cambridge. I'm not sure where. I think Warren set her up with an apartment."

"Are they seeing each other?"

Jim smiled as her rapid-fire inquisition.

"No, I believe Warren is faithful to his wife."

"Don't you find it difficult working with her? I mean, with her unnerving silence?"

"Americans are often uneasy with quiet people. Asians are accustomed to that behavior. Some Chinese people feel their loyalty and time are supposed to be dedicated to the mission at hand. I know it's a bit old fashioned, but perhaps Lan was brought up that way."

She watched as Jim reached into his brief case and produced a zip-locked bag. He opened the bag and offered its contents to her.

"For you," he said. "I baked these last night."

She stared at him and took a cookie. "Last night? You mean after you got home from that pizza tavern?"

Jim slid off of his chair and positioned it in front of his workstation.

"I couldn't sleep," he said, "so I baked."

"Oh," she replied, feeling her face flush again.

She felt an awkward silence fill the room but smiled when she visualized Jim bustling around a kitchen baking cookies.

The silent office air came to life with the echoing of Warren's loud, melodious voice. He was approaching their office singing another aria. This time she recognized the aria. It was from *Madame Butterfly*. As he stepped into the office, his singing continued.

Carrie was prepared for the bizarre interruption this time. Warren nodded only to Jim and pointed toward the conference room, without skipping an operatic note. He walked behind Jim while singing the final bar of his song.

By Warren's buoyant mood, she felt confident there must be positive news about Jim's incarcerated brother.

A few minutes later, they both came out of the room.

Carrie noticed a definite look of relief on Jim's face, which created a pleasurable wave of empathy inside her.

Now it was Warren's turn to pull up a chair and sit down next to her.

"And how's our American scientist doing this morning?" he said in a smug tone.

"I'm fine, Warren, especially after such fine entertainment from our Under Secretary of State!"

He chuckled. "It's not professional, but it's a gift from my Tang dynasty relatives."

Though she was quite sure where he was going with this, she politely asked, "Oh, how so?"

"Carrie, the Tang people, my ancestors, were a very special lot. They introduced many innovations to the Chinese people. Not only did they create inventions and advanced technologies, but they also were well educated in the arts. Each generation encouraged children to take up an artistic skill. These people studied all over the world and produced some of the best artists, singers, and musicians who ever walked the earth. Since I'm a direct descendant of the Tang bloodline, I'm blessed with these artistic skills in my genetic make-up."

She deliberately kept her feigned, interested expression while she reflected on what Jim had told her last night. She now saw that Warren's racial pride, and perhaps his prejudice, were still present. She wondered if that pride still carried the anti-white and anti-black attitudes that he once held. She thought how the background and purpose of this project was too convenient for someone with a racial bias.

"That's good to know. Are there any other talents that I haven't seen?"

"We Tang people are full of extraordinary talents. We all have leadership, strength, intelligence, and courage. You don't know about my personal achievements, but not only was I a decorated F-16 pilot, I later created my own computer networking company on the west coast. It was my startup company that helped launch wireless networking that all of us use today. You see my bloodline has been good to me and it's helped the United States in some small degree. Ah, but enough about me. Is Dr Ying in the office today?"

Jim answered, "No. Lan left for Saratoga this morning. She's refining her testing procedures. We think she'll be doing some field testing in a few days. We sent her up with a preliminary batch of agent yellow."

"Yes, you're testing for the Mongoloids first. I still find it disappointing that clear directions weren't followed. At least field testing is a positive sign of progress." His mouth spread into a thin line. He shrugged, saying, "I'm off to Washington again. My boss, Zachary Hinton, beckons me once more. I wish I could fly my own jet back and forth. It would save a hell of a lot of time."

Turning to leave, he looked back. "Did either of you hear about the mysterious virus incident on Pakistan's Astola Island?"

"Yes. I read about it in the Globe this morning," Carrie answered.

"Let's hope that that wasn't some local testing done by the SAN. If it was, you can expect to be working around the clock on Project V."

Warren left the office, his singing again echoing down the hallway.

Jim shrugged his shoulders without any comment to Warren's statement.

"Aren't you going to do it?" Jim asked her.

"Do what?"

"Try my cookies. I baked them just for you."

She blinked, a little surprised at his personal admission.

For me? That feels nice and different simply having someone do something for me. That rarely happened during my first marriage. And up until now, it hasn't happened since.

She bit into the cookie and found it filled with dark, bittersweet chocolate chips. She purposefully moaned with pleasure, which put a grin on Jim's face.

THIRTEEN

Jim gave her a slight wave and left the office area to meet with the other research staff. Carrie continued processing data at her workstation while thinking about what Jim had told her about Lan Ying. She understood the loyal, quiet discipline after having witnessed it herself while a student in Beijing. And now she felt relieved the woman's anti-social behavior wasn't aimed at her.

When Jim returned an hour later, Carrie stopped him before he got into his own work.

"Will you take a look at this? I'm running into some kind of problem with my simulation program. Maybe there's something I'm missing in the DNA software data files."

He sat at her computer and scrutinized the data displayed in cryptic format only a computer programmer could decipher. After scrolling back and forth for about five minutes, he chuckled out loud.

"Is there something funny you found with my protocol program?" Carrie said, with some defensive sarcasm.

"No. But you definitely found something. You found a latent bug in the software linkage routine."

"Really? Are you sure?"

"I'm absolutely sure. And not only did you isolate the faulty software logic, but you also showed me something that I hadn't tried before. I think your simulation using these particular synthetic compounds is interesting. This new algorithm coupled with this particular chain of organic cells can be promising."

"Thanks."

She felt an immediate glow from his heartfelt praise. It was a welcomed boost to her confidence in her work on the project.

"But how do we get the software bug fixed?"

"I'll call it into the CDC. They authored this program. It should be an easy fix, and I can download it to our file server as soon as they have the patch."

"Good, I'll alert the others that maybe we can prepare for tissue testing soon."

"You're doing good work, Carrie." He paused. "Now I have an important question for you."

She stared at him. Her heartbeats quickened.

"Sure. What is it?"

"How does second row behind the dugout sound?"

"Excuse me?"

Was this some sort of secret code? Had she missed something? Or is it some joke the man is trying to tell me?

"I managed to get my hands on two box seat tickets in the second row behind the Red Sox dugout for tonight. Would you like to go with me?"

She smiled, blushed, and blurted out shamelessly, "Are you kidding? Yes, I'll go to Fenway Park with you."

"Why don't we leave here from work and get a bite to eat before the game."

"I didn't ask earlier, but I take it Warren had some good news about your brother?"

"Yes. Warren contacted his Beijing connections and made arrangements for Jiang Ming to stay in the same detention facility until his release."

"So you'll be staying?"

"Of course, I'm staying."

She looked at him with a simple reply. "Good."

She glanced up at the digital clock and noticed it was almost three o'clock.

"I'm going outside for some air. I'll be back shortly."

* * *

"Barbo! I hope you can talk. I got your instructions."

"Yeah, I've got a little time. First, how are you settling in up there?"

"Great! It's all good. I've got nothing for you yet on Warren, but he is definitely an interesting character. He has still not met with the Beijing contingency since I've been here, but I'm sure there will be some meetings soon."

"I was disappointed that Dr Josef Marotsky wasn't cleared to be Project Leader. He had some ties to the Russians that our intelligence officers didn't like. Top-secret security clearances can be tough to get at times. I understand that there is another Chinese man assuming his role."

Carrie sensed the President's discomfort with more Asian participation on the project.

"He's Chinese American, Barbo. Jim Chen is a senior research scientist at the CDC in Atlanta. I think he's a good choice."

"Okay. Is there any indication that Warren knows about your background in Chinese studies at Yale and your living in Beijing years ago?"

"No. He seems to be a person filled with himself. There's no room to bother with anyone else."

"Hmm. What about the feasibility of the bioagent? Anything on that?"

"Much too early for that, Barbo."

"I'm still getting sketchy reports on that event on Astola Island in Pakistan. Do you think there's any connection with those researchers who died and what you're working on?"

"I don't know. Warren seemed concerned about that also. Hey, I have a thought. Can your intelligence guys get me a photo of the crew of the *Stuttgart* before they died?"

"I'll look into it. If so, I'll have my staff email it to you."

"I wanted to ask you something else. Did you know about the actual subject testing for Project V being done at Saratoga State Prison?"

There was a long pause before any response.

"Carrie, there are some things the President should *not* know."

"Oh."

I'm in a whole different league here. I've still got a lot to learn in this fucking cloak and dagger game. This is going to be one helluva challenge to tell the President about some things but not about others.

"Carbo, if ever you want out of this, let me know. I realize this role is very different from academia, but as I told you, I need you on the project and very pleased you're there. I've got to get going. Use the purple phone whenever necessary."

* * *

The night game ended early at Fenway Park. It turned out to be a pitcher's duel with the Red Sox coming out on top 2 to 1. Since it was still early, there was time for a cab trip to Boston's North End, which was famous for its Italian cuisine. They planned on coffee and dessert.

Jim ordered a rum-soaked pound cake to have with their cappuccino. As they sat in a corner of the dimly lit restaurant, Carrie steered the discussion back to their work.

"You know what really bothers me? I don't understand why you, and now me, are working on developing the viral agent, while Lan is charged with testing our samples before working on a vaccine formula. Doesn't that bother you?"

"I'm not sure I follow you."

"Why doesn't Warren have all three of us working as a team? You know, with all of us trying to first create the lethal virus and then testing it. We, all three of us, could move forward as a team to develop the vaccine for the infectious bioagent."

"I'll be honest, Carrie. I don't spend much time thinking about Warren's overall strategy of the project. I'm focused on what I have to do. Don't forget, I reluctantly joined Project V. If it weren't for the deal to release my brother, I wouldn't be here at all. From the day I started, I've focused all my energy on developing a racially discriminating virus. The sooner I discover it, the sooner Jiang Ming becomes free. Then I can return to the CDC and get on with my life. It's as simple as that."

"I understand that now. But looking at it from a distance, some things don't seem right to me. Also, it seems Warren has Lan reporting to him almost on an equal and separate line from you."

"I assume it's because it might take some time for Lan to develop the vaccine in Phase II. That'll begin after I've left the project. And don't forget, she also does all the dirty work, the field testing up at the prison hospital."

"But where are the checks and validation procedures? How do we know what she does when conducting her tests? How do we know she's administered the tests correctly? How do we know where she is on developing a vaccine?" Carrie paused. "In other words, Jim, how the fuck do we know what Lan *is* doing?"

Jim laughed at her mini-tirade. He seemed entertained with her fiery emotion and her unique style of asking rapid-fire questions.

"She really gets to you, doesn't she?"

Carrie took time to bite into the rum cake. "Yeah." She smiled back at him. "I guess it's because I'm close to another Chinese woman who lives twelve thousand miles away. Her name is Wei Xing. She's open with me about everything, as I am with her. Now I'm working twelve feet away from another woman who, by comparison, seems robotic and impersonal."

"I really don't have the answers for you," he said.

"Have you ever accompanied Lan to the test site?"

"No. Soon we'll begin scheduling real-life testing."

"Do you ever think about the people, you know, the subjects who will be used for the testing?"

Jim put his head down for a moment as though hesitant to answer her probing question. He finally looked up.

"Yes, I do think about the subjects. I can't dwell on it because it's something I'm morally against. Considering what we're developing, there is no other option. We'll never know if what we create in the lab kills humans until it actually kills humans."

"Do you know where the subjects will come from?"

"I know that they are volunteer prisoners transferred to Saratoga Prison Hospital after being screened. They're all convicted criminals facing the death penalty for horrendous crimes. They come from prisons across the country. Most are multiple offenders. They're serial murderers, rapists, pedophiles, terrorists, and the like. Many of them want to die, to escape the wait, I suppose."

"Do they know what they're facing when they arrive at Saratoga?"

"They only know that they're participating in a medical research project. They have been made aware of the risk of sickness and possibly death. If they survive, they have an option of being reassigned to a different secure prison or to return to their originating lockup."

"How is the testing of the subjects organized?" Carrie asked before sipping her cappuccino.

"One part of the subject population consists of ethnically pure Asians, pure Whites, and pure Blacks, as we know them today; or subjects who clearly have dominant gene clusters for that race. You've heard of the expression DNA 'junk.' We bypass the 'junk' part and look for predominance of genetic clusters. Obviously this applies to dominant and not recessive genes that may have mutated through generations."

"...which could prove that once upon a time we were all one original race but over millions of years have had cell mutations to adapt to our regional environments."

Jim simply nodded and continued with his description of the testing process.

"The other part of the subject population consists of mixed races of all kinds.

"During the screening process, all subjects are validated for DNA identity and screened for infections. That takes a few days. If a subject qualifies, he or she is transferred to the new, secure testing ward within the prison hospital. After Lan arrives, she'll administer, along with her staff assistants, the bioagent to the subjects. This will be done with the test subject drinking a beverage with our ice cubes floating in a liquid. She'll wait for the outcome and record her findings."

There was a long silence as the waiter brought them complimentary cordial glasses filled with Sambuca and the traditional three coffee beans added for "Good Luck."

After the waiter left, Jim's eyes focused sharply on a middle-aged man who sat at the bar sipping a cup of espresso. He was alone and reading a copy of the Boston Herald. He wore a light gray suit with an opened dress shirt over his large, athletic build. He was about fifty years old, with a thick head of curly brown hair. There was a distinctive, thin facial scar that stretched from earlobe to chin flawing his well-tanned complexion. Such a scar when caused by a sword was called a "Heidelberg scar" and was once considered a badge of honor among fencers.

Carrie caught Jim staring at the stranger.

"What is it? Do you know that man at the bar?"

"No, but I recognize him from the ballpark earlier tonight. Do you remember when that foul ball flew over our heads? I turned to see where it landed. That man was sitting in the row behind us. It struck me as odd that a man would wear a business suit and dress shoes to a ball game. I figured then that he had come in from a day's work at his office. Now he's at the same restaurant in the North End as us, and that bothers me."

"Do you think we're being followed?" Carrie asked in a whisper.

Jim looked into her eyes then smiled. He shook his head in the negative.

"No, I doubt it. It must be coincidental. Besides who in hell would want to follow us?"

His answer was convincing to Carrie.

They each sipped the cordial and savored its licorice-like flavor. No other words were spoken as they enjoyed quietly glancing at each other.

Then Carrie did something that surprised even her. She instinctively reached out and gently grabbed Jim's wrist and held it. His skin felt pleasantly soft and warm to her touch. It felt good to touch another human, especially him. He made her feel good, and she hoped he felt the same.

"Look, Jim, I don't mean to put a damper on such a nice evening with all my questions. I enjoyed the baseball game. And coming here afterwards was special. I want you to know how much I enjoyed tonight."

Jim smiled back at her while turning his hand in hers and gently squeezing her fingers.

"I enjoyed tonight, too. I enjoyed it because I shared it with you. To be completely honest, I didn't care if the Sox won or lost. Either way, I would've still been happy."

The tender moment hung between them as they finished the last of their cordial. As they approached the door to leave the restaurant, the maitre de offered to call a taxi for them.

While they stood outside the Italian restaurant watching couples of all ages strolling about, Jim took her arm and gently pulled her closer to him. "Carrie," his voice was soft, "let's have the cab driver drop me off first before bringing you back to the Elliot House."

Her heart immediately sank. She thought how he must be protective of his personal reputation as a married man. Being seen in public with another woman could damage his reputation and whatever was left of his marriage.

"Of course."

After stepping into the back seat of the Boston Yellow cab, the silence had changed the atmosphere.

"I wanted to protect..."

"I completely understand," she interrupted. "You're a married man; and if people who know you saw you escort me back to the Elliot House, there could be rumors. The security people, the house staff, or whoever we might bump into. I totally understand your decision."

Jim reached out and gently squeezed her hand in his. He spoke to her in a soft whisper.

"No, that's *not* why I suggested this. It's *you* I want to protect. You are still a personal friend of the President of the United States. If any rumors started, it's your reputation that would be damaged. I told you I have a non-marriage, and that I'm asking for a divorce. I couldn't care less about what people said or thought about me. It's you who I'm concerned about. And I certainly don't want to derail our relationship. I don't want it to die on the vine, but rather to see it grow to fullness."

Nobody had paid attention to them getting into the cab and leaving the historic district with its quaint, narrow streets, except for one person. He was the scar-faced man who stood in a nearby alley and watched their every move.

Carrie silently looked at the man beside her, the man who had exposed his heart, the man who was so full of surprises. The smooth skin of his high cheekbones intermittently reflected the overhead streetlights and neon signs along Boston's historic Hanover Street.

When the cab made sharp turns through the narrow streets, she wanted to fall into his coal-black eyes. His hand gripped hers more tightly when he leaned towards her.

Slowly she closed her eyes and waited for the moment his lips would touch hers. When she felt his mouth on hers, she tasted a hint of the sweet liquor. With the essence of coffee and moistness of his lips, her heartbeat accelerated. She felt a stirring deep inside her that she hadn't felt for a very long time.

For some reason, this man moved her like no other had.

The gentle kiss ended much too soon and left her wanting more. As Jim pulled away, she raised her hand behind his neck to bring him back towards her. This time she leaned in to initiate the kiss and pressed her mouth on his, hungry for him. She felt his arms wrap around her and pull her body closer to his own. She teased his lips with the tip of her tongue, which soon penetrated and tasted him with a flicking against his tongue and inner mouth.

When they finally broke apart, she leaned her head against his shoulder. They didn't speak until the cab slowed to a stop outside of Jim's house.

Before she could say good night, he brought his finger to her lips, removed it, and brushed his lips against hers. He then slid out of the rear seat and was soon headed up his walkway and unlocking his front door.

As the cab turned around, Carrie contemplated what had just happened.

They had crossed a line, certainly, and she would have to deal with it sometime. But not tonight. Tonight she gave herself permission to simply enjoy the moment, put off the analysis of what was happening between her and her married project boss, at least until tomorrow.

* * *

Back inside her apartment, she noticed her desk phone blinking with a voice message. She pressed the button to listen while she brushed her teeth inside the bathroom. She immediately recognized Wei Xing's voice.

> Hey, Girlfriend! We have to talk! I'm tired of keying in text and not being able to chat. Give me a call when you can. I hope you're doing well. Love you always, Wei Xing.

After hearing her voice, Carrie recalled how she and Wei Xing hadn't drifted apart. It was something they promised each other not to do. But recently her father's illness, her teaching job, and now this top-secret research project had all but consumed her. She owed a lot to her Beijing girlfriend. Wei Xing had helped Carrie meet her academic goals while a twenty-year old student in China. She helped her become immersed in the Chinese culture and language by hanging out with her everyday.

Later in bed, Carrie reflected on the year and a half she had spent in Beijing. Her friend took her to the theater, lectures, Beijing opera, and the local markets in various villages outside of the city. They played tennis, jogged, drank wine, and bathed nude together in some luxurious sulphur-water baths inside beautiful spas. They shared their most intimate thoughts and personal hopes for the future.

Although Carrie's academic training at Yale was extensive, Wei Xing picked up for Carrie where the classroom training had ended. The two young women had begun a routine still carried out to this day. Carrie would speak Mandarin to Wei Xing and Wei Xing would speak English to her. Carrie became proficient in the Chinese language, including mastering its tonal reflections. When she spoke on the telephone, Beijing natives mistook her for a young Chinese woman.

As she drifted off to sleep, she made a mental commitment to reply to her long-distance, best friend's message soon.

The next morning, Carrie was surprised to see Jim already working in the office at eight thirty, about half an hour earlier than his usual arrival time.

"How is Carrie on this beautiful summer morning?" he asked with a beaming smile.

"Wonderful. And you?"

"I'm fine. And how was your evening?"

"Last night? It wasn't bad. And yours?" A smirk filled her face.

He walked towards her, stood within inches, and stared into her eyes. "Last night was one of the best nights I've ever had in my life!"

She stifled a giggle before responding.

"Really now? And why was last night so good for you?"

"I tasted the best rum-soaked cake I've ever had in my entire life!"

The look in his eyes was smoldering with passion, and she knew he wasn't thinking about last night's dessert. She smiled at his subtle joke and punched him lightly in his stomach.

"Yeah, that was the highlight of my evening too," she replied.

Jim's face took on a more serious look as he sat down next to her. "Look, I downloaded the software fix from CDC late last night. If you could, I would like you to resume the protocol testing you were conducting yesterday. I really believe you're on to something with your algorithm. Your creative formula might bring us closer to discovering a viral agent."

"Sure. I saved my programming routines on the file server, so it'll be easy to pick up where I left off."

"I have to leave the office for a few hours. There's an old colleague of mine visiting Boston from his native Sweden. I'm not really into those social, 'good ol' buddy things, but he's a guy I worked with on an epidemiology project briefly in Europe. We plan to have lunch together. You have my cellphone number if you need to contact me."

"Okay, I'll see you after lunch."

Carrie logged onto the lab network to continue her simulation testing. The arrival of an intranet email from Washington was signaled by a small pop-up message. Carrie opened the email and then an attachment to the email. Before Jim left the office, she called him over.

"Jim, take a look at this. I asked around if I could get a copy of a photo of the crew aboard the research vessel *The Stuttgart*."

"You mean those German researchers who died off of Pakistan? What's it look like?"

Carrie tilted her screen so Jim could see the photo. Each man's smiling image was tagged with their name and project title.

"Look, they were zoologists, paleontologists, and marine biologists according to the labels on the photo. With two exceptions, the tall, lanky man standing in the back row and that short guy sitting in the front row. The tags for them show that one was a cook and the other an assistant. The tall man is obviously black and the shorter man Asian. Among the exploration team, they were the only survivors of the mysterious virus that plagued the ship. The victims were all white men and women. They were all Caucasians."

"Shit! This is not good, Carrie, not good at all. We've got to let Warren know. Be prepared. You and I will soon see the urgency of Project V escalate as soon as he hears this information."

She was surprised at Jim's reaction. It was the first time that he had shown any anxiety about the research project since they had met. He placed his hands gently on her shoulders, though still with a serious look on his face. He then handed her a large manila envelope, clasped and taped closed.

"Here, I want you to have this."

Carrie hesitantly took the large envelope from him.

"Carrie, after I leave, please open this and follow the instructions that I've outlined inside. It's very important to me."

Still not understanding what was going on, she managed a slight smile.

"Sure, Jim. I'll follow your directions. You needn't worry."

His face lit up with his boyish grin, the one that sent her knees quivering. His hands gently squeezed her shoulders in a gesture of affection.

She watched as he rose, grabbed his brief case, and left the office.

Carrie stood alone still holding the sealed envelope.

What instructions could he possibly have inside? I know how to run the simulation testing. Was there something else he was going to teach me? Was there something more sensitive about the project that I didn't know?

She put her emotions aside, dropped into her professional persona, and faced her computer screen. Tapping on her keyboard, she re-launched her previous simulation tests. After initiating the programs, she walked over to the side counter and poured herself a cup of coffee. She couldn't delay the mystery any longer. It was time to open the mysterious envelope. Returning to her bench chair, she picked up the envelope and cut it open with a pair of scissors.

The tips of her fingers pulled out a folded piece of paper with computer printed text on it.

She glanced at the top of the paper. The first line made her heart beat faster. The text read:

"Dr Carrie Bock—For Your Eyes Only" was printed in large, bold letters. Underneath was the mandate: "Follow these sequential instructions. It is important."

Alone in the office, she read the instructions aloud: "One. You are to leave the Elliot House at 6:00 pm today. Two. You must wear comfortable clothes. Three. After leaving the gate, head towards Route 158 South. Four. Continue for three miles and then turn left onto Timber Lane. Five. Turn at the third right onto Rockwood Ave. Six. Pull into the opened garage at 98 Rockwood Ave. Seven. Enter the house. Eight. Be prepared! Be prepared to have a clambake of steamers and baked lobster."

Carrie couldn't contain herself from letting out a spontaneous burst of laughter. She read the text over again, this time in silence. She now understood this man. Along with his intelligence and dry wit, she now appreciated his sensitivity and sense of humorous surprise. He had actually been listening when she told him that steamed clams and lobster were the things she missed the most living a solitary life.

She returned to her technical tasks, but now with a lightness and joyful anticipation. Excitement built within her about how their next date at his house might turn out.

FOURTEEN

The rest of the day crept by for Carrie even though she kept busy running her simulation tests. She created a series of genetic engineering algorithms for the tests.

Without Jim or Lan around, the office was quiet. Although focused on the simulation tests, she wished someone was there to share her excitement.

From the printed test results, she saw how the simulated virus invaded and attached itself to only those organic cells with Mongoloid characteristics. Using the "lock and key" paradigm, the lock opened only when it found a match with the programmed genetic codes. The virus then attached to the cells of the Mongoloid host. For cells from people of the other racial groups, the simulated virus would not attach.

Her heart beat stronger and faster. She read the computer copy over several times to make certain she hadn't overlooked something. She took in a deep breath and exhaled audibly.

It now struck her that she may have developed a racially targeted influenza algorithm.

She folded the computer report and placed it inside a hidden compartment in her handbag to take to Jim's house that evening. If she wanted to show Jim the indisputable proof of her findings, she would have to sneak it past the security guards. After putting away her files, she signed off from her workstation and soon skipped up the stairs to her apartment.

After showering, she called down to the kitchen and asked for the kitchen staff to have a bottle of chilled Chardonnay put aside. She didn't want to go to Jim's house empty-handed.

She slipped on a pair of navy blue shorts and a short sleeved, white eyelet top with a deep V-neck front. She looked in the mirror as she brushed her hair. Was she ready for this? It certainly felt like the next step in their relationship. She shivered a little as she wondered exactly what might happen between them.

While brushing her naturally highlighted, auburn hair and looking into the mirror, Jim's words echoed in her mind: "a non-marriage, with divorce imminent." Could she believe that enough to be with this man?

At the security station in the foyer, the guard waved the metal detector wand around her and then checked her handbag. When the man noticed the bottle of wine and personal objects inside, he smiled and waved her past.

Following Jim's directions, she easily found the way to his modest house. She drove her Harley into the opened garage as instructed.

Jim was standing at the door waiting for her. He looked handsome and casual in white linen shorts and a dark blue, silk Hawaiian shirt.

He kissed her gently on the cheek and took the bottle of wine from her. He gave her a brief tour of his three bedroom, Cape Cod-styled house. It was decorated in a Spartan manner, with minimal color and function overshadowing fashion. She stepped out onto the rear deck. There she found a candle lit dining table. Soft music played in the background through outdoor speakers.

They sat and chatted for a while over a glass of wine. Jim told her of his friend's reunion and their luncheon meeting.

"Sounds like you had a good day, Jim. But I think I had an even better one."

His face lit up. "Your simulation algorithm?"

She returned his smile and excitedly told him everything. She detailed how she had set up several simulation tests that produced the surprisingly positive results.

"You seem surprised. You developed the formula, why shouldn't it work?" He assured her it was the most encouraging report since Project V had begun.

"I brought the computer reports with me." She reached down and pulled the folded pages out of her handbag.

"How the hell did you get them out of the Elliot House?"

"Look!" She opened her handbag wide and pointed to a slit in the liner. "I have a secret compartment. I folded the pages and hid them inside. Besides, the guards are so used to me by now that their security shakedown is very cursory when I leave."

Jim's eyes scanned the data on each page. A broad smile lit up his face.

"God, Carrie. This is so exciting! If the lab's tissue tests come back with these anticipated results, we can conduct our first real field test."

"But *Lan* will conduct the first test," she corrected him with an exaggerated tone to her voice.

Jim smiled at her. "Enough about work. Let's get our dinner prepared."

As the twilight sky faded to black, they ate their steamed clams and baked stuffed lobster dinner on the deck. They purposely avoided more shop talk. They shared their personal histories, including places they had visited around the globe, different jobs they had held, and family stories.

The summer night was warm, but a slight breeze made it comfortable. They finished one bottle of Chardonnay and started a second one when Jim suggested they go inside.

In the living room, they put their wine glasses on the coffee table and sat down on the couch close together.

"I missed being with you today," he whispered softly in her ear as he threaded his fingers through her hair.

His touch immediately warmed her. As she turned her head to speak, Jim's lips met hers. At first the kiss was gentle but became more intense with tongues erotically dueling. Their pent up sexual hunger instantly became unleashed.

Carrie felt a natural heat surge within her as her hands slipped up under his silk shirt. Her palms felt his hard and flat chest. Her fingers could feel his rapidly beating heart.

Rolling her body toward him to be closer, she felt his hand glide smoothly up her leg into her loose shorts.

She could feel his strong hand gently kneading her soft flesh with a slow, heated rhythm. Their kiss deepened and became more passionate as her breathing became more rapid and excited.

More than anything, she wanted more. She needed more of this amazing man. She stood up and pulled him up from the sofa. Within minutes they were in his bedroom frantically helping each other out of their clothing.

Her fingers trembled as she struggled with the buttons on his shirt, with wanting to see more of him, to feel more of his skin. She pulled off her top and bra. She quickly stepped out of her shorts and panties and stood completely nude ready to fall into his arms.

As Jim lay down on the bed, he said, "Wait. Let me look at you."

His eyes caressed every inch of her, admired her breasts, and lusted at the juncture between her thighs. They panned back up to her sparkling blue eyes and glossy auburn hair. His shifting eyes teased her and made her tingle with sensual anticipation. She liked that he was looking, really looking at her. Finally, he spoke. "Come, come to me."

She fell beside him and soon they hungrily kissed and explored each other's bodies wantonly, unashamedly. As he kissed her breasts, she reached down to feel his desire and grasped him gently. Her hand moved lightly up and down with her fingers playing on his most responsive and sensitive areas.

They were both completely aroused. She pulled him on top so he could glide into her. She wanted him inside her, for him to feel her warm, moist welcome.

Soon every inch of his manhood was thrusting into her. And with each thrust, she felt something grow. She sensed a rapturous wave within her building slowly at first and then cresting and causing her to shudder in ecstasy. Another wave followed, and another. The sounds of pure passion were reignited deep inside of her. Repressed within her for so long, it now flooded out in uncontrolled moans and cries.

She grabbed his buttocks and squeezed hard as another wave climbed up and cascaded throughout her body. As she moaned in gratification, she felt Jim's release. His throbbing triggered one more incredible, delicious shudder throughout her body.

Then it was quiet. Everything stood peacefully still. Not an ounce of pent up tension was left within her. She felt light, as though she were floating outside of her body. While her labored breathing slowed, her whole being became completely relaxed. It had never been like this for her before.

They both lay still while staring up at the spinning ceiling fan. No words seemed appropriate, or necessary. She smiled, completely satiated. While her breathing normalized, she felt herself drifting into a welcomed sleep.

The morning sunlight peeked into the bedroom through the eastern window, and Carrie slowly opened her eyes. It took a moment for her to get her bearings. It was then that her eyes identified the shiny glass face of Jim's wristwatch on the nearby dresser. With a variety emotions, she recalled the prior evening, from the delightful dinner to the erotic lovemaking. She smiled to herself as she rolled her body onto one side.

Where was he? She was surprised that Jim wasn't still next to her. Immediately missing his warmth, she sat up while modestly covering her breasts with the bed sheet.

"Jim, are you still here?"

"No. I ran away. I'm not here anymore," he replied from somewhere outside of the bedroom.

"Get your cute little butt back in here," she commanded with a giggle.

Jim, dressed in a hunter-green silk robe, entered the bedroom carrying a bed tray with steaming cups of aromatic coffee and what smelled like freshly baked croissants.

"I thought you might like this."

"You, kind sir, are a man after my own heart."

He sat down on the bed and placed the stand up tray on top of the bed sheet. They enjoyed their light breakfast in bed, with bites of the pastry between soft intermittent kisses.

When they finished, Carrie showered and got dressed while Jim scanned the morning paper.

"Jim, I don't want to wait until our research assistants come in on Monday to test the tissue samples. If we think we're onto something here, we should get started as soon as possible. Besides with this Astola story, there is going to be much more pressure on us to get some results soon."

Jim nodded and put aside his newspaper. "I'll meet you at the lab in an hour."

* * *

After changing her clothes, Carrie stepped out of her apartment and jogged down the stairs to the bottom floor. When she met Jim inside the lab, he had already taken tissues and frozen sections from the yellow, black, and white freezers. She watched as he methodically set up the electronic microscope for them to conduct the next series of tests. These tests wouldn't be simulated. They would be done on real human tissue from Whites, Blacks, and Asians. They hoped to see different results, with only the Mongoloid tissues showing a viral attack and subsequent infection from the agent while the other specimens remained unaffected.

After a quick lunch, they returned to the glass incubators to observe the early results. The preliminary tissue tests showed that they were on the right course of action.

It had been a wonderfully successful day.

Later, while cleaning their desk areas, Lan burst into the office. She couldn't hide her surprise at finding the two of them in the office on a Saturday afternoon.

"Hello, Lan. How did the site visit go?" Jim casually asked.

She walked over to her workstation without a word and then turned to face both of them. Her frown told the tale.

"The testing crew made a few procedural mistakes that I corrected immediately. They have to be more thorough in their preparations for the subjects. It was progress, nonetheless."

Jim nodded. "How did the segregation process go?"

"We have that pretty well set. I have the African American staff working as a team, the Chinese working as a team, and the Caucasians working as a team. They have no clue as to why, but I'll control which team gets the bioagent. I need to insure that they're not handling the lethal agent targeted for their own race. If we don't segregate them, they'll become infected from the subjects and they too will die."

Jim continued the interrogation. "And the Saratoga hospital wards are sealed off, correct?"

"Yes, Jim," Lan answered coldly. "But we can't test any subjects until you provide me with the lethal virus. I won't return to Saratoga again until I have the frozen agent to test my killing the prisoner subjects."

A cold, steely bolt of energy shot down Carrie's spine. The phrase "my killing the prisoner subjects" rolled off of Lan's lips as if she looked forward to watching the men and women die before her eyes.

"And that could happen soon, Lan," Jim said. "We, or rather Carrie, has discovered something that's very promising. There was a bug in the software when we produced that last local test here in the lab. But now everything is working, and the new agent looks promising. That's why we're in here today performing some tissue tests. If things look good on Monday morning, you'll be making the trip back up to Saratoga soon."

"Not a problem, but I think the drive to Saratoga takes too fucking long. I hope we can get access to a helicopter to shuttle me back and forth from the Elliot House. It would be much more efficient since I'll be doing lots more tests in the near future."

It was evident to Jim and Carrie that the Asian scientist actually enjoyed her role in running the field tests on human subjects.

The thought sickened Carrie, and she remembered Jim's own ethical reservations about the morality of the tests. But he was right. There was no other option for final testing of a killer virus.

"Let me know when you have it, and I'll pack for my return to Saratoga."

She picked up a few folders and walked over to the office supply cabinet. She withdrew something small from a box on the shelf, dropped it into her handbag, and closed the cabinet door.

Lan managed a smile as she looked over at Carrie.

"I came in here to pick up a few things. See you two on Monday morning," Lan said, apparently anxious to leave for the remainder of the weekend.

After Lan left, Jim took a few steps closer to Carrie.

"Can I see you again tonight?"

"Yes."

"Can you come by about seven? We'll do burgers on the grill with a salad."

"Perfect." As she turned with the hope that he would kiss her, a bellowing operatic voice echoed in the hallway. She stepped away from Jim as Warren came through the office door with his usual over-the-top theatrical entrance.

He finished the last few bars of his aria in dramatic fashion. "I bumped into Lan in the hallway. She told me you would be here," he said.

"We thought we would get a jump on next week's testing," Carrie said.

Warren looked at Jim and smiled.

"I hope you're not working our President's friend too hard, Jim. She's only been here a few weeks and already you've got her coming in on a Saturday."

"It was my idea, actually," she interjected. "The sooner we get this done, the sooner we can all get on with our real professional lives." She hadn't quite meant the words to come out as they did.

Warren's eyebrow arched and then relaxed.

"Carrie, you know you can move on anytime you want to. Remember it was President Bowa who wanted you assigned to Project V."

Great. Lift foot. Insert into mouth. It's time for me to backpedal.

"I understand that, Warren. And I do want to be here. What I meant was that we all know it's a temporary project, and therefore we would all like to speed it up."

"Most definitely," Jim chimed in to support her.

Warren, in his self-centered way, seemed to ignore the response.

"I'm going to be staying overnight tonight, Carrie, and I wondered if you'd like to meet me for dinner in the dining room."

"I would love to Warren, but I'm going to visit my dad tonight and won't be staying here."

Her quick thinking and response was not overlooked by Jim.

"Why don't we meet for breakfast on Monday morning? I have a conference call with some of the Beijing people at nine. How about we meet at eight?"

"Yes. Breakfast on Monday morning would be great. I'll meet you in the dining room at eight."

"You two have a good day, or at least what's left of this fine weekend." He smiled at the two of them. "And remember to have some fun. All work and no play. You know the rest."

After Warren left, a relaxed silence filled the office.

Carrie threw a few things into her briefcase and let out an audible sigh.

Her emotional ambivalence concerning her role in the project was returning. The directive from the President was to be his "mole" on Project V. To do that, she would have to spend time with Warren so she could report what he was up to with their Chinese allies. Then she must determine whether the ambitious young man was truly loyal to the goals of Project V and to the United States. But now she was also committed completely to the stated goals of the project.

Carrie felt a tension headache coming on. She walked to the office supply closet when she remembered that she had seen a bottle of Tylenol on the top shelf. While she dropped two tablets into her hand, she saw a box of 256 GB flash drives on a lower shelf. There were nearly three dozen drives. Outside the box was a taped handwritten label: "Lan's flash drives, DO NOT TAKE!"

So that's what Lan took out of the closet earlier. Why the hell does she need so many? Each drive could back up a large computer's contents, including both created files and programs. And we all back up our files centrally to the Project V server. Nobody could get a disk out of here with the security checks at the foyer and the front gate. She must store it somewhere, and apparently she does this on a routine basis.

After closing the cabinet door, she turned and looked into her lover's shining eyes. She immediately forgot about the mystery woman, the human subjects at Saratoga, and the incredibly egotistical Warren.

"I'll be at your house at six o'clock, not seven. Have a Dewar's Scotch on the rocks ready for me. And I'll have cheese on that burger," she said.

He was surprised at her outburst but still laughed at her direct and controlling tone.

* * *

Upstairs in her apartment, Carrie packed an overnight bag with cosmetics. She would drive over to see her father for a brief visit before heading to Jim's house. She prepared to leave the Elliot House grounds about 4:30. The sun was still high in the sky, which kept the afternoon temperature still hovering around ninety degrees on the Saturday afternoon. After being checked at the front gate, she adjusted her helmet and drove her motorcycle along the serpentine driveway leading out to the main road. The driveway, hidden by dense forest and vegetation, seemed particularly tranquil on this late June day.

After pulling onto the main country road, she accelerated to hear the powerful sound of her Harley unwinding.

Another sound, almost an echo, came from behind her. She glanced in her rear view mirror and spotted another speeding motorcycle behind her. There were no cars on the road. The bike must have been doing more than seventy as it came closer.

Within a few minutes, the bike caught up with her Harley Softail and pulled alongside.

She identified the motorcycle as one of the best money could buy. It was a high end, loaded BMW R 1200 RT. The road machine was popular for its high powered and efficient engine and its well appointed leather and chrome exterior. The driver's handlebars were elevated to a high position, and the bike's fuel tank had a hand painted yellow lightning bolt. The empty rider's rear seat was elevated a few inches. This model had minimal chrome and a sleek, black body.

Carrie couldn't identify the tall driver. The rider's helmet had a full pull down, sun glare visor with a dark, smoky-gray tint. It hid the driver's face completely. The mystery driver kept pace with her, while occasionally looking over at her. With a loose fitting, black jacket, blue jeans, leather boots and gloves, she couldn't determine whether the driver was male or female.

When she glanced over, the driver simply nodded at her. Just before accelerating, the biker gave the universal thumbs up sign and sped away. The sudden, mysterious encounter left her with an uneasiness in the pit of her stomach.

FIFTEEN

On Monday morning, Carrie picked up the New York Times inside the dining room. She checked her watch before sitting down at one of the cloth-covered tables.

A waiter served her a cup of hot coffee.

Scanning the paper, her eyes caught a catchy headline. She read an article in which the journalist attacked the new President, Bartholomew Bowa, for being condescending and seemingly aloof with the national press and reporters. The article compared his presidential style with that of his predecessor, who had held frequent press conferences despite their disagreeable content.

While holding the newspaper in front of her face, she soon sensed there was someone staring at her. Lowering her newspaper to the dining table, she looked up and saw the Under Secretary of State smiling.

"Warren! Good Morning. Please sit down."

After some small talk and ordering their breakfast selections, Warren started right in with his agenda.

"I trust you're getting along well with Jim Chen and Lan Ying."

"Hell, yes. No problems so far. And with Hans and the other researchers, you've assembled quite a research team. The list of names on this project reads like the 'Who's Who' of the Scientific American magazine."

She knew her syrupy patronizing would set the tone for an amiable discussion.

"Yes. I agree. I think we have the best minds working on this, and I'm personally pleased to be leading the group. And we are improving our alliance with Beijing with this top-secret, bilateral effort. It might be one of the most important events in the history of SinoAmerican relationships."

Not wanting to hear more of his hubris, Carrie let the statement go without commenting. She decided to change the subject.

"I enjoy your singing. I didn't know I would get such an entertainment bonus while working here."

The man chuckled at the flattery. "It's not professional, but I've enjoyed singing since I was in high school. Enough about me. Are you feeling more confident these days about meeting our goals *soon* on the project?"

His emphasis on time was noted.

"It's much too early to say, but I'm more open to the feasibility. The SAN could indeed have something. I would never have guessed that a military strategy for genocide could be based on a virus combined with racial profiling."

"Carrie, this concept is not new; only the technology is more capable. You should do some research into the history of this strategy. The concept was explored many years ago during World War II. It in fact gained significant momentum in the 1940s."

"It did? I've not read anything about that."

"Not many people have. It was top-secret information at the time, and only a few aspects of the project are declassified even today."

"You mean we have access to Hitler's secret strategies and we still haven't published them?"

Warren shot a condescending eye at the attractive woman and personal friend of the President.

"It wasn't *Hitler's* idea to develop a racially targeted bioweapon."

"Oh? Who was the author of such of novel and depraved idea?"

"It was the United States of America. The government leaders, including a select group from Congress, wanted to develop such a weapon. Their objective was to bring the war to a quick and climatic end, even if millions of innocent people died in the process."

Carrie's hands immediately went limp and lifeless. She nearly dropped her coffee cup.

"I don't believe it. We, the United States, wanted to create a genocidal bioweapon during World War II?"

"Yes. It's quite an interesting story that most Americans haven't heard about. It was kept secret for a very long time. Even now, it's not discussed freely except in prestigious academic and political science journals. I understand some professor has a book coming out soon on the story. The bioweapon was targeted at Asians, in particular the Japanese."

"Who was working on that project?" she asked, still surprised at Warren's revelation.

"Back in those days, there was no such thing as the Central Intelligence Agency. Its predecessor, known as the US Office of Strategic Services, or OSS, had formed a team of expert scientists. They convened secretly, much like I've done with Project V here. The team was made up mostly of anthropologists, with some medical doctors, research scientists like you, and so on. They all worked intensely on the project for quite some time. There were a few conscientious dissidents who dropped out at the beginning, though most could separate their professional research from the morality of the project, as scientists must always do."

Carrie looked into the Under Secretary's gray eyes. She rewound her mental tape to replay his words. Was there a message for her in there?

"Yes, as we scientists must always do," she parroted back with a mimic of Warren's tone.

They both stopped talking when the waiter arrived with their food. Neither was as interested in the food as their conversation.

Warren continued. "They looked at everything. The anthropologists examined anatomical and cultural characteristics unique to that racial sub-group. It was rumored, but never proven, that the popular anthropologist, Margaret Mead, was also consulted by the OSS on this project."

"They brought in the heavy hitters?"

"Yes, but they had no clear plan. They studied Japanese hygiene, diet, physical traits, and social characteristics that might lead to some weakness unique to that group of people. The US had thoughts of contaminating their rice paddies so that the disease would spread as part of the daily Japanese diet."

"That is astounding! But with all of those bright people, they still couldn't create a weapon."

"True, but don't blame the researchers. The top-secret project was aborted. Don't forget it was another group of research scientists who abruptly ended the war with the Japanese. The Manhattan Project gave us the atomic bomb and that was readily available."

She considered what he had said, her mind reflecting on the catastrophic bombings in Hiroshima and Nagasaki.

"I guess the thinking was that if we couldn't find a virus to kill them off we could bomb the shit out of them," Carrie commented.

"That's why the project ended. Today we have—as does every nation—access to the Human Genome Database, in addition to highly advanced technical knowledge of DNA, cell biology, and biophysics. That's something that was unavailable during World War II. Current technology has apparently made truly selective weaponry possible."

"But weaponry that can only be aimed at a major racial group with a selected pedigree of gene clusters," Carrie corrected.

"Yes, for now. We can always adjust and refine as we progress in the new field of biological weaponry. There's no limit to what can be done as the algorithms that you and Jim develop get fine-tuned over the years."

What he just said is interesting and perhaps has some technical merit. If a biological weapon can be refined and fine-tuned, it might be able to target only a subset of cultures, like blue eyed, red headed Irish, or only men of Middle Eastern genetic characteristics. This fucking weapon is the most heinous concept ever conceived by mankind. And I'm on the leading edge of developing it!

"I believe that the American leaders have matured in their perceptions of other ethnic cultures and today would never dream of abusing prisoners or others because of their race as they did with the Japanese."

"Really? Tell that to the Guantanamo Bay detainees."

God, this guy is intense! And it's not clear which flag he salutes every day.

"According to President Bowa, your Chinese sources reported that the Pakistani terrorist group already has the weapon."

Warren leaned back in his chair before he spoke.

"Yes, through me, the United States has been told by Beijing that such a bioweapon is either ready or nearly ready for deployment. We still don't know the exact status of it. And that mysterious incident that took place on Astola is very troublesome. That may have been one of their live testing efforts. What is equally troubling is that we still don't know the delivery system they'll use. If the SAN terrorists have the agent, they could use missile launchers to spread airborne pathogens. If the agent doesn't dissolve in water, they might choose to contaminate drinking sources or other consumables. There are many ways it could be delivered."

"I know all that from Jim. What is daunting is not only the work in Phase I, that of developing the viral agent, but also the work in Phase II, that of finding the preventive vaccine or antidote. I've got to tell you, I still think it's quite a bold undertaking."

"Yes, but Lan will become more focused on Phase II. For now, you and Jim must be concerned with developing or duplicating the agent now held by the terrorists."

She wanted to raise her concerns about Lan working on that final phase by herself, but thought it best not to raise adversarial issues at this time.

"It still sounds to me as incredibly ambitious," she said. And trying to put a positive spin on their conversation, she added, "though, as I said, I am much more open now to the possibility."

A soft cellphone tone came from inside Warren's suit jacket.

"Excuse me, Carrie, I'll step away. Please finish your meal."

Warren walked away from the table, but the phone conversation could be heard easily with the echo in the empty dining hall.

The Under Secretary spoke in Mandarin apparently in the belief that he couldn't be understood.

Carrie mentally translated every word of his side of the spirited conversation while she continued eating.

Warren paced as he talked.

"I know, I know. I understand. It was a decision the scientists made without me involved. They chose agent yellow first because they told me it was easier," Warren's tone was defensive.

There was a pause before he continued.

"I am sorry. But this sequence will help us develop the agent black and agent white viruses sooner."

He became silent again while listening to what seemed to be an angry voice on the other end of the communication.

"Yes, yes, I can guarantee it!" Warren spoke into the phone.

The bold statement caused Carrie to nearly choke on a piece of toast.

This was followed with another period of silence. Warren continued pacing around the dining room without saying a word. He quietly listened to his caller. As he stepped in undefined circles, he moved further away from Carrie's table, which made it more difficult to hear and to translate the discussion spoken in Mandarin. She heard some words and phrases that made some sense.

"...yes, I remember discussing that...I can work on that. I return to Washington tomorrow and will see Zachary Hinton. Yes, he is the man. I can handle it. Yes, yes, I will get back to you by the end of the week."

Warren folded up his cellphone with a loud snap and returned to the table. His expression spoke of his preoccupation with a problem.

"I hope your eggs aren't cold," Carrie said, in between sipping her coffee.

"That's all right. I got a call from my contacts in Beijing. We have to move on this project. They got more intelligence reports. My informant told me those Germans who died aboard the vessel, *The Stuttgart*, were victims of a real test of the SAN's new biological weapon. Now we know the terrorists' agent works."

Carrie looked over at the man as he methodically used his fork to tatter the poached eggs on his plate.

She reflected on the photo of the smiling faces of *The Stuttgart's* crew.

Yes, but if that is true, we know that the SAN bioweapon works only on white people. Or at least it works only on white people for now.

SIXTEEN

"Looks like you're going to be left alone again today," Jim said after she entered the lab office.

"What's up?"

"Lan went home to pack for Saratoga."

"So soon?"

"The lab tissue tests are finished. They looked so promising that I thought we should conduct a field test right away on human subjects. Lan will return, take the ice cubes from her freezer in the Cold Room, and put them into a portable cooler with dry ice. Then she'll head up to the prison."

"That's great! How soon will we know the outcome of the testing?"

"Probably by tomorrow or the next day."

"You said I would be alone today. So where is Dr James Chen going to be?"

"I have to fly back to Atlanta for the weekend. There's an annual Epidemiology Conference that I must be at. I'm one of the CDC panelists at a session for tomorrow afternoon. We're hosting the conference, and I had told Warren that I had committed to this two day obligation long before I came on board with Project V."

"I wish I could be there, but I'll hold down the fort 'til you get back," she said jokingly.

"How was your breakfast with Warren?"

"It was okay. It's clear he wants us to advance this project more quickly. And I think he's still pissed off at you for rearranging the order of agents. Seems he really wanted agent white, agent black, and agent yellow developed in that order."

I better leave it at that. I can't let on to Jim that I overheard and understood the phone conversation in Mandarin.

"Hell, I explained the rationale to him about that."

"He also gave me a history lesson on international politics and the attempts at bioweapons in the past."

Jim took off his lab coat and hung it up. He then slipped on his sport coat.

"My flight leaves early this afternoon. I'll give you a call when I get settled."

Carrie walked up to him and threw her arms up and around his shoulders. She kissed him warmly on the lips.

"I can't wait 'til you get back."

Minutes after Jim closed the office door, the purple cellphone rang from inside Carrie's handbag.

"Carbo, can you talk?"

"Yep. I'm all alone. I came from a breakfast meeting with Warren."

She told him about the session, including the phone conversation in Mandarin and the reference to Secretary of State Hinton. She underscored how Warren still had no idea she understood Mandarin.

"That is interesting. I'm curious about why they mentioned Zachary Hinton's name in the phone conversation. Why would they need to talk about my Secretary of State? Besides, I have Hinton flying back and forth to the Middle East to calm down the continuing conflicts over there. He hasn't any work on his current agenda for China."

"Don't know, but I might find out more. He's still here until tomorrow when he flies back to the Capitol."

"Great! Listen Carrie, I still haven't received any confirmation that the incident in Astola was caused by terrorists. The public news is that the crew may have had some form of food poisoning."

"The black man, who was a lab assistant, and the Asian cook weren't harmed, and neither was the ship's crew. Your news lines might be a little clogged, Barbo. It's seems strange that only white people died."

"Yes, it does. Keep me posted on anything you pick up."

"Will do."

The call ended, and Carrie resumed her work at the computer.

Half an hour later, Lan came into the office.

"Carrie, I'm going into the Cold Room to take out the agent yellow ice cubes, and then I'm off to Saratoga."

"Can I join you?"

"To Saratoga? No. That's my territory and is not according to the plan."

The plan?

"I meant can I join you in the Cold Room?" Carrie replied in a dry, stinging monotone.

"Oh, sure. You can come in with me and see the samples if you like."

Carrie followed her into the refrigerated room without saying another word.

Lan slipped on a pair of insulated gloves. Carefully, she took out rectangular blocks of dry ice from a utility freezer and used them to line a portable cooler. She walked over to her horizontal freezer and stood in front of the digital keypad so that Carrie couldn't see which combination of keys she punched. After she stood back, the horizontal cover lifted.

Carrie watched closely while Lan reached inside for the stainless steel cylinder of ice cubes. She noticed a label affixed to the container with the handwritten Chinese character *huáng* [yellow].

It is her freezer, so I guess writing in Chinese isn't a problem. Besides the mystery woman doesn't know I read the language as well as I speak it.

Lan placed the container inside her portable cooler. After she closed the freezer lid, the two women left the Cold Room, still without a word.

"I'm off to Saratoga now. I'll meet with my assistants tonight, and we'll do the test tomorrow some time. See you when I return."

She pivoted and with cooler in hand left the office.

Carrie spent the rest of the morning at her computer developing new algorithms for agents white and black. She modeled each formula after the initial one for agent yellow using the same gene clusters though with modifications for the black and white racial attributes. If the agent yellow field tests were successful, testing the succeeding agents in the lab and field would soon follow.

At one thirty, she left the lab and drove her bike over to the Holly House to see her father. After a brief visit, she went shopping for a surprise birthday gift for Jim. She knew he would be back in town for his birthday, if he even remembered that special day.

At the South Shore Plaza, she headed directly for the Harley Davidson store. She parked in an area specially designated for motorcycles, although at midday she was the only one parking there. She hopped off her bike and stored her helmet.

She found the perfect gift for Jim, a pair of black leather riding gloves with the Harley Davidson logo stitched across the wristband. After leaving the store, she decided to buy something for herself. It felt good to do something for herself, which she did so rarely. She walked along the inner shopping mall while peering at the window displays. She stared at the life-like manikins in one particular store. Liking what she saw, she marched through the doorway of Victoria's Secret.

Later, when she returned to the parking lot, she noticed another motorcycle now parked next to hers. As she hopped onto her bike. she looked over at the sleek, black BMW R 1200 RT. It had a small yellow lightning bolt painted on the fuel tank. Carrie knew it belonged to the same biker who had pulled beside her with the friendly hand signal.

That's pretty freakin' coincidental. Is this someone who is stalking me? Who the hell owns this BMW bike?

She decided to let it go and sped off from the shopping plaza. Later, while walking up the stairs to her apartment, she was met by Warren on his way down.

"Hi, Carrie! I don't know if you have plans for dinner tonight, but if we're both going to be alone, I would love to have you join me in the dining hall."

"Yes. That would be nice. I thought you'd be back in Washington."

"No. I really have to wait until Secretary Hinton returns from the Middle East. It seems he got delayed. Let's meet about seven."

Inside her apartment, Carrie put away her shopping items. She stripped down naked and padded into the shower. While shampooing her hair, she thought how she must tease out more information from Warren at dinner. It was her mission, the primary reason why she was here in the first place.

I can't imagine what the hell is in this whole thing for him. Is he working for Beijing? Was all this shit manipulated, starting with that bizarre call to his house some months ago? But for what reason? Who wanted what from this top-secret project? The United States and PRC will eventually share the vaccine once it has been proven effective. That's a win-win situation and a no-brainer. No, I think Warren is into something, and I've got to find out what the hell it is.

Carrie entered the dining room a few minutes past seven. Warren stood with a mixed drink in his hand while looking out through the Romanesque-styled windows. The view of the grounds was magnificent on this late summer evening with the emerald green grass and the manicured landscape.

"Hi, Carrie. I decided on a drink before dinner. I'll get Raul to make you one."

He waved to the dining room's head waiter.

Raul took the order and returned with her Dewar's Scotch and water.

"This really is such a beautiful spot. It's close to Boston, yet hidden from the noise of traffic and the rest of a bustling society."

"When I learned that Elliot House was on the market, I jumped at the chance for us to use it. It's hidden and conducive to seminars and retreats. I don't know if you saw it yet, but there is a huge lecture hall on the first floor. This dining room was a plus.

"In the beginning, I lived here for several weeks, but it wasn't fair to my wife and children back in Maryland. So now I only come here when it's absolutely necessary."

"You've done a lot with this project in a very short time. You set up a state-of-the-art lab, assembled some great research professionals, and now have all pistons running at once."

"Yes, yes. I was a little disappointed when Marotsky couldn't head up the project, but it seems Jim has stepped up to the plate and is well respected by the others."

"Yes, recruiting Jim was a good move. He's very knowledgeable about viral *vaccines*."

Warren's eyebrow arched slightly at Carrie's emphasis on the word "vaccines."

"That was a good recruitment from the CDC. President Bowa's recommendation was a good one also. I hear good things about you from the others—though since Bart said you were good, I never thought otherwise. I respect him and his judgment."

"President Bowa is bright, and I know he'll be a good leader as his administration moves forward."

"It is his courage and perseverance that got him the Presidency, but what I like most is that he's a trailblazer for the rest of us."

Before they sat down at the table, Warren removed his sport coat. He wore a short sleeved dress shirt, and the dense hair on his arms caught Carrie's attention. She knew that most Chinese and other Asians have little body hair, but Warren's forearms were thickly covered with wispy strands of black hair.

Raul brought their meals. He served each of them a rack of lamb with wild rice and a spring salad. He poured wine for each and left the bottle on the table.

"You mentioned that the President was a trailblazer for the rest of us? What did you mean?" Carrie asked while placing her napkin on her lap.

"Being the first non-white President sitting in the White House is ground breaking. He's the first American leader of color. After his administration, voters will more easily look beyond the color of one's skin or the fold in one's eyes."

"I clearly can see that your ethnicity is Chinese. Excuse me for being bold but your eyelids don't have the single fold characteristic of Asians. In fact, the color of your eyes isn't the coal black found in most Chinese; more like a light charcoal gray."

"You are observant. Do you know why I have these physical characteristics? Of course not! They are typical of the Tang dynasty and its descendants. I told you the Tang were a special breed. Many of them had the double-folded eyelids that gave them the appearance of rounded rather than slanted eyes. And I saw you staring at the hair on my arms. Not typical of a Chinese person, eh? Again, I was told at an early age that men of Tang lineage had hairy arms like those of Western men."

"That's interesting, and something I'm sure most people don't know."

"The most outstanding characteristic is that we Chinese, especially us Tang, are bright and courageous. And that's what the rest of the United States will soon learn. Because of our forty fourth President, 1600 Pennsylvania Avenue is no longer open to only white men. With a man of color now sitting in the Oval Office, people will begin to realize that skin color and physical characteristics don't make the President. Someday, perhaps soon, Asian American men like me will be considered qualified candidates for the White House. The American people who had previously been beaten, cheated, and misled by stereotypical, white, wealthy men will realize that color, race, and ethnicity are not important. Someday, we will not only see a woman in the Oval Office but we will also see an Asian."

"Have you considered running for a higher office? I know you were a Congressman from California for one term. Do you have higher aspirations after working in the Bowa administration?"

"I don't *think*, Carrie, I *know*. And I will run for President someday. This project, Project V, will give me a high enough national and international visibility to make that possible. Once we have this project behind us, Zachary Hinton has promised me I'll get the due recognition and credit across the country. Think about it! We're protecting not just some nations but perhaps vast segments of the human race from becoming obliterated. That's why I'm working hard and driving you, Lan, and Jim to reach our goals soon. It's important for all of us to find out more about this virus, and most important to find the prevention. And now with this Astola Island incident, we know the SAN are moving ahead. They aren't using derelict prisoners as we are. Those bastards are testing the agent in the public human laboratory."

Carrie thought about how she had just learned a lot about this intensely driven man. He had been jerked around by a young, attractive WASP woman in college who was the first true love of his life. Later he harbored hatred and disdain for non-Asians for a period but got his life back on track. He served in the Armed Forces, knows about running a successful business in America, ran successfully for political office in California, and now serves as the Under Secretary of State. Project V coming to fruition with a prophylactic serum will give him global recognition. It will clearly provide a launching pad to higher political office.

While drinking coffee after their dinner, Carrie felt better about her assignment. She now could tell the President that there were no overt signs of disloyalty by Warren. Despite his ambition and intensity, the Under Secretary apparently still has the protection of the United States as his ultimate priority.

"By the way, Warren, I saved the best news for last. Lan is up in Saratoga this evening. She'll conduct field tests tomorrow for agent yellow."

Warren's face lit up.

"That's good news! The sooner we get all of these tests over with, the sooner we can work on the vaccine to prevent any genocide biological agent."

"Yes. That will be led by Dr Ying," Carrie responded.

"I'm off to Washington in a few days. Zachary Hinton will be back from the Middle East, and I have lots to tell him."

They walked out of the dining room together and parted on the elevator at the third floor level where Warren got off for his room.

Carrie glanced at her watch. It was a good time to call her friend, Wei Xing. With Beijing twelve hours ahead, it would be nine fifteen in the morning at her office.

"You told me to call you so we could chat. And that's what I did!" Carrie instinctively spoke in Mandarin as she always did with her friend. And Wei Xing replied in English, with the correct use of contractions that had taken Carrie many hours of patient tutoring to teach her.

"Carrie I miss you so much. When are you coming back to China? You haven't been back here in almost two years."

Carrie thought how caring for her father had taken its toll on all facets of her life. Nonetheless, she was happy that she could look after him and insure that he had the best of care. She would have to put vacations and other things on hold for a while.

"I know, Wei Xing. I will get over there one of these days. And the next time I get there, I am staying for more than just a few weeks."

Wei Xing talked non-stop for over fifteen minutes. Her topics covered her job, her insolent boss, her latest romance, and her planned trip to America the following year.

Carrie interjected a question as her friend was winding down.

"Wei Xing, what do you know about the Tang Dynasty?"

"What do I know about the Tang Dynasty? Not very much. That's because the Tangs weren't in power for very long. There wasn't a helluva lot recorded about them. I think they were noted only for their emphasis on childhood education and the arts…you know big on music and artsy-fartsy things."

"I know that. I met someone today who is very proud of his Tang Dynasty heritage. Among other things, he told me that the Tang people had physical characteristics different from those of other Han Chinese. Do you recall reading or hearing anything about that?"

"Physical characteristics? No, that's strange. Like what?"

"A variety of things, like more body hair, great singing voices, and so on."

"That's right, Carrie. Now, I remember. The Tang men were well known for their enormous dicks. It was something passed down from generation to generation. And of course they were very popular with all of the Chinese women. Does that answer your question, girlfriend?"

Carrie burst out laughing. Her old Beijing friend hadn't lost her sense of humor. It felt good to have a bout of "girl talk" again.

They continued to talk on the phone for almost an hour. Carrie still didn't tell her about Jim, and the only thing she shared about

Project V was that she working on a special and sensitive government research project. Wei Xing didn't ask any more about it. It was the nature of the relationship they had. If one or the other wanted to talk about something, about anything, she would bring it up. Neither pried nor prodded the other.

SEVENTEEN

Carrie arrived in the lab early on Monday morning. She was surprised to see Lan already at her workstation typing in text at a rapid rate.

"Good morning," Carrie greeted her with her perky, early morning voice.

Lan stopped typing and swiveled her chair towards her.

"Hello, Carrie. Let me finish keying in this text, and we can talk."

The Chinese woman turned back to her computer and resumed keying in a large amount of text. She then scanned the screen to proofread what she had just typed and closed the file.

"I have some good news. I was going to wait until Jim came in this morning to tell you both but, Carrie, your bioagent test sample worked!"

She couldn't believe her ears and felt an overwhelming wave of shock: she had developed a lethal, racially targeted flu virus.

"Agent yellow worked? Tell me about it."

"Tell you what?" Jim interjected, as he stepped through the doorway.

"Good! You're both here," replied Lan. "Get your cups of coffee while I finish writing up my notes. We should go into the conference room, and I'll give you both an update on my field tests."

The three convened in the conference room.

Lan described in detail how the field testing went. She told them that there were still some minor hitches in the procedures, but the end result was positive.

"The Mongoloid bioagent, agent yellow, killed the Chinese prisoner subjects. The non-Mongoloids and mixed race subjects were unscathed after ingesting the beverage chilled with our lethal ice cubes."

As she listened to Lan, Carrie mentally pulled away from the depressing news of the deaths and allowed herself to appreciate her role in advancing the project. Now with Dr Carrie Bock, friend of the President of the United States, assigned to the Project V research team, they had made significant progress. And that's all she concentrated on at the moment.

"How many specimens, ah, subjects, were used in your test?" Carrie asked.

"There were only sixteen subjects for this initial field test. We had four Whites, four Blacks, and four Chinese. In addition, we used four mixed race subjects, two who were White-Black, one White-Asian, and one Black-Asian. They included both sexes and a wide range of ages."

"And all were administered the agent yellow ice?" Jim asked.

"Yes. We didn't use any placebos in this first test."

"And how was the agent administered?" he asked.

"I transported the agent in the ice cube form to the prison hospital. It remained frozen within the dry ice packs as planned. I held a meeting with my assistants in the sealed ward. At the planned time, each screened subject was given a six ounce cup of apple juice with the ice cubes melting in each of the cups."

Carrie mentally visualized the calculated murders taking place while Lan spoke proudly.

"Each subject drank the complete six ounces of the chilled apple juice. The non-Mongoloids had no serious reactions, although each of them coughed slightly. They all reported a mild irritation in their throats. There was no change in body temperature and no dermatological signs of any viral infection. Within half an hour, they all said they felt okay and had no discomfort."

"And the Mongoloid subjects?" Jim asked.

"The onset of illness took between ten and fifteen minutes. They all died within thirty minutes."

"Symptoms?"

Lan looked directly at Jim first and then at Carrie, a slight grin forming on one side of her mouth. The sinister smile sent a shiver up Carrie's spine.

"Each subject began perspiring within a few minutes. They soon developed a strong, raspy coughing spell. Their body temperatures spiked at one hundred and two. Facial complexions became pale.

They also experienced labored breathing in the last few minutes before death. Some lost consciousness while others became mildly delusional prior to expiration. All of the Mongoloids were dead within half an hour of ingesting the agent yellow."

"Just ten minutes seems very soon for the viral infection to compromise the subject," Jim said as he rubbed the base of his chin.

Carrie was working hard at separating herself from the morbid reality of the work Lan described.

"Were there any other outcomes, like color changes in finger-nails, blotches on the torso, anything like that?" Jim asked.

"Yes, there was one unexpected result. Each of the subjects had a small stream of blood coming from each nostril as they died. There wasn't much blood, a trickle, barely enough to reach the mouth. They must have experienced ruptures of the nasal capillaries."

Carrie looked over to Jim for his reaction to Lan's description.

"That must be part of the upper respiratory damage. My guess is that this occurred as a result of the high concentration of the agent. Did you monitor the subjects' blood pressure as the trial went on?"

"No, but we can certainly do that," Lan replied. She appeared embarrassed that she hadn't thought of that basic clinical procedure.

Carrie asked, "What was the concentration?"

"It was one part agent per eighty million parts water."

"I started there," responded Jim. "But now I can adjust the ratio before making the next batch of ice cubes. I suspect we won't get the nasal bleeding, but the subjects may survive much longer than half an hour."

"How long?" Lan asked.

"I don't know. That's what this testing is for, right?"

Lan nodded, with a gesture more of politeness than agreement.

Before ending the meeting, Jim stated that he would soon have a more diluted batch of the agent for Lan to test.

Not needing or wanting to hear these details, Carrie left Jim and Lan in the conference room. She was still feeling proud that she had developed the complex algorithm that resulted in a racially sensitive virus. That was her assignment, or at least one of them. She also felt confident that if the Mongoloid virus continued to test positive developing bioagents for the other two races wouldn't be far behind.

She still had ambivalent feelings about what she was doing on Project V. She would much rather be working on the antidote or virus vaccine. The job she wanted was to invent the solution rather than create the problem.

What bothered her most were the roles each of them played on the project. It still didn't make sense to her that Jim, who was world renowned for his work on vaccines at the CDC, was not leading that critical phase. From her own perspective, developing the racially targeted virus was probably the easier job. It could take months or perhaps longer before a vaccine was developed. Or, worse, maybe there was no vaccine for the insidious virus that she had just developed.

She slid onto her workbench chair and let the computer scan her retina. The "Welcome to the Network" message appeared on her screen. As the software programs loaded, she mused about all that had happened over the past two months.

I, like Barbo, had doubted that Warren's intelligence data was accurate about the Pakistani terrorist group. There has not been any official verification that SAN had the bioweapon, though the Astola Island incident appears to have validated that. But here I am investigating one that apparently works based on genetic cluster profiling. When we find the viral configuration for Caucasoids and Negroids, the first phase of Project V will be complete. The next phase, finding the vaccine, would fall totally under Dr Lan Ying's responsibility. Jim's obligation to the project would have been met, and his younger brother released from his incarceration in China.

Carrie's mind kept rushing into the future.

Jim will leave and return to his career at the CDC. He'll resume his high level position and lead research scientists in creating beneficial medicines. And me? What the hell will I do for the rest of my life?

Her personal thoughts kept racing through her brain and created a slight headache. She walked over to one of the cabinets and shook two Tylenol tablets from a bottle. After tossing them into her mouth, she swigged down a half bottle of chilled water.

Walking back to her workstation, she glanced at Lan's empty workbench.

What is the story with this mystery woman anyway? She never lets anyone know about her freakin' personal life. She's all business when she's with Jim, and me, and the other researchers. She obviously enjoys her work, that of testing the virus and killing human beings in field tests, albeit they're the scum of the earth.

Why did Warren handpick her? And why was this ice woman selected to perform the testing and to solely spearhead developing the vaccine? There are too many unanswered questions attached to the young, attractive, Chinese scientist. Is she capable of leading the next phase of Project V? Can she create a vaccine and test it thoroughly? How will I ever know? How will anyone ever know?

Her thoughts were interrupted when Lan stepped back into the office. Jim followed and offered her a slight smile.

"How does it feel to be considered one of the world's super scientists?" Jim asked. "You created something that had been thought about for many years."

Carrie smiled. "You mean I'm the second person to create it. Don't forget why we're here. The SAN terrorists came up with it before me."

"Perhaps, perhaps," he replied with a stoic expression. "My gut tells me that if they really had the agent *and* an effective delivery system, they would have deployed it by now."

It was the first time a discussion like this was held inside the office. Usually their conversations concerned technical problems. They hadn't yet talked openly about the reason Project V existed.

Carrie probed. "Explain."

"The terrorists may or may not have a bioagent, but there is also the challenge of an effective delivery system, which must be simultaneous and widespread. If not, we, and certainly other countries, would retaliate with massive invasions or bombings of suspected sites where the terrorists were developing the agent and put an abrupt end to the horrific threat of racial genocide."

Lan's head shot straight up as she listened to the conversation on delivery systems. It was time for her to ring in.

"The important thing is that we still have a lot of work ahead of us," she commented. "We need to refine the agent yellow and continue testing. We can then focus on developing agent white and agent black. The delivery system is not our concern. We can leave that to the powers that be."

Carrie was surprised at Lan's emotional directive on the topic. It was uncharacteristic of their quiet, focused colleague. But what she said was accurate. They weren't involved with delivery systems.

Her words were a signal that they should all get back to work. Not another word was spoken for hours. At eleven thirty, Jim left for a prearranged meeting with the staff scientists.

While he was gone, Carrie's cellphone rang. It was Warren.

"Carrie, I heard the good news. I congratulate you. I understand it was your formula that developed agent yellow. Good work!"

"Did Jim give you a call?" She was surprised he would have heard the news already.

"No. Lan told me. She was so excited that she called me very early this morning."

Carrie's skin prickled with a sudden rush of anger.

The bitch had gone around Jim to inform Warren first of the news. In fact, Warren knew it before I did.

With the phone to her ear, she glanced over at Lan concentrating on the text displayed on her computer screen.

"I'm coming back to Elliot House for a few days. I would like to spend some time with you. How about we meet for dinner again?"

Her special assignment from Barbo surfaced in her mind. She was supposed to work on the project and bird-dog the Under Secretary of State.

"I would love to, but I do have a lot going on with my father and some personal things. Why not let me call you when I know we can meet?"

There was a short pause before the Under Secretary responded. He wasn't used to rejection of any kind.

"Sure."

At lunch, Jim met Carrie on the patio. He chose a table in a far corner so that their conversation couldn't be overheard. Carrie immediately told him about Lan's updating Warren before reporting to them.

He nonchalantly focused on his food.

"I can't believe you're not pissed off. How dare she call Warren and tell him before you or me. For God's sake, you're the overall project leader who reports to Warren. And what about me? It was *my* formula. I mean, what is wrong with this weird ice woman?"

Jim's smile at her anger only added fuel to her fire. She watched as he salted his turkey sandwich in a calm, routine manner.

"It's not worth getting angry about. Lan calling Warren really doesn't bother me. In fact, it tells us a little more about our mysterious colleague."

Jim bit into his sandwich.

"What do you mean?"

After wiping his mouth with his napkin, Jim took a sip of milk before responding.

"Look, Lan called Warren on her own because she has some need for personal recognition. She needs to feel positive attention from people of authority."

"But she had little to do with the agent development other than administering the field tests."

"She may be mentally assuming the role of project leader in her own mind. She wants to be the bearer of good news to our immediate boss. It probably helps her tender ego."

Carrie finished her fresh tomato stuffed with tuna salad while trying to understand how he could be so calm, so rational when she wanted to rip the woman's head off.

"I'm not sure about that. I still wonder what the relationship is between Warren and Lan. I still think they might be having some kind of secret affair."

Jim laughed leaned forward and whispered. "You mean like us?"

Carrie made a funny face and stuck her tongue out at him. She did appreciate that he was trying to cheer her up and defuse her foul mood.

"Maybe I'll find out more later," she added. "Warren and I are going to have dinner again this coming week. If you're good, I'll let you know what I learn."

She winked at him as she stood up to leave.

EIGHTEEN

Carrie walked into the dining room at eight fifteen. Warren was again standing alone and looking out through the windows. He appeared to be in deep thought. She spotted Raul and ordered a double scotch on the rocks. She hoped to numb the pain from her earlier visit with her father. It had been more emotionally deflating than usual.

"Hello. Sorry I'm a little late."

Warren turned to her with a nearly empty cocktail glass in hand. "No problem. I hope your day went well, and your father is comfortable."

A sigh came out louder than expected as she took the drink from the waiter. "Alzheimer's disease is well…it is what it is," she replied, and then sipped her drink.

"Come, let's sit down. They had two entrees tonight, lemon-buttered swordfish with capers or a New York strip steak. I took the liberty of ordering you the fish."

It's happening again. This egocentric bastard has to control everything. He even made a decision on what I'm to eat. The swordfish entree did sound appetizing, but I'll send him a clear message from Carrie Bock.

Carrie waved her hand for Raul to approach their table.

"I'd like to have the steak tonight, Raul. Could you please change the order?"

She turned to face the Under Secretary who was motionless with his mouth open.

"So how was your trip back to the Capitol?"

"It went well. I spent a lot of time with my boss, Zachary Hinton. He was excited to hear the news of our progress. With this new spirit of a Beijing-Washington alliance, we're moving to take the bilateral relationship to the next level."

"What does that mean?"

"The PRC is well aware of the criticism their country has received over the years with their industrial and commercial pollution. For the longest time, they ignored foreign criticism and carried on business as usual with polluting their air and water supplies. Several countries fought back with an embargo on selected Chinese imports. Beijing's new goal is to learn from our own Environmental Protection Agency. They want to emulate the EPA policies and procedures we've implemented in the US."

He took a swig of his cocktail.

"That sounds like a positive move."

"Since international environment issues fall under the aegis of the State Department, they asked that I present a new cultural exchange program to Zachary, which I did. Bilateral talks have already taken place, and news of an Environmental Exchange Alliance will hit the press in a few days."

"That sounds interesting, Warren, and fast. I didn't know something like that could happen so quickly. And I'm sure this program will help your own political career."

Warren waved for Raul to bring him another bourbon and water.

"I want to help Zachary Hinton too. He loves to showcase programs like this. He has told me it's a pleasant change from the work he's been doing in the Middle East."

"From what I understand about your boss, Zach Hinton, he likes to showcase himself as well as the programs," Carrie commented.

Warren smiled at the playful remark directed at his boss.

"There's no question Zachary likes the publicity. He misses the limelight that he enjoyed during the presidential primary campaign. But he'll get a lot of mileage with this new and exciting paradigm of SinoAmerican relations. It's a win-win situation all around; and again, I'm glad I could play a role. The Chinese scientific community gets closer to our country, and they learn how to implement cleaner air and water systems for the rest of the planet. What could be wrong with that?"

Carrie reflected on the phone call she had overheard during which Hinton's name was mentioned. Now she and the President know what that was all about.

As they ate their dinners with wine, Warren was feeling good about things in general. Significant progress had been made on

Project V, he had helped his boss get some international publicity, and he had appeased his Beijing contacts by arranging an Environmental Exchange Alliance. These events and the volume of alcohol in his bloodstream made him feel very good.

Carrie thought the time was convenient to get some information from this ambitious dynamo. Her confidence in speaking with her target was high now. Discovering agent yellow gave her a newly found popularity and proof of her station on the project team.

"Warren, now that we're moving forward, I still look back a bit on the beginnings of Project V. I know that you recruited Jim because you have known each other for years. What about Lan Ying? How did you find her and determine her qualifications?"

"I had nothing to do with recruiting Dr Ying. Lan came highly recommended by my Beijing contacts. She was a post-doctoral candidate at Qinghua University and has worked in several successful research labs in China."

"So you didn't interview her?"

"No. In keeping with the spirit of the alliance, I took the testimony provided to me and went with it."

"I take it your choice for Project Leader, from Duke University, was Josef Marotsky. It's too bad he couldn't get the clearance."

Warren paused before responding. He sipped his wine and picked up the bottle to pour more into Carrie's wine glass. She stopped him by placing her hand over the rim. He refilled his own glass.

"That's not really true. Beijing knew a lot about Josef, about his work at Duke and his experience before that. He was recommended to lead up the project. He's an American, a renowned scientist, and certainly qualified. It wasn't me who recommended Dr Marotsky, it was the General."

Carrie's ears shot up at the mention of the title.

"The General?"

"General Peng. He's my counterpart on this project. He facilitates much of what's needed. He pays the bills, and gets me what I want to move Project V forward. Without his influence and deep pockets, we would still be scrambling around for resources of all kinds. He'll be coming here from time to time. Not often lately, though when we were just beginning he was here almost every day. I'll introduce you the next time he's here."

"So General Peng recommended Josef Marotsky to head up the project?"

"Yes. He thought having an American scientist leading the project would be helpful. Marotsky was a great choice, and I agreed."

Although she was tempted, Carrie knew enough not to ask any delicate questions about Lan Ying. If she asked another follow-up question, Warren might become suspicious of her focused interest. Besides, she had learned a great deal already.

Warren hadn't selected Lan for the project as Jim had speculated. Also, Lan's research background was limited. Now I need to find out more about General Peng. He's an important piece to this puzzle.

"Does General Peng have a vested interest in America with this project?"

Warren had a puzzled look on his face as he tried to decipher what Carrie's meant with her cutting statement. He took another sip of his wine before responding.

"I know you came recommended by the President on this project because of your twenty or so years in clinical and medical research. But let me give you some education about the Chinese language and culture."

Good Lord! This self-absorbed idiot is now going to bore me to death. If he only knew how much I had studied the Chinese language and culture and how much time I had spent in China. He astutely diverted the topic, even though he's getting quite drunk. I'll give him that.

"General Peng, like me, has a high regard for our beloved country. Do you know the Chinese word for 'America'?"

She knew the answer, but replied, "No. Why would I know that?"

"America is called *Měiguó*. The translation for the Chinese character, *Měi*, is beautiful. And the translation for the Chinese character, *Guó*, is country.

"So for centuries, the Chinese have called America 'the beautiful country'," Carrie commented while trying to sound naïve.

"True. Do you know why the Chinese people called America the beautiful country?" Warren asked his question in a slow, deliberate tone to avoid slurring his words. He had drunk a lot of wine on top of his bourbon cocktails.

"I presume it's because America *is* beautiful, with snow-capped mountains, vegetation of all types from tall trees to the grassy plains, and deep blue water in our rivers, lakes, and shorelines. You know, the song, America the Beautiful."

Warren took on a serious look again as he responded. He raised a finger in the air to make his point. "Not so. The Chinese call America 'the beautiful country' because of its natural resources. No other country on the earth has the water supply for drinking, agricultural, and industry; the forests for building; the oil, coal, and minerals for industry; and the arable land for farming. In other words, the country naturally provides what people need to survive and thrive. That's why the Chinese think America is truly *the beautiful country*."

"It takes people to use those resources effectively or else the country wouldn't be regarded as so bountiful."

"Yes, but the people who inherited those resources didn't have to be white Anglo-Saxons. They could have been Africans, Icelanders, South Americans, or…"

"Or golden-skinned Chinese people with a single fold in their eyelids?" Carrie finished his sentence.

His grin was difficult to decipher as he peered at her across the table.

"Yes. The Chinese people could use this country's natural resources as effectively, or more so, than other races and ethnic groups."

Warren looked away, paused for a moment, and seemed to be in deep thought before turning to face his dinner companion.

"Carrie, I'm sure you understand that when people say that 'it has nothing to do with money,' they *always* mean it has to do with money. You can replace the word 'money' with the word 'race,' because when people say that 'it has nothing to do with race,' they *always* mean it has to do with race."

Carrie wondered what he meant by these statements. She knew

he was drunk and dismissed it as some free associative thought he may have confused within his logical brain this evening. However, his statement about the white Anglo-Saxons was disturbing. It suggested that he still harbored anger from being dumped by his former fiancée and the rest of her family.

Carrie noticed Warren's eyes becoming more glassy as Raul set another opened bottle of wine on the dining table. She brought the topic back into focus for him.

"It's too bad Dr Marotsky couldn't take on the job. He's such a legend in our field. I would have liked to work with that man."

"Between you and me, I think his clearance getting squashed was a bunch of bullshit! Josef has an impeccable record and is no threat to this country's security. Just because some uncle is still over in Moscow shouldn't have created any concern. For God's sake, the uncle is in his late seventies and is soon retiring from a career in academia."

"Was he a scientist too?"

"His uncle? That I don't know," Warren replied and then poured wine into his empty glass.

As Carrie sipped a decaf coffee, she thought she may have tapped out all that she could get from an inebriated Warren.

"I have an early morning tomorrow, so I'm going up to my perch and turn in for the night."

Carrie stood up and shoved her chair towards the table.

"I'll be heading up soon too. I want to make a couple of phone calls and get some sleep. I'll probably see you for breakfast."

Carrie simply waved goodnight as Warren pulled out his cell-phone from his leather belt holster.

After locking her apartment door, Carrie stripped down and washed up for bed. She owed her long distance friend, Wei Xing, a phone call.

When they connected, Wei Xing said, "You're a hard person to catch up with these days. How much longer is this project going to last? I miss talking to you. Email doesn't cut it for us."

Carrie finally disclosed her relationship with Jim Chen, and how their romance had progressed. She didn't mention that he still had a wife back in China, and only told her how Jim was a colleague and her project boss.

Wei Xing told her how she was making plans to come to America next April. She hoped her boyfriend could join her on the trip.

"Wei Xing, what do you know about a PRC government official, a high, mucky-muck by the name of General Peng?"

"General Peng is a highly respected leader here. In fact, he was once considered a candidate for President of the PRC. He's kind of a milksop-looking character, but he's supposed to be a brilliant tactician."

"Tactician? You mean as in military combat?"

"That too. Now he's retired from the Chinese Army and heads up the MSS organization."

"MSS?"

"It stands for the Ministry of State Security. It's like your CIA and FBI combined with your office of Homeland Security. It's where our sneaky spies work. All intelligence gathering, whether national or international, goes directly up to Peng. He's a very powerful man in our country."

"He's the head of Chinese Intelligence?"

"That's right. When I was the temporary Minister of Education, I met him at some social functions. But I don't know him. He seemed nice, not impressive looking."

"Not impressive looking?"

"I guess I'm not being so polite. He's a chubby little guy about five feet tall, and has a boyish grin even though he's in his sixties. And he still wears those retro, thick black horn-rimmed eyeglasses. At times, he could be mistaken for our previous premier, Deng Xiao Ping. Why the sudden interest in General Peng?"

"I learned tonight that our Under Secretary of State, Warren Lee, and Peng are acquaintances."

"That makes sense, I guess."

Carrie couldn't tell her friend more. She had shared earlier how she was working on a sensitive project for the advancement of virus prevention, but didn't dare violate the confidentiality of the project.

NINETEEN

Carrie skipped her routine morning run because she wanted to sleep in a little longer than usual after her late night. She popped into the dining room on her way to the lab. She had expected to find Warren there but he wasn't. She ate half a bagel and drank a cup of coffee while enjoying the solitude.

When she arrived downstairs, she found Lan alone in the office. They exchanged some obligatory pleasantries while Carrie slipped on her lab coat.

Carrie plopped down in front of her workstation waiting for the retinal scan to give her network access. The usual "Welcome to the Network" message didn't display. The monitor's screen remained black. She reset the power button, but the screen still didn't respond with the standard series of log-on messages.

She swiveled the monitor around to see if something had become disconnected. As she did so, she caught Lan's reflection on the darkened screen. Without Lan realizing that she was being watched, Carrie kept her eyes riveted to the screen. Lan was staring at Carrie, as she had some weeks earlier. A chill ran down Carrie's spine as the Chinese scientist continued to stare at her without saying a word.

What the hell is wrong with this chick? She stares at me when I'm not looking. I wonder if she suspects that I have a double purpose with this assignment. But she doesn't know me. She couldn't have met me when I lived in Beijing, and she has to be about ten years younger.

Carrie turned to face her. As she did so, Lan immediately turned around and acted as though she had been busily working on her computer. It was the same reaction that Carrie had observed the previous time.

"Something's wrong with my workstation. Was your computer all right this morning?"

"I had no problem. Mine came up after it scanned my retina as usual. Did you check all of the cables?"

"Yeah. They're all connected tightly."

Lan came over to help diagnose the problem. She was only inches away from Carrie while she inspected the system.

"I'm sorry. I'm not much help with this stuff. Ask Jim when he comes in. He knows a lot more about computer hardware."

Lan lightly brushed Carrie's shoulder as she returned to her workbench.

Carrie pulled out the hardware manual but her reading was interrupted.

"That's really nice. Is it lavender?"

Puzzled at the comment, she turned to face her colleague.

"What? I'm sorry, what did you say?"

Lan looked at her with an unusually shy smile on her face.

"I meant your scent. It's lovely. I asked if it is lavender."

"Yes, it's a lavender body wash. Thanks."

The interaction was so surprising that she almost forgot what she had been doing. Now a little rattled by the computer malfunction and the personal question from Lan, she decided to leave the office until Jim arrived. She stepped outside the lab for another cup of coffee on the patio.

She met some of the other researchers also having coffee or tea before they returned to the microscopes, Petri dishes, centrifuges, and other tools of their trade.

She joined the wide bodied, famed geneticist, Hans Hartman, who was sitting alone.

"You're looking well today, Carrie. Riding your Harley must be relaxing for you."

"Yes, riding gets my mind off of things, and I enjoy the exhilarating feeling of freedom."

"As all us bikers do!"

Carrie leaned back in astonishment.

"Hans, I had no idea! I haven't seen you with a bike at the Elliot House."

"I do my riding during my off hours. I'm fussy with my new machine and won't ride in the rain or along the heavy traffic roads of Boston."

"I can understand that. I would never drive every day from Boston to here either. What kind of bike do you have?"

"I just upgraded to a new BMW. It's a beauty!"

"A brand new BMW bike! That's quite an investment."

Carrie reflected on the image of the mysterious biker who drove next to her with the hand signal. She remembered seeing that same bike in the mall parking lot standing next to her own Harley."

"What model BMW..."

Just then a shadow blocked the morning sunlight on the patio table.

"Carrie, I hate to interrupt, and I do apologize." Jim came closer to the table. "I need to see you right away about something important."

"Sure Jim. Excuse me, Hans," Carrie said. "We'll talk later."

As the two walked back into the laboratory, Jim was visibly concerned.

"Lan tells me your workstation isn't working. I need to look at it with you present. It's strange because Lan's machine is okay and mine booted up right away. Were you working on it late last night?"

"No. I was with Warren until the time I went up to my apartment."

When Carrie again faced the retinal scanner, nothing happened to enable her access to the computer network.

"Come with me. I want to check out the file servers."

They walked down the main corridor until they came to the door with a sign: Computer Room. The security system scanned Jim's retina, and the door opened. Carrie followed him inside.

Jim sat in front of a six foot high metal rack holding twelve computer file servers resting in individual slots. He scanned lines of cryptic text presented on one screen. After paging by several screens, he stopped and stared at one message. He shook his head in surprise at the text.

Wkstn 18 disabled at 06:00 by Admin.

"That's strange. Your workstation was disabled from the network at six o'clock. I can enable it, but I don't know why it was disconnected this morning. According to the computer generated message, the network systems administrator did that. That function can only be done physically from this central computer, because none of the networked workstations have access to the administration software. Somebody had to log onto this server and intentionally disable your device."

She watched him tip-tap the keyboard with instructions for the operating system.

Satisfied he had restored Carrie's workstation onto the network, Jim led her out of the Computer Room.

Carrie sat down at her bench and had no problem logging on with her first attempt.

Lan looked at the two of them.

"Looks like it's all right now," Lan said. "What was the problem, Jim?"

"I'm not sure," he answered cautiously without looking at her.

All three quietly resumed working on their tasks for the remainder of the morning.

Later that afternoon, Jim asked both Lan and Carrie to join him in the Cold Room.

"I want to go over our procedures for Carrie. We need to show her in detail how we create test batches of the bioagent," he explained. "I also want to show her the security checks and balances we have built into it and how the process works. We won't be in here too long, so I don't think you'll need extra coats."

"I'll take your word for it," Carrie said as she shivered in anticipation.

The three of them entered the chilly room.

"Okay, some weeks ago we set this system up, so it will be redundant to you, Lan, but I want Carrie to know how and why we developed this procedure."

Jim led them toward the center of the frigid chamber. He turned and stood in front of the industrial sized ice-making machine. Jim pointed to the hopper and feeder to the ice maker.

"This is where I feed in the bioagent liquid that I prepare in the lab. Before the hopper door will open, I must key in an access code on the keypad on the side of the machine. Only I have that access code, which means that only I can start the process. I created a new batch of concentrated agent yellow last night. It is in this special beaker. Notice how it's been securely capped from its creation in the sealed incubator. This prevents us from inhaling liquid fumes and becoming infected."

"That's reassuring," Carrie quipped dryly.

"As I said, the hopper won't open until I key in my access code. After I do so, it will open and I'll place the beaker inside. The hopper door then closes automatically. There's a robotic arm inside the machine that opens the beaker and pours the agent into the ice maker. I then set the agent to the distilled water ratio I want before processing."

Jim demonstrated by keying in the access code on the digital key pad. The hopper door opened, and he inserted the glass beaker. The door closed, and a mechanical noise soon started.

Carrie looked at the machine and glanced around at other storage freezers after Jim spoke. The sound of ice cubes falling into a container broke the silence. The three moved closer to watch as a series of ice cubes were ejected from the machine.

"Because the virus is in a frozen state, it is inactive. It is inert and completely powerless. It's safe for any one of us to handle the cubes, though with rubber gloves. The virus compound doesn't become viable until it begins to melt near room temperature, as it did with Lan's subjects drinking the apple juice. Only after the melting ice is ingested will the viral compound perform its function."

"It doesn't have to be apple juice; it can be soda, coffee, water, or *even scotch*," Lan interjected with a grin.

Was that comment aimed at me? How the fuck does this mystery woman know that I drink scotch? This woman is really getting on my nerves.

Jim smiled politely before continuing.

"This new batch has been diluted at a higher ratio than the first batch. Until tested, we won't know how lethal it is, if at all. My calculations indicate it will work as well as the first batch, but it will take longer for the subjects to die than just half an hour. My guess is that it also shouldn't be strong enough to cause those nasal capillary bleeds."

"I really don't think that's a problem," Lan said. "They're dead anyway."

An awkward silence again filled the room.

Lan was clearly showing another side to her during the demonstration. When she spoke, she had an almost childish, one dimensional attitude. Her remarks were unlike those of any other seasoned scientist Carrie had ever met.

Breaking the awkward silence, Jim continued.

"This is important, Carrie. We immediately transfer the batch of ice cubes into Lan's storage freezer. When she's prepared for the next field test, she'll come in here, key in her access code, and leave for Saratoga with the containers of our bioagent in a dry ice pack."

Jim lifted the output container of ice cubes from the ice machine and filled a stainless steel container labeled agent yellow.

Lan stepped over to her storage freezer and in similar fashion to Jim keyed in several numbers on the keypad so neither Carrie nor Jim could see which digits she pressed. The freezer lid opened. The container was then carefully lowered inside. She closed the freezer lid, which automatically locked.

Jim turned and directed his words to Carrie.

"This routine works for us and provides simple checks and balances in terms of security. Only the three of us have access to the Cold Room. But I have access to the ice machine's hopper, and only Lan has access to her storage freezer. So we have to work together when creating and transferring the lethal agents. Any questions?"

"I've got it," Carrie replied with her teeth chattering slightly from the frozen air.

"Good," he said. "Now let's get the hell out of here and get warmed up."

* * *

Just before noon, Lan announced she was headed home to pack for her stay at the prison hospital.

"I'm curious. Isn't the Saratoga Prison Hospital an old, dilapidated site?" Carrie asked while Lan copied her computer's data onto another flash memory stick.

She watched Lan perform the same ritual each day before leaving the lab. The memory stick was some sort of backup for her. Or more. She must be so paranoid that someone might hack into her workstation that she erased all files resident on her computer after the transfer to the flash drive. Where she put the flash drive's backup files was a mystery. She couldn't take the drives home because she would be stopped by the Security Guards. No official material was permitted to leave the top-secret laboratory.

"It's an old prison, but when Project V initially got launched, I worked with contractors to renovate the hospital wing. I had new equipment brought in, and sections of the ward are now partitioned with glass walls so that my assistants and I can administer the bioagents at the same time. There are cameras positioned throughout the ward so I can monitor the activities and reactions of all of the subjects. I can also do that from a building adjacent to the hospital through my computer webcam. I have my own bed in that building as well, since this testing process takes so long. We'll do post-mortem autopsies in the morgue after each successful test to learn more. So it isn't a one day process."

Carrie watched Lan as the curvy, attractive, Chinese woman quietly pivoted to face her desk, now with her back to Jim and Carrie. She picked up her black leather handbag from the floor and sat it on top of her desk. She pulled out a shiny brushed-gold tube of lipstick. She then faced Carrie with a smile.

"I'm going to the Ladies Room to freshen up before heading out. See you guys in the morning."

She was soon out of the lab office.

"Jim, we've got to talk," Carrie said, as soon as the door closed.

Jim nodded but kept a watchful eye on the door.

"How about tonight? Can you come to my place?" he asked in his usual soft voice.

"I don't know. I feel a little nervous with Warren staying here. How about meeting on the top of Big Blue after work? At least we can talk up there, and I can return in time to see Warren in case he wants to meet again."

"I'll be there about six."

"I'm really pissed off about my computer being disabled from the network. That had to be done manually, right?"

"Definitely. It was done manually, and it was done at precisely six o'clock this morning."

"Who has access to the Computer Room and the file servers?"

He turned to look at her. The furled brow told her he was troubled with the mystery.

"Right now, only three scientists have retinal access. In addition to me, one of the research associates. But he's in Europe on a funeral leave. And of course Lan."

"Is that it? You mentioned only three scientists. Is that it?"

"No. One other person has access to that room."

Carrie knew who that might be but waited to have her guess verified. "Is that other person, Warren Lee?"

"That's right. Warren Lee, Director of our top-secret Project V."

After Jim left the office, Carrie thought about her underestimating the Under Secretary of State. She wondered as she picked up her bag, what the intense self-centered man was really capable of doing. It still wasn't clear what his goal and motivation were on this project.

The door opened and Lan burst into the office. She looked at Carrie with a hurried smile.

"I forgot to lock my desk."

She took a set of keys out of her pocket and locked the center drawer. She pivoted sharply and left the office again.

The sudden entrance and whirlwind exit didn't surprise Carrie. Something else did catch her attention. Lan had left earlier to freshen up with the little gold tube of lipstick. Yet she had no lipstick on when she returned.

TWENTY

As Carrie had anticipated, Warren called her with another invitation to join him for dinner. Though reluctant, she accepted because each time in his company was an opportunity to learn more. Barbo would want an update soon.

"Sure, on one condition."

"And what's that?"

"I select our meals, and the time."

There was a silent pause before the characteristically male chauvinistic and proud Asian responded.

"Fair enough," he said.

"I'm busy until early evening. I'll meet with you at eight o'clock."

When she hung up the phone, Lan walked into the office.

"I thought you were on your way to Saratoga."

She stared at the woman's ice cooler that was labeled with the "hazardous material" logo on each side.

"I dropped by to tell Jim…" She stopped speaking when he walked into the room. "Jim, my plan is to administer this batch of agent yellow first thing in the morning."

He nodded. "Yes, but remember the onset of its effects may take longer. Keep a watchful eye and meticulous records. I want all of the details."

Carrie watched as Lan's eyes narrowed to signal her personal offence at Jim's apparently unwarranted remarks.

Just before six that evening, Carrie gunned her Harley up the highest incline of The Blue Hills. As her bike hugged the last curve, she saw Jim standing beside his bike. His helmet was off, already hanging from his handlebars. There was another couple parked nearby in a black VW Jetta convertible with the top down.

After setting her bike's kickstand and removing her own helmet, she walked over to him. They stood close to the parking lot guardrail and embraced quietly.

Carrie felt better with Jim's arms around her, with him holding her, making her feel safe and special. When their lips finally came together, their kisses tasted of a sensual hunger that pained both of them.

Finally drawing apart, Jim spoke first. "Do you know how many times I wanted to reach out for you at work, in the office, to hold and kiss you?"

Her eyes answered for her, but her audible sigh couldn't hide her own frustration.

"I think we're doing a great acting performance in front of Lan and the others, but it sure as hell isn't easy," he said.

"It has to be this way for a lot of different reasons. Your wife, your marriage, our working together, and everything connected to that. We can't be public, at least not now."

As they stood still holding hands, she hoped her words sounded logical to Jim, that he could see that their relationship was not without inherent dangers. She was even more frustrated for not being completely honest with him.

She desperately wanted to reveal to Jim her real assignment, that she was a "mole" for the President of the United States assigned to Project V. She wanted to tell him that she was trained in the Chinese language, which made her more qualified for her assignment than simply her microbiology credentials. He deserved to know she wasn't simply working on the bioagent research, but was bird-dogging Warren Lee to determine whether he had any subversive connection to China's MSS.

At times, she felt as if she were cheating on him, though she knew that telling him about her actual role would be a serious security compromise. She had to continue her ambivalent situation.

Jim looked out at the tall pines and leafy oaks blanketing the high hills.

"I want to tell my wife about you, about you and me. She knows our marriage has been a farce. It was from the very beginning. If she has any feelings for me, she'll grant me a divorce right away."

Carrie was surprised that he had brought up such a sensitive and private topic on a mountaintop parking lot. She moved closer to him and snuggled her head underneath his chin.

"Do you think that's wise?"

"It may or may not be, but that's what I want to do. I'm falling in love with you, and I don't want to lose you. I'll do anything to have you for my own." Still staring out beyond the hilly Massachusetts terrain, he underscored his feelings. "Carrie, I've never been so happy in my life, and it's because of you."

His sincere words echoed like a carillon ringing in her mind. It affected her immediately. Her eyes welled up, and a warm feeling seemed to emanate from her heart and spread throughout her being.

She abruptly turned away so Jim couldn't see the tears on the brink of cascading down her cheeks. Unable to hold them back, she turned to face him and raised a quivering hand up to his smooth face. Her fingertips traced his jaw line as her tears began their race downward.

She kissed his soft lips. Whether she wanted to or not, she too was falling in love. And it was becoming harder and harder not to fully commit to him. She found herself embracing him quietly without speaking for several minutes.

When she regained her composure, she took a tissue from her jeans to dry her eyes. She changed the mood when she began chuckling out loud.

"What's so funny?" Jim asked, with surprise in his voice.

"When the President told me about joining this top-secret project, he told me there would be a lot of tension and excitement and hopefully some pleasure. He was right, but I thought he was talking about finding the agent and vaccine, not falling for the project manager."

They both laughed at their unexpected situation.

Carrie still wanted to talk business before returning to the Elliot House for dinner. Their walk led them onto a wide hiking trail and took them along a shady path under the late day's sunlight. She breathed in the sweet acrid scent of pine and cedar trees with each step.

"I'm really concerned about the network hack job done today. Some bastard deliberately took out my computer this morning."

"It bothers me too. The whole thing makes no sense. Why would anyone do that? The technical problem was resolved in minutes once I determined what had happened."

"I think it has to be someone who wanted the code for the virus algorithm stored on my machine. He, or she, couldn't log onto my workstation since my retinal ID prevented that. The perpetrator must have known that and getting onto the file server directly was a way around that. Even though it's early in the project and we've only investigated Mongoloid gene clusters, this person could copy my software code and model it later for Whites and Blacks. It wasn't me, and it wasn't you poking around with the network early in morning. That leaves only Lan or Warren."

Jim stopped walking and turned to her with a serious expression on his face.

"Did you store a backup version of your algorithm programs on the file server?"

"I did. But I saved it with the encryption software that I always use. Without knowing which encryption package I used, no one could decrypt it to make it readable. My decryption software is only on my workstation and is activated when I download to the server. If someone had successfully hacked into my files on the server, they wouldn't be able to make any sense of them."

A broad smile expanded Jim's face. He put his arm around her shoulders as they continued to walk.

"That's it. When the files showed up encrypted, this person got angry and left the Computer Room before resetting your workstation online."

Carried pondered his guess.

"You might be onto something. I think from now on, I'll do what Lan does each day. She makes a copy of her data on a flash memory stick and locks it up. Then she erases everything on her workstation. She reloads it each morning when she comes into work. I think I had better start doing that."

"I agree. It makes sense. As we informed you when you came on board, we have a secure network here at the lab. We have our own intranet inside these walls rather than general access to the world wide web. We are linked with CDC and Washington, and that's it. She can't send backup files through the internet to any other computer. We have an ironclad firewall that keeps us safe from outside hackers or hacker wannabes."

"I'll begin that routine tomorrow," Carrie said, as if she were talking to herself.

"What the hell do you think she keeps on those memory sticks?" Jim asked.

"My guess is she records every damned thing. If you ever watch Lan carefully, she compulsively makes notes of everything and keys the text into her workstation. I think it must be like a diary or some journal of everything that goes on. Hell, I bet she even records what we all eat and drink at the Elliot House."

Jim shook his head. "I noticed that, but didn't think more about it. I guess she reports all of it back to someone."

There was a silent pause with only the soft sound of breaking pine needles below their feet.

"Do you think that that someone could be Warren? Or do you think it was Lan who broke in, and she's acting as an informant for Warren?"

A chilly feeling overcame Carrie as she spoke the words.

Just a few months ago, I was correcting undergraduate microbiology tests. Now I'm steeped in a top-secret project and using words like hacker and informant. Instead of reviewing student lab books, I'm trying to figure out who is screwing around here by breaking into computer files.

"I don't think so," Jim replied. "Even though it's his project, he doesn't seem to ask you or me for much technical details. Our status meetings with him are pretty much a sham. All he wants to know is when we're going to be finished with each phase. And we know that Lan calls him directly with updates on our progress."

"Warren is one of the brightest people I've ever known. He could do or be anything he wanted with his intelligence and charm.

Even during his depression, he never appeared to be malicious or clandestine in anything. I believe that he trusts me and you. He doesn't need a mole, as you imply. One thing about Warren is that you always know his opinions and what's on his mind, even if his ideas are unpopular."

"He also has great ambitions," Carrie added. "He wants to become President of the United States! That goal is not unusual, except with him. I get the feeling that his desire is based less on ego than on vengeance. He wants to show that a Chinese American can sit in the position of ultimate power in the United States."

"If you're right, you know where that anger came from."

"From his former fiancée, Allison Wellington?"

"You bet."

Carrie went on to tell Jim about her previous evening with Warren. She told him how Lan had actually been handpicked by the MSS head, General Peng, and not by Warren. She explained how Warren had revealed that he didn't know who Dr Lan Ying was before Project V got started.

"That's news to me. I had always guessed he picked her as he had recruited me. I don't know much about General Peng, though in the early days of the project he spent a lot of time with Warren here. He also accompanied Lan to the prison hospital a few times."

"I'm feeling more uncomfortable with this crap. Nothing is clear. And I still have my doubts about Lan Ying. Warren told me her experience and credentials are only from the academic arena. Do you think she's even qualified to develop the vaccine for our bio-agents?"

"Working in academia is not a bad thing. She talks the talk and walks the walk, but I haven't pressed her for details on how she'll develop the vaccine. Once we finish the agent yellow test phase, I can learn about her approach and review her planning protocols for creating and testing the vaccine."

"Can you do that?"

"Sure. I would think that she would begin with chicken embryos before moving on to human tissues and finally live subjects. It's the conventional protocol."

"I would like to know more about her, sooner than later."

"For now, all we can do is keep our heads down and bring the first phase of Project V to completion."

Carrie checked her watch. "Hell, it's getting late. I have to go."

He didn't respond verbally, but the expression on his face spoke volumes to Carrie.

They circled back towards their bikes. They embraced once more with their longing goodbyes. Both ached to spend the night together.

A few moments later, the two lovers sped down the serpentine road from atop Big Blue.

TWENTY ONE

Carrie was the first to arrive at the dining room. She was met by one of the waiters who made her a scotch and water. Before he turned to leave, Carrie had a question for him.

"What do you recommend for tonight's dinner for Mr Lee and me?"

"Dr Bock, we have pheasant with wild rice or medallions of pork with a light currant sauce."

"I would like each of us to have the pheasant."

"Yes, ma'm."

Within minutes, Warren made his entrance. His bright, cheery smile showed him to be in a good mood. He looked in better form than he had on the previous evening. Tonight he wore a long-sleeved, navy-blue sport shirt with light gray slacks.

Carrie mused that the Under Secretary had grown sensitive about his hairy arms while in her company.

"What kind of day did you super scientists have in the lab today?" he asked as he headed towards the bar.

"Actually pretty good. Jim prepared another sample of agent yellow, and Lan should already be in Saratoga. More testing will take place tomorrow."

"I wanted to meet with all three of you for a project status meeting before I returned to the Capitol. If Lan is away, we'll have the meeting with just the two of us."

"I can call Jim, and he'll come here within a few minutes."

Warren looked directly into her eyes. He wasn't giving any clue to what he was thinking, and that bothered her.

"No. There's no need to spoil Jim's evening."

They both took the same chairs as they did the previous evening. Tonight Raul came into the dining room with garden salads and an array of homemade dressings.

As they sipped their drinks, Warren asked more detailed questions about the testing procedure. She was surprised how little he seemed to know about Lan's testing. She wondered if he might have been purposely teasing out the details to see how much she knew.

"Explain to me again why the testing agents are frozen for the test," he asked. "Why do you use ice cubes?"

"Because the agent is inert while it's in a frozen state. We can travel with it as long as it is packed in dry ice. After the ice melts, the pathogen becomes viable; and since it is insoluble in water, it doesn't dissolve but rather becomes a lethal liquid."

He took a sip of his drink. "I guess what I really wanted from you, Jim, and Lan isn't technical details but a project timeline."

"A project timeline?"

"Carrie, I'll be very candid with you. I was the one who found out about this terrorist bioweapon some months ago. When I spoke with certain people about it in Washington, they doubted such a racially targeted agent could be developed. Your team, and especially *you*, discovered that it can be done. It is now possible to aim a lethal virus at a race, and literally obliterate it from the face of the earth. This could soon become public information around the world. If we can develop these agents and their vaccines, they will be sought after by every country."

"But..." Carrie tried to interrupt, but Warren wouldn't let her. He held his hand up.

"Please let me continue and be quite candid. I'm trying to build my own political resume and garner some public recognition. I already have the military, business, and limited political credentials. Project V can put me over the top. It can make me the most prominent Chinese American politician who the voters deeply respect across the nation. I would like to be running in either the next election or the succeeding one. This project is emblematic for me and for other people of Asian blood. Just as President Bowa broke the color barrier for the Oval Office, I can be the first man of Far Eastern ancestry to lead the United States. The sooner the project is completed, the sooner my professional and personal reputation becomes public knowledge. In politics, surprising names often pop up. The former Governor of Alaska, Sarah Palin, is a good example."

"Warren, I think that your political ambitions are great, but....

The Under Secretary of State interrupted.

"So that's what I need to know from you, a timetable for your group to discover the agent for all three races and their respective vaccines. Jim will not be involved in Phase II, but with your experience you should be able to give me a ballpark estimate of when you can finish Phase I."

Warren's tone blatantly spoke of urgency, but not for the right reasons.

Carrie's mind raced to consider the complex situation concerning Warren. She didn't know if she could trust this wonder boy from the State Department. She questioned his emotional stability because he had his eye on the prize for all the wrong reasons. And she hadn't yet dismissed the possibility that he may have been the one who attempted to steal the software formula from her computer.

"It was unfortunate that Lan called you and got you so energized about our first test. It is still premature. Jim and I would have preferred telling you after more testing. Yes, my formula does seem to work. We've found a way to identify the Mongoloid gene clusters and can produce a lethal influenza-like virus to attack hosts with those clusters. But there's much more work to do, not only with the bioagents yellow, white, and black, but also with the vaccines, which Lan hasn't even begun to work on yet. The vaccines are what we're ultimately after, aren't we?"

She stared at Warren and paused so that he knew that her question wasn't rhetorical but carried a stinging message.

"That is the goal," Warren replied.

"We have lots of work still to do. At least for now, I can't give you a timetable."

"What about a rough estimate? Can you say one month, two months, or something like that? This project can't go on forever. If the SAN are testing their agent now in isolated pockets, it won't be long before they unleash it around the world. We—the US government, if you like—*must* have an idea of when the agents and vaccines will be available."

It was obvious Warren realized that he had foolishly put forward his personal agenda. Now he was sidestepping it by underscoring the real urgency for the United States to meet the goals of Project V as soon as possible.

She sighed audibly. "I don't play hypothetical games. We need to assess our work, adjust our plans, and keep working. I can't speak for Jim or Lan, but it's obvious that we all have much more work to do, *as I have said*. I found the agent yellow quickly and, to be honest, probably with a great deal of luck. We have no idea if the others will come to fruition as easily."

The conversation ended as the waiter entered the dining room with their meals.

"Pheasant! Carrie, you make excellent decisions." He gave her one of his signature smiles and held his wineglass at the stem while the waiter filled it.

They ate dinner without any more discussion about the project.

"I've got to turn in early tonight. I wish you continued luck on the project. Please keep me posted on your progress. I don't know when I'll return here, but don't hesitate to contact me if necessary. I will call Jim periodically."

As soon as Carrie returned to her apartment, she considered riding her bike out to Jim's house to spend the night with him. He had been on her mind the entire evening. After stifling a long yawn, she thought better of that and decided that an early night was the prudent choice.

As she slid under the covers, her purple cellphone rang.

"Hi, Carbo, it's me," President Bowa said.

"What's up?"

"I have heard from my Directors of the CIA and NSA. I had earlier asked them to research their network about the SAN terrorist organization or any group that may have developed a racially targeted bioweapon."

"And what did they tell you?"

"No surprises. Their networks say that many terrorists groups have discussed such a bioagent, but none of the scientists could put it together. They believe that no such weapon exists, but don't rule out the possibility of one being feasible. They say that the SAN terrorist organization doesn't have the collective brainpower and resources to effectively use the Genome Database or DNA sampling sources."

"Do you think the Beijing intelligence sources misled Warren?"

"Not sure at this point."

"What about the deaths on Astola Island? All of the White people died, but the Black man and Asian man apparently survived."

"That is perplexing, and we should get more intelligence on that soon. Everything else so far is unsubstantiated. Our operatives are working through British clandestine agents. The Brits are actually more embedded into that part of the world than our agents.

"Carbo, despite the apparent likelihood that the SAN don't have a bioweapon, I think we should continue. The vaccine will be a good defense if, or when, such a bioagent is developed. With the progress you're making, I don't think we should abort Project V. Do you?"

"No. That's not what I'm saying. I think the project must continue. We're learning a lot on several fronts."

"There was some intelligence that the NSA picked up that tweaked my curiosity, however."

"What was that?"

"Supposedly several years ago, the Russians and Chinese had secretly allied to form a group of esteemed scientists to develop bioagents, but the project fell apart through some petty political negotiations. They couldn't agree on who would get what out of the clandestine effort."

"That's interesting. Do you know who the principals were?"

"Let me walk over to my desk. I scribbled some notes. Here it is. The Russian lead person on the project was a bioscientist, some guy by the name of Vladimir Trotchekov. And the Chinese participant was someone called General Peng Dehuai."

"General Peng!" An icy shiver went through her body.

"Do you know him?"

"No, but I may be meeting him soon."

"What does that mean?"

"I'm not sure right now, but I'll get back to you on that."

"That's not why I told you about this. Peng's Russian contact, Vladimir Trotchekov, has ties to the United States. Guess who his nephew is?"

"Could it be our beloved research scientist, Josef Marotsky?"

"That's right."

Carrie recalled Warren telling her how Dr Marotsky had been General Peng's recommendation to lead Project V. Some pieces of the puzzle were now fitting together. But she had to keep all of this to herself and not tell Jim because of her role on the project.

"Carbo, before we hang up, what's your impression of how Warren's been acting these past few days?"

"Right now, I'm not sure. I told you Hinton's name was mentioned in that phone call."

"That must have been about the Environmental Exchange program that he's spearheading. I doubt it goes beyond that."

"Tell me more about the exchange program. Is it something to do with university students, particularly budding, young scientists?"

"No. It's nothing like that. Hinton is arranging a large scale exchange of experienced environmental engineers and scientists to visit each other's countries. The program will last several weeks, with our experts visiting China and evaluating their industrial and manufacturing systems that need improvement. The purpose is to protect their air, land, and water resources from pollution. At the same time, a large group of Chinese engineers will spend time in the United States to learn how we implement environmental systems to protect our natural resources."

"And this came originally from Warren, right?"

"Warren brought the proposal to Zachary, and he jumped on it. He sees political opportunities with the national and international press. It is something that can improve SinoAmerican relations. And the other world leaders are solidly behind it. Hinton believes that facilitating such a project will help the United States regain global approval after the Bush-Cheney isolationism of the past eight years."

"And your Secretary of State gets a little boost for his next Presidential campaign."

"No doubt that was his motive. I was a little pissed off that he went so far with this before letting me know the details. Hinton is still struggling with not being in charge. This was an opportunity to slip one by me. We had some words, and I don't believe anything like this will happen again. His wings have now been clipped real short."

"I can see Hinton getting some good press on this one. But what bothers me is that it came through the back door so to speak. I know Warren works for the State Department, but it should have been arranged through normal diplomatic channels."

"That bothers me too. It's similar to the way Project V began. Sometimes the person sitting in the Oval Office has no idea what's going on with multiple agendas. But I can't get too reactive over that right now."

Carrie recalled a sensitive conversation they once had had before breaking up.

"If I recall, Barbo, I told you over twenty years ago why I hated politics. I told you to be aware of the sharks and barracudas who would eat you up and spit you out."

"Ha! I do remember that conversation, Carbo. I remember it well. But I've learned how to identify the sharks and barracudas who swim around the Capitol. It's those damned piranhas that are hard to see. When you finally spot them, they've already taken a big bite."

He chuckled over his metaphor.

"Just be careful if you want to survive your first term in office."

There was a brief, awkward pause before the President spoke again.

"Carbo, you're an expert in Chinese culture. Can you tell me something? Is this a typical method in getting things done? You know, as you said, using the back door to get things done?"

"I'm not an expert on Chinese political or tactical strategies, but the Chinese are famous for using the backdoor—what they call *hòumén*—to get things done."

"I'll keep that in mind," the President replied and then changed the subject.

"What's your take so far on Mr Lee? Do you think he's got some subversive blood running through his veins? You know what I'm asking. Do you think he's more loyal to his ethnic motherland than the good old United States of America?"

Carrie exhaled an audible sigh.

"God, Barbo, there's so much to this man. I need more time with him. I'll give you a report when the time is right."

"There's one more thing. In my daily intelligence report, I was told that there is definitely an operative mole working within the Elliot House lab. I presumed it was Warren, but so far they haven't provided me a name. The operative may be working directly with the Chinese MSS. All we know is that he or she is not to be considered a loyal allied participant."

"Okay," Carrie said softly while trying to hide her anxiety. She restrained herself from telling him more in case her speculation was wrong.

"I've got to go, Carbo. But wait! Something else came up from Hinton that I need your counsel on. Hinton's hosting a birthday party for his Under Secretary, Warren Lee, in a few weeks. He asked if I could make an appearance. I probably won't do that, but I do want to get him a gift for all the work he's been doing. You know, he's still innocent until proven guilty. I would like you to think about some unique and appropriate gift since you know him better than I do. I gotta go; the press is waiting. We'll talk again soon."

Carrie hung up with a myriad of thoughts running around in her head.

Peng, the Russian scientist, Marotsky, Hinton's insubordinate ways, Lan, Astola Island, and now a special birthday gift for Warren Lee.

Carrie felt a migraine coming on.

* * *

While showering the next morning, she was amazed again at how the human brain works. So often she would go to bed internally troubled with a problem. She would stress herself trying to find the solution and begin to manifest a headache before dropping off to sleep. Somehow after a nap or a good night's rest, the solution became clearly etched in her brain.

As she dried off, she thought over and over how this morning's epiphany would help solve some of the issues within Project V. She now felt she could protect the project and keep it on the fast track while she could personally control how the outcome was handled. She needed one other person to help with her plan. That person was Jim.

When she stopped by the dining room for a breakfast roll, she saw one of the house staff, Amy O'Brien, serving coffee to Warren. She knew that Amy, a diminutive Irish immigrant in her late sixties had worked at the Elliot House since MIT owned and operated the facility. The woman knew the facility well and had an outgoing personality. She wasn't surprised that Warren had allowed her to continue to work at the isolated retreat center.

Warren's gaze caught hers as Amy poured some tomato juice into a crystal glass for him.

"Good morning, Carrie. Would you like to join me for breakfast?" he asked after sipping the juice.

"I'm sorry, I can't. I stopped by just for juice and a roll. I want to get to the lab early."

She eyed the full plate of poached eggs, toast, and potatoes with a side dish of fresh fruit sitting in front of Warren.

"Too bad."

"It looks good, though. And it looks like you've got one helluva healthy appetite today."

Warren smiled. "I'm really quite famished this morning."

Amy set a tray of jellies near his plate.

"That's true, Dr Bock, but I thought Mr Lee didn't care for our food all of a sudden. He missed breakfast altogether the other day. I found he was still sleeping. I had to wake him up about eight thirty in the morning. He's usually up and dressed by six!"

Her Irish brogue was heavy with a story-telling, endearing character.

"Yes," he replied bashfully. He affectionately raised his eyebrows at Amy and then turned to face Carrie.

"I really overindulged the night before during our dinner. I apologize. It was truly out of character for me. Sleep is the best remedy for that. I was glad Amy woke me or I would have slept past nine," he confessed with a sheepish tone.

"No apology is necessary," Carrie said, as she grabbed her juice glass and croissant before scooting out of the dining room.

As she stepped down the flight of stairs, she thought about Warren sleeping off a hangover the other morning.

He got up very late according to Amy. If that were true, he couldn't have been the one who disabled my workstation at six o'clock in the morning. Lan is now the only one left who could have hacked into the system. She couldn't get at my software algorithms because of my encrypted programs. That must have angered her enough to forget to reenable my workstation.

TWENTY TWO

When Carrie walked into the office that morning, she felt a sense of relief. It was more comfortable with Lan in Saratoga conducting the second round of field tests. It was something she couldn't easily identify, but she often felt uneasy with Lan quietly working with her in the same room, especially when it was the just two of them. The woman had too many mysteries attached to her.

Carrie walked over to Lan's work area. She wondered whether any personal items could provide clues about this eccentric researcher. She dismissed any guilt of privacy invasion and pulled on every drawer in Lan's desk.

As I expected, they're closed up tight, just like the mystery woman herself.

Her body jerked when Jim hailed her from the doorway.

"Good Morning! I see we're alone today."

"Yes," she answered, as she stepped back towards her own work area.

"Good."

Jim walked directly over to her, placed his hands gently on her shoulders, and kissed her warmly on the lips. It was the first intimacy they had shared in the office. It caught her off guard.

For a moment, she forgot everything, her mission to spy on Warren, her misgivings about Lan, and everything about Project V. She simply enjoyed the moment and the moist, gentle kiss.

They slowly distanced themselves from each other.

"By the way, sir, do you and I know each other?" she asked as she backed away from him.

Jim laughed at her joke.

As they settled into their work, Carrie was more eager to tell him of the plan that had come to her that morning.

Unable to restrain herself, she finally broke the silence.

"Why don't we go out somewhere for a long private lunch today? You know, instead of joining the others on the patio."

Jim looked at her with a curious smile. "Sure. What did you have in mind?"

"Let's go to a nice seafood restaurant. We could find one along the shoreline in Nantasket or Cohasset. I would like some place where we can be alone for a change."

He nodded.

"I drove my Mustang to work this morning since they're calling for thundershowers later today. I'm going to be in the tissue lab all morning, so let me know when you're ready."

At noon as they drove along the shoreline south of Boston, she told him what she had learned about Warren's sleeping in the previous day. Interspersed with her story, she gave him driving directions to their destination.

"I really doubt he was in the Computer Room at six in the morning. I was told he slept past eight o'clock. It had to be Lan. Why in hell does she want to steal a copy of my agent yellow formula? After all, we're supposed to be a freakin' team. If she had asked me for the programming code, I would have probably given a copy to her."

"She doesn't know that. She might think you and I would keep the formula and turn it over only to Warren when the project ended. She doesn't comprehend the concept of teamwork. She's an individual who treats everyone else as an individual."

"I don't get it. But I'll tell you one thing. I'm going to get to that witch and understand what the hell makes her tick long before the project is completed."

"You can try to get to know Lan, but I don't think she'll open up. She has one of those stoic Chinese personalities." He smiled and turned to wink at Carrie. "I called her at the Saratoga before we left and asked if she needed any of my vendor contacts to begin testing for the vaccine. In particular, I asked if she needed names of reliable chicken embryo vendors."

"And what did she say to that?"

"I think I caught her off guard. Or she hasn't done much thinking or planning to develop the vaccines. She answered by asking me to provide her with a list of vendors that we use at the CDC. Beyond that, it didn't sound like she had done much preparation at all."

"We have to get more involved with her role in this project."

At the end of the country road, Jim pulled into the parking lot of Hugo's Lighthouse, an upscale seafood restaurant overlooking a picturesque water inlet.

They opted to sit outdoors at a dockside table since it was a beautiful late summer day with a cool breeze coming off the ocean.

"So what made you wanted to get away from the lab?" Jim asked.

Carrie knew she had to present her overnight epiphany very delicately. Her plan would not only affect Project V, but also their relationship. Before she spoke, she inhaled the salty breeze wafting inland. The scent sharpened her senses and revitalized her inner confidence.

The waitress took their orders and left.

"What I'm going to tell you is an idea, a plan of sorts. I came up with it this morning, and it involves you. I want you to simply listen to me and not react until I've fully proposed my idea. Is that okay with you?"

Jim nodded. His expression told her that he was anxious about her disclosing something that he didn't want to hear.

"What's your plan?"

"First, I must start with my latest theory. I now believe, *strongly believe*, that discovering the elusive grail of this project, the vaccine, is not the top priority of China's MSS. Nor was it ever their goal, as it is for the American government. I also don't believe that it's Lan's top priority. Rather I think that they only wanted the bioagents. And they want to get their hands specifically on the agent white and agent black algorithms. That's why the original directive was for us to develop and test agent yellow last. I'm convinced that Lan's mission is to get her hands on the algorithms for developing the white and black bioagents."

"Now, Lan and you…"

"Wait! Whoever has the formula controls the world, and it could potentially change the configuration of the human race on every continent. It could wipe out the entire humanity of some countries."

She stopped speaking when the waitress appeared. The young woman placed their lobster rolls and a dish of coleslaw in front of each of them and retreated inside the restaurant.

Carrie continued. "I want us, you and me, to take control of Project V from within. I want to make finding the vaccine our priority. To hell with Lan! I still maintain the project can't be considered complete until the vaccine is discovered and ready for mass distribution. I can tell you that's what the President is expecting. Now, here's my plan. I'll continue to work on developing the next two viral agents. I feel that I'll have agent black and agent white ready for testing in a short time. I'm sure I can model it after the agent yellow formula."

When Jim raised his eyebrow, she wondered if he was surprised at her confidence.

"And?" he interjected.

"And, if I'm dedicated to finding the last two racial viruses, I want you dedicated to finding the vaccine. This is your expertise and background. You may have to network with some of your colleagues at the CDC. Nobody will know what we're working on, especially not Lan. As I develop the bioagents and give her samples to test, you'll be secretly testing for the vaccine. In this way, we can assure that the vaccine will be developed at the same time as the viral agents."

"But..."

"Please let me finish. I know what this means for you. You were planning to leave as soon as the agents for all three major races were developed, and then your brother would be freed. But now, and I hope you agree, it's doubtful Lan could ever come up with any prophylactic serum. What I'm telling you is, I'm not sure she *ever* intended to do so. I don't think she knows a damned thing about developing vaccines for any organism, let alone for an organic-synthetic viral agent."

She took a bite of her lobster salad roll and washed it down with a sip of iced tea. She then continued without losing any momentum.

"Warren also knew if anyone could figure out a way to develop a bioagent based on race, it was you, his ol' college buddy. Do you see where I'm going with this? If the MSS want only the lethal agents, their mission would be done when your mission is. If they really wanted the vaccine, they would keep you on a short leash until such a vaccine was developed."

Jim looked at her in disbelief. "I don't know…."

She cut him off.

"I know I'm asking a lot of you, Jim. I know how badly you want your brother released from prison as soon as possible. I also understand that you wouldn't have agreed to join Project V if his freedom wasn't part of the deal. And if you agree to develop the vaccine, Jiang Ming's release will be further delayed. If we work hard, long days and nights, I think we can accelerate the time it takes to reach our goals."

After another sip of iced tea, she looked directly into his eyes from across the table.

"If you aren't involved in finding the vaccine, there may never be one." She continued staring at him to see if he had absorbed all of what she had said.

"I didn't expect this to be our little 'luncheon chat' today. You've made quite a proposal to me and I need time to digest it before I respond."

Not surprised at his answer, she was content that he wasn't immediately negative about her plan. She reached across the table, grasped his hand in hers, and squeezed it firmly. She had to be totally honest with him.

"Jim, there's more. I'm also being quite selfish. I'm not looking forward to you returning to Atlanta. With the original agreement, you could be heading south in a matter of weeks. I want to be with you as long as I can. I'm aware that with my plan, your stay up here will be extended, and that makes me happy, happier than you probably know."

Jim squeezed her hand without saying a word.

After coffee, the two returned to Jim's Mustang and headed back to the Elliot House.

As they drove along, Carrie decided she wanted to amend the discussion she had had with Jim. She now had a personal plan to make that happen.

"I have a proposal," she said, reaching over to take his hand again in hers. After we get back to the lab this afternoon, I'd like to ride over to your place and prepare a nice dinner for us tonight. I'll have it ready for you when you come home. "

Jim smiled as he drove. "Sounds like a bribe to me."

She smiled back at him. "No, not at all. I haven't done that for you. You'll have time to think, and we can discuss this more over dinner tonight."

"Oh shit!" Jim shouted. "I just missed my turn back onto the main road." Jim's head swiveled around. "If I take this side street, I can turn around and get back on track. See, you've got me all flustered."

Carrie giggled. "I have that effect on you, eh?"

Jim turned the Mustang onto the side street. He drove about a hundred yards through the residential neighborhood before pulling up into a driveway. Before putting the car into reverse, another car, a black Mercedes sedan, slowed and nearly stopped near the driveway entrance.

Jim could clearly see the driver's face in his rear view mirror as it peered out at his Mustang. The Mercedes then sped away.

"Look! Did you see who was driving that Mercedes?" Jim asked as he backed down the driveway.

"Who was it?"

"That was the same bastard I saw at the Red Sox game and later sitting at the bar in the Italian café."

"You mean that guy with the long Heidelberg scar?"

"The same guy. And he has been tailing behind us. Being in this little seaport town at the same time that we are is not just another coincidence."

Jim looked both ways then carefully pulled out and resumed driving back to the lab.

They drove in silence before Carrie asked, "If we're being followed by the scar-faced guy, who the hell is he working for?"

"I have no idea, but I'll tell you one thing: there's a helluva lot more to this project than you and I know."

* * *

Back in her apartment, Carrie packed an overnight bag and checked her email. One message was from Wei Xing, who asked her to set a date and time for their next phone call.

She keyed in a response, a suggestion that they connect in the evening in two days.

The Homeland Security guards carefully examined her overnight bag at the checkpoint before she exited the Elliot House grounds.

She made one stop at a local market and bought two Porterhouse steaks and fixings for a salad.

As she rode the rest of the way to his house, rumbles of loud thunder rolled in the background. With any luck, she would beat the rain and avoid getting soaked.

Once she arrived, she found the hidden house key that Jim had told her about. She looked around to make sure nobody was watching her and then let herself inside.

TWENTY THREE

In Jim's kitchen, Carrie found everything that she needed to prepare dinner. After setting the table, she turned on the TV, sat down on the sofa, and switched the channel to CNN. The station's White House correspondent was providing a remote report to the anchor person from the West Lawn.

> Today, Heidi, the Secretary of State, Zachary Hinton, has broken new ground in the historically fragile Chinese American relationship. The colorful and energetic member of President Bowa's cabinet has initiated a cultural exchange program with Chinese environmental engineers. They will infiltrate the United States in the next couple of months to learn how we protect our environment with regulations, procedures, and processes. The Chinese are especially anxious to learn how we control and prevent air and water pollution. Simultaneously, we will send hundreds of our environmental engineers and scientists to China to recommend how Beijing can implement new programs to protect their air and water resources.

As the reporter narrated, Carrie watched the background video taken earlier in the day.

The Secretary of State stood in front of the Capitol with nearly a hundred Chinese engineers. One short, chubby man stood in the front row with a serious expression. He kept panning the reporters and photographers as though he were uncomfortable with the public commotion. He was distinguishable from the others by his rotund frame and a red wine birthmark that stood out on his left cheekbone.

The visiting group of engineers seemed to be all male with the exception of one tall, slender woman. She stood out with her salt and pepper hair tied up in a bun. She appeared to be about sixty years of age, but had supple skin and a warm, alluring expression. The cameras caught her charismatic smile, but also revealed a shot of her right arm, which had been amputated at the elbow.

The other members of the group ranged in age from mid-twenties to late fifties. All were smiling with apparent excitement at being in the United States and learning more about American environmental technology.

Secretary of State Hinton effectively used the news media by taking all the credit for the innovative, international program. He told the public that "this is only the genesis of many peaceful, progressive alliances between our two global superpowers."

He then paused and smiled for all of the photographers and news cameras.

The CNN newscaster continued.

> As the Chinese proverb goes, "A journey of a thousand miles
> begins with a single step," though we'll have to wait to see if
> this journey continues as planned for the Bowa administration.
> And now back to you, Heidi.

Carrie shut off the TV when she heard Jim come through the doorway.

"I could get used to coming home to a beautiful, sexy woman preparing my dinner."

Carrie laughed as she enjoyed her own fantasy. This could be the first of many dinners she would prepare for him; and on some nights, he would cook for her.

She watched him as he opened a bottle of red wine and filled two glasses. Allowing him a few minutes to unwind, she didn't jump immediately into their planned discussion. He had a lot to think about since lunch.

"Jim, that guy who stalked us today is making me feel creepy. I'm thinking about contacting President Bowa and having the FBI check him out. What the hell would somebody want with you and me?"

"I don't know. I can't get it out of my mind either. Who would want to stalk us? Maybe he is tailing only *one* of us. I really don't think it's Warren, unless he's curious about the two of us and wants to know more about our personal relationship."

"What about Lan? Maybe she assumes that if we become close we'll plot against her. She seems like someone who wants to know everything that's going on so she can record it in her journal. I wouldn't put it past her to hire someone to tail us."

"Or someone else hired an agent because they can't keep a guarded eye on you and me and our relationship. It may be for protection of some sort."

"Like who?" Carrie asked.

"Like President Bowa."

The shock of hearing this allegation created an awkward pause. She hadn't thought about any political effect of their secret affair.

"What do you mean by that?"

"I was just thinking that maybe your friend in the White House is worried about your personal safety and has assigned someone to look after you, a bodyguard of sorts. I presume his intention is benign."

"I never thought about that." Although Carrie was amused and somewhat disappointed with the idea that Barbo would provide her with protection without telling her in advance, she would rather that be the case than someone spying on her for political gain."

"Let's go into the living room," he suggested. "We can relax on the sofa for a while. I want to know how your afternoon went without me being around."

"Did you miss me?" Carrie asked in a girlish tone to help change their mood.

They sat on the sofa and made small talk in-between sips of wine. For her, the alcohol and casual conversation served to whet her sexual appetite. She wondered if he was having similar thoughts.

While gently laying her hand on his thigh, she asked, "Are you terribly hungry? If you are, I can put the steaks in the broiler now."

His enlarged pupils seemed to reveal what she had hoped.

"No, I'm not hungry now. I need to work up an appetite for dinner."

He leaned into her relaxed body and kissed her with such heartfelt passion she never wanted it to end. Within minutes, they both stripped and entangled on Jim's bed.

Loud rumbles of thunders echoed outside as her hands explored his body, her mouth not leaving his. When she reached for his expanding manhood, he moaned in her mouth while she stroked him intimately.

Afterwards, as they lay perspiring on the bed, Jim reached for the remote control and turned on the overhead fan. It soon whirred at high speed cooling their exhausted and heated bodies.

Without speaking, she raised her hand to slowly rake through his wavy black hair. As she gazed into his coal-black eyes, she brought her hand down to his face. Her fingertips gently traced his cheekbones, the tip of his nose, and finally his full lips.

Trying to stare into his warm and gentle soul, she wanted to tell him how she felt deep inside her own heart, but knew she had to restrain herself. She was still assigned to an important, top-secret mission, and he was still a married man.

Jim's eyes grew larger as he looked over to her. He spoke softly.

"Carrie, I have to tell you something."

Her immediate reaction was that he had made his decision. She felt her heartbeat accelerate with anticipation. But that wasn't his message at this time.

"I called my wife in China last night."

A surprising curve ball was just thrown at her. She had to mentally regroup. "And did you tell her about me? About you and me?"

"No. But she had news for me."

"News? Was it about your brother?"

"No, it was news about her father. She told me how he is seriously ill. He's expected to die soon, perhaps within weeks or even days. I asked her if she would grant me the divorce after he died."

"And?"

"She agreed. She knows the burden the marriage has been on me, on the both of us. It had been a mistake, but she could never hurt her father with a divorce while he was still alive."

A role of thunder rocked the house and was followed by a torrential downpour.

Carrie was overwhelmed with joy at the surprising news. It was certainly not what she had expected to hear.

"That's good. I'm happy for you."

"You mean you're happy for us. Soon we can be public about our relationship. We'll no longer have to creep around in the dark and hide our love. We can share our love without worrying about malicious gossip hurting you or your friend, the President."

Both got up and dressed.

Carrie held back from asking about her new plan for Project V.

Later, when they sat down to eat dinner, the subject was still not raised. After they had washed the dishes, Jim made a pot of coffee and gestured for them to sit on the couch.

"I've given a lot of thought to your plan."

She sipped her coffee and waited. It seemed right to let him to take his time.

"First, I think you're right about what's going on here. I initially thought Lan to be a strange and introverted person, but now I'm more suspicious of what her motives are. Or perhaps what General Peng's motives might be relative to Project V. If we're right, you and I are indirectly developing genocidal bioagents only for the PRC. I also believe Warren was duped into this project unwittingly. I believe that despite his personal issues and dormant vengeance he would never sell out his country. I don't think there's any connection between him and Lan working for the PRC. I also agree with you that the objective of finding a vaccine must be met. It's *our* ultimate goal."

Although she felt greatly relieved by what he had said so far, she wanted to hear about the extent of his personal commitment.

"You know how I feel about my younger brother, Jiang Ming. He's the only family that I have, and I want him freed as soon as possible."

Carried listened and anxiously awaited his climactic decision.

"I have total confidence in you, Carrie. I feel that you can come up with the black and white bioagents soon, while I concentrate on developing the vaccines. As you said, if we work closely on this, with long hours, it will work. I'm willing to stay on to develop the vaccine. And it isn't just the project for me either. I also want to be with you. Not during the life of the project but for the rest of my life. I hope that might be forever, but I'm willing to take one day at a time.

I told you that I love you, and I meant it. I love you more than anything, and making these sacrifices is only a small way for me to prove it."

Carrie set her coffee cup down on the table. Her hand trembled slightly. She quietly moved closer to him so she could wrap her arms around him and hug him as tight as she could. When she eased away, she kissed his lips as her hands caressed his face with tears of joy running down her cheeks. There was a newly charged energy, an energy of happiness that surged throughout her body.

"Jim, I love you so much."

And she did. It seemed as though all of her pent up emotions were suddenly released. It was in that moment that she completely gave her heart to the man she held so close.

He gingerly broke their embrace. His face was now more serious. It was Dr Jim Chen with his analytical, strategic expression.

"We need to strategize. All afternoon I've thought about it. Listen to my idea. The vaccines must also be made into ice cubes, so we can test it in a similar fashion with the prison subjects. But they must be kept away from Lan so that she's unaware of their existence."

"How the hell can we do that? All of the ice cubes go into her private freezer."

"I'll make different batches for each vaccine without her knowing it. As soon each batch of vaccine cubes is produced, we'll sneak them upstairs into your kitchen freezer."

Carrie thought about the proposal. "That'll work. But you're talking about multiple batches."

"Yes, I am."

"Are you thinking one vaccine for agent yellow, one for agent white, and another for agent black?"

"Yes."

"I see it differently. I now know how the racial gene clusters are identified. I also know how the lethal agent reacts when the genetically coded information is found after looking for a match. After it is found, then and only then will the virus attack the cells."

"What's your point?" Jim asked.

"What if our vaccine merely fakes out the agent, or any of the agents? What if the vaccine's only purpose is to transmit back that there is no match. It will be unable to identify the Mongoloid, Negroid, or Caucasoid gene clusters. The vaccine then becomes a blocking agent for *all* racial viruses."

Jim's eyes focused intensely on her as she spoke. "Keep talking, I'm getting it."

"With a universal lock and key model, we'll set the lock to be unable to open under any circumstances. If the vaccine lock doesn't open, the attacking viral agent is stymied. It will die off and no longer be viable. We already know that if it can't find its intended racial gene cluster, it dies off before infecting the body's cells. Like most vaccinations, once the human body has absorbed it, it will be effective for years, perhaps a lifetime. This way we need only to have one anti-viral vaccine for all of the bioagent viruses. Think about it. It's like a super-vaccine to protect against *any* racially discriminating virus. Regardless of an individual's genetic makeup, he or she will be protected."

Jim stared at her. It was obvious his mind was processing the technical machinations of what she had said. Soon a broad smile brightened his face.

"That makes sense. It really does! I have one important question."

She was more than ready to engage in a scientific and academic debate with him. She respected how his analytical mind worked and was prepared to defend her hypothesized solution to their monumental problem.

"What's your question?"

"How am I so lucky to be in love with someone so beautiful, and so sexy, and so freakin' brilliant at the same time?"

She laughed and then playfully punched him in his stomach.

That evening began a bonding relationship much deeper than Carrie had ever shared with any other person, including her ex-husband years ago.

They had more coffee and discussed how future testing might be done on both agents white and black while Jim simultaneously produced vaccine samples, all of which had to take place without Lan's knowledge.

They also discussed the troubling problem of Lan single handedly conducting the field tests. Both agreed that something had to be done about the mysterious scientist from Beijing.

TWENTY FOUR

The next day seemed to last forever for Carrie and Jim inside the office. They waited to hear from Lan and the progress of her field test at Saratoga. There was no call from the perplexing, insolent woman on that hot last day of July.

"I left a message for her to call us. I've got a meeting at the Harvard Medical School with several former colleagues to discuss some state of the art techniques that could help the project. I'll check in from Cambridge."

"I'll text you as soon as she reports in."

Before he left, he turned and kissed her lightly on the lips.

"What would you like to do tonight? It's Friday, and we should kick the weekend off right. How about a long bike ride and then dinner out? Whatever you're in the mood for, I'm game."

Without thinking, she answered with what she really wanted.

"No. I want to do something different tonight. I want you to come upstairs to my apartment around six o'clock. Lan is still away and Warren has returned to Washington. Nobody will pay attention to you using the rear staircase to come up to my place."

"Okay, if you're comfortable with that. What can I bring?"

Carrie looked at him with a deliberately seductive expression. "Nothing, absolutely nothing."

* * *

The day went on without any word from Lan and her progress at the Saratoga Prison Hospital.

Carrie set up software routines for agent black and agent white. She then prepared a series of overnight computer tests before leaving the office for the day.

At six that evening, she heard Jim's knock at her apartment door while she was teasing her hair in front of a mirror.

"Come in. It's unlocked," she called out from the bedroom.

The window shades had already been pulled down. There were several lit candles scattered around the living room to create a relaxed and romantic mood.

She stepped into the room wearing a blue silk, Chinese embroidered robe. In one hand, she carried a festively wrapped gift.

She greeted him with a soft kiss, but when their kiss threatened to go further, she broke away to hand him the wrapped present.

"Happy Birthday!"

"Happy…how did you know?"

"Don't you remember when you told me the saga of Warren's old girlfriend, Allison? You told me you two shared a birthday. And I recalled that the date of that special day is tomorrow, August first."

Jim was pleasantly surprised and reached out to take her into his arms, but Carrie broke away again in anticipation of him opening his gift.

"It's nothing big, but I thought you could get some use out of them."

While his fingers tore at the colorfully wrapped package, the happy glow on his face hinted at what he must have looked like as a young boy. He took out the black leather gloves. His hands stretched them out while pulling them on.

"You don't know what this means to me, Carrie. I haven't really celebrated a birthday in over thirty years."

His statement surprised her.

How can people not celebrate their birthday? I won't question him on that. I don't want to change the mood.

"I didn't bake a cake, but I did light some candles."

"So I see."

"Come, there's more in the next room."

Carrie grabbed his hand and led him into her bedroom. The darkened room had several more candles on the night stand and bureau. They flickered softly in the dark.

"So romantic. I like it very much," Jim commented.

"When I was shopping for your gift, I bought something else. But it's for me. Would you like to see it?"

"I'd love to see it."

Her eyes stayed fixed on his face while she slowly untied the belt to her robe and let it quietly slide to the carpeted floor. She was naked except for a light blue silk thong. She twirled around so he could see all of her and then paused with her back facing him. She leaned slightly forward while turning her head over her shoulder to glance back at him. She enjoyed watching his excited expression. His lustful look tingled her with a shot of warmth between her thighs.

Jim moved toward her and wrapped his arms around her from behind. A wide, anxious smile lit up his face.

"And I thought you and I would be riding on our Harleys tonight," he said with a gentle kiss on her cheek.

She gave him a coy smile with her uncensored reply.

"We will, darling," she whispered as she reached down to the crotch of his pants and squeezed gently. "Tonight, I'll be on your Fat Boy and you can ride my Softail."

Desire flared in his eyes at her suggestive invitation, and soon they were in each other's arms. They entangled hungrily on her bed and celebrated Dr James Chen's most memorable birthday of his life.

After their lovemaking, his relaxed state changed and suggested to Carrie that he was deep in thought. She chose to leave him for the moment and go to the bathroom to wash up.

As she turned to sit up, Jim's hand shot out and grabbed hers. His sober eyes looked deeply into hers with a serious glint. His expression told her he didn't want her to leave him.

She sat back down, rolled over towards him, and let her soft breasts fall onto his hard chest. She gave him a soft kiss on the lips. He responded and raised his hands to cup her face.

"Carrie, I love you."

She understood that he was free to love her, and he was clearly caught up in the moment. After all, she had created the perfect setting. But whatever it was between them would have to be enough for now. She still had another overriding commitment. And that commitment sent a surge of guilt through her once again. She couldn't disclose to Jim her background in Chinese studies, her past personal relationship with Bartholomew Bowa, or her top-secret assignment to watch Under Secretary Lee and report back to the White House. She couldn't be as honest with him as he had been with her.

She kissed her own index finger and placed it over his lips as if to seal them shut.

They both fell asleep in each other's arms.

At two thirty in the morning, something woke her. She looked over at her lover as he lay beside her. By the dim candlelight, she could see that he was also awake. She leaned towards him and whispered softly into his ear.

"Do you know what we should do? We're both wide awake now, but the rest of the world is asleep. Let's go for a ride and watch the sun come up!"

He turned to her and smiled. "Sure, but where?"

"How about heading down to Cape Cod? If we leave now, we can be at the eastern side of Chatham and catch the dawning sun come up over the United States. I've always wanted to do that."

"You're right! Let's get out of here. If we stayed around here today, we would probably end up back in the lab working."

"Perfect. Let's pack up some clothes and stay the weekend."

After showering and dressing, they were soon outside on their motorcycles. They stopped at Jim's house to grab a few things before heading to the Cape in the darkness before dawn.

TWENTY FIVE

When Lan entered the office the following Monday, she appeared physically exhausted. She had spent four days at the prison hospital conducting tests. Over the busy weekend, she hadn't communicated with Jim or Carrie on the progress of the second round of tests on agent yellow.

Carrie stared at mystery woman. Her hair was disheveled and not neatly pulled back in her usual fashion. Her eyes had a tired glaze to them.

Without saying a word, she tilted her head for Carrie and Jim to follow her.

The three of them, armed with cups of coffee, assembled quietly in the conference room. Before speaking, she cleared what sounded like a dry irritated throat.

"The agent is still working effectively," Lan began. "All of the subjects who ingested the agent had the same symptoms and results as before. The exception was that the diluted samples took longer to take effect. And believe me, they took too much longer."

There was no attempt for the Asian scientist to veil the anger in her voice.

"How long did it take for the onset of symptoms?" Jim asked.

"It took almost four hours for each Mongoloid to die. In each case, the subject was comfortable for the first hour, but then came down with symptoms of an upper respiratory tract infection. There was discomfort with a sore throat, increased coughing, and a low grade fever. The symptoms gradually increased in intensity. Eventually their body temperature reached forty degrees Celsius. There was mild perspiration followed by drowsiness and extreme lethargy. This continued until the subjects began expiring. Again before death, some became delusional, while others merely drifted off into a coma, never to recover."

"What about the sinus cavity bleeding? Was there any more of that?" Carrie asked.

"Yes. In every subject, a light trickle of blood came from each nostril. So that symptom wasn't due to the volume of the viral agent, but rather a characteristic of the virus itself."

"The dilution only delayed the critical onset of the virus and had no other bearing on the infection," said Jim, as though thinking out loud.

"What about the other subjects? How did they respond?" Carrie asked.

"The Whites and Blacks who had been given agent yellow experienced only a mild cough. There was no elevated body temperature or perspiration. The Mongoloids who had been segregated and given a placebo of course had no symptoms."

"Was there any difference between the males and females?" Jim queried.

"None. Both sexes responded the same."

Jim inhaled deeply and looked at Lan with a serious expression. He raised the tone of his voice to emphasize his next point.

"Lan, I think you've done some great work. Now we all need to move more aggressively, and we know that Warren wants us to do likewise. We're getting a lot of pressure to advance our progress. I want to modify the testing procedures so that Carrie and I can participate more closely. We will soon be joining you on your trips to Saratoga. It will help us to move more conclusively when we test agent white and agent black."

The color of Lan's pale complexion instantly changed to a fiery crimson. She was obviously disturbed and believed that her ordained project responsibilities would become usurped. Her tired eyes instantly took on a piercing look. She mustered strength to articulate a response, cleared her dry throat again, and raised her voice sharply.

"I believe we all can work faster to develop agent white and agent black. Agent yellow is working well, and if I can get a copy of the viral formula, I can assist you two in creating agent white and agent black."

Jim and Carrie briefly exchanged looks. Lan's revealing statement was tantamount to confessing she was the one who broke into the Computer Room.

Aha, the duel begins! Lan wants to get her hands on my software formula, as she tried to do surreptitiously. Jim was right about her. She may be sneaky, but she's not smart or mature enough to cover up her hidden intentions.

"I'll take that under consideration," Jim answered calmly without looking at Carrie. "I'm not totally satisfied that we've concluded the first wave of testing of agent yellow as our model. Like any good scientist, we need to observe."

Carrie was impressed with Jim's cool, authoritative reaction to Lan's unveiled request.

"Are there any more questions about this last field test?" Lan asked in a disinterested tone.

Neither Jim nor Carrie responded.

Lan slammed her brief case closed and stormed out of the conference room.

Back in the office, the tension hung in the air while the three of them worked on their tasks without saying a word. Lan sat at her workstation tippy-tapping feverishly non-stop.

Carrie knew Jim had already downloaded the new software that he had acquired from the CDC. It was a library of current programs used to develop vaccines for infectious diseases, such as the H1N1, bird flu, SARS virus, and many other potentially lethal viruses. She felt comforted that he was actually working on her plan right now, even while Lan was in the room with them.

Lan left the office early in the afternoon without saying another word to Jim or Carrie. It was obvious that she was still angered with Jim's suggestion that he and Carrie participate in the field testing.

Carrie and Jim worked late into the evening with only a brief break for dinner. It was almost ten o'clock before they finally left the lab.

When Carrie got up to her apartment, she remembered that she had told Wei Xing that they would talk that evening.

"How's everything in Beijing?" Carrie asked after connecting with her friend.

"It's a beautiful, late summer morning here in the capitol of China. Do you want the temperature, wind speed, and relative humidity as well?"

Carrie laughed at her friend's dry sense of humor.

"No, silly! I want to know how *you* are doing. How's your love life?"

Wei Xing talked excitedly about her latest romance. She went on for five minutes non-stop.

Even though they were in their forties, Carrie realized how much she had missed their light and easy girl talk. At the present, she needed to shift gears and dig for some information.

"Wei Xing, have you ever done any genealogical research?"

"Genealogy? That's not really my thing. What did you have in mind?"

Carrie now began a fabricated story that she had already crafted in her mind before the call.

"You remember my love affair with Bart Bowa during my days at Harvard. He contacted me recently from the White House. He asked me if it would be all right that he mentioned my name in his future memoirs or autobiography. Evidently someone is working on the manuscript already even though it won't be released until years from now. I told him it was perfectly fine to mention my name and our relationship during that period."

"Wow, that's so cool! It must seem weird to have had such a special relationship with a man who is now the President of the United States. And I think that it was sensitive of him to get your permission and approval before the book comes out."

"I know. In the course of our discussion, he asked if I had any personal contacts still in China who could do some quick genealogical research. It's going to be a surprise birthday gift for his Under Secretary of State, Warren Lee. He's the person connected to the Tang Dynasty that I was inquiring about. I'm sure it's something Warren doesn't already have, and it would make a great gift. I thought I would just run it by you. If you could email me his ancestral information, I could have a formal Family Tree designed here."

"Sounds like fun! I suppose I could do it. Email me his birthday and whatever else I might use to get started. If he comes from a noble family, the records were usually well kept. It shouldn't take long, and I still have some connections in the PRC's Records Department."

"Perfect. I'm going to need it by the end of the month."

During the rest of the call, Carrie described her growing romance with Jim and his imminent divorce.

* * *

When Carrie arrived at the office the next morning, she was surprised to find herself alone. Neither Jim nor Lan had come in yet, although it was nearly nine o'clock. She was eager to run her simulation test for agent black. The test would prove whether she was able to model other agents by reconfiguring the yellow formula with minor modifications. If it appeared successful in the software environment, she could test tissues in a few days. If the field testing went well, the formula could be remodeled again to develop agent white within a week or so. Her innate positive attitude hoped for the best scenario.

After she finished initiating the programs, her phone rang.

"Carrie, it's me," Jim said. "I was on the phone late last night with my colleagues at the CDC. I want to fly down there today and do some work off-site. It's a great opportunity to work with one vaccine specialist who I greatly respect. My hope is to come back in a day or so with some additional software routines to develop the vaccine."

"Okay, if you think it will advance our goal, it makes sense."

"I'll miss you, but we'll have lots of time after I return *and* after Project V is completed."

His reassuring words put a smile on her face. "Remember, I love you."

"I love you too. I'm assuming Lan is out of the office."

"She hasn't been in at all morning. Based on yesterday's session, she may not show up again. I think she's still mad at you. When you told her we would be involved with her field testing, the Great Wall went up immediately."

"I know. But now I want to be there at Saratoga to observe the tests. I trust her reports are accurate, but observation is necessary for us to know exactly how the agents are working."

As soon as she heard his words, an idea flew into her brain.

"Jim, what if we install remote monitoring? It would save us all that freakin' travel time, which we really can't afford. There are already video cameras in the hospital ward. All we need is a communications link and a TV monitor installed in our office. We can watch how the agent is administered and the progressive reactions of the subjects. This way we can have real-time observation without leaving the lab and interrupting our own work."

"I like your idea, and I think that for a while it might be useful. When I said that I wanted you and me to be on-site for the testing, I had my own plan in mind. I thought that we might test potential vaccines by secretly administering them before Lan administered the bioagents."

Carrie knew that Jim's idea had merit, but she shuddered at the thought of actually witnessing the deaths in person. Sooner or later they would have to be directly involved in administering vaccines; and it would have to be done without anyone knowing it, especially Lan.

"Let's think about it," she responded. "Please call me from Atlanta. I miss you already."

"I will. I'll call tonight."

As she hung up, Lan entered the room. Her mood had certainly improved. She was grinning today and gave a friendly greeting.

"Where's Jim?" Lan asked, after sitting at her computer.

"He just called in. Seems he wants to consult with some of his colleagues at the CDC. I guess he'll be gone for a couple of days."

Lan's smile testified to her happiness that Jim was out. Carrie turned to continue her simulation testing of agent black. She mused whether this would be the perfect opportunity to get to know her colleague better since just the two of them would be together all day. She decided to catch her by surprise and initiate a non-project conversation.

"Lan, have you seen any good movies lately?"

It took a few seconds for the unexpected and innocuous question to make sense to her colleague.

"Me? No, I haven't. I've only seen a few of those action thriller movies since I've been in America."

"Is that what you like to watch, action thriller films?"

"Yes and no. I don't like most American dramas. They don't seem real to me. If I'm going to see a movie that isn't real, it might as well be something way out there."

"I agree. There's a new mystery movie coming out next week," she said as she turned the knob to office door. "Maybe you and I could see it together one evening."

Without waiting for an answer, she stepped through the doorway and headed for the Cold Room with a smile over catching her mysterious colleague off guard. She hoped that if she could meet with Lan outside of their work environment, she might learn more about this strange, unknown woman.

In the Cold Room, she collected frozen tissue samples taken from Black males and females. It was the next step in her testing process. She would provide one of the research assistants with the tissue samples who would concoct a new viral agent based on her latest software formula. The research assistant would record cell activity without knowing that it was Negroid tissue being tested.

About an hour later, Carrie returned to find Lan making a cup of hot tea. Her rare smile signaled a hidden warmth in her associate's persona. It appeared that the ice woman may have begun to thaw.

"Carrie, I would love to go to a movie with you some evening. It would be fun."

"Great, I'll check the listings, and we'll pick a date."

"I was a little angry with Jim's comment yesterday, about you and him getting more involved with the field testing. I have nothing to hide, and I always give him and you very accurate reports of what took place. I was angry with him assuming that if you two got involved, somehow the testing would move more rapidly. That made no damn sense to me."

"To be honest, Lan, he surprised me with that statement also. I had no idea he was thinking about getting involved with the field testing," she lied.

Carrie looked directly at her colleague as she spoke. She noticed how Lan accepted her last statement with some relief on her face.

"What do you think is on his mind?"

"I'm only guessing, but there is some stress and urgency to developing and fully testing the agents. It's frustrating not being able to see the actual test results. Although I haven't said anything, it bothers me a bit also. I'm sure you can understand that."

"In time…"

Carrie cut her off by saying, "I have an idea. Is there any way we can network the cameras in the hospital wards so we can observe the subjects from here?"

"And have you hooked up with a viewing monitor?" Lan asked.

"Yes, I think that'll work. We could put the monitor in here so Jim and me, but nobody else, could watch."

"Except for Warren. He could watch since he has access here."

"Yes, Project V is his pet."

She watched Lan's eyes. Her pupils immediately shrank, as though she were zooming away from the conversation with other thoughts about who really owned the pet.

"Yeah, it's his project," she replied with a disinterested tone.

"I'm not sure that we can do this communication link. I personally have no objection to having the cameras feeding images here. Let's give it some thought and run it by Jim, shall we?"

"We'll run it by Jim," Lan replied.

And whom else would she run it by? There will surely be a call to General Peng.

* * *

Just before lunch, Carrie decided to continue to cultivate a positive relationship with Lan.

"How about joining me for a motorcycle ride at lunchtime? We can get a hot dog or a sandwich at the shore."

Carrie could see that her colleague was caught off guard again. *I'm two-for-two surprising the ice woman.*

"Who, me? I've never been on a motorcycle. I was brought up on plain old fashioned bicycles, you know, the ones you pedal, and nothing more," she chuckled.

"C'mon, it'll be fun. You can sit behind me and hold on as tight as you need to. I have an extra helmet."

Lan seemed happy with the invitation. "Okay, let's do it!"

Once she secured Lan's helmet, she donned her own. Soon they were riding through the Elliot House gates waving back to the uniformed soldiers guarding the only entrance. The day was cool and overcast with a threat of afternoon showers. Lan tightly held onto Carrie's waist, her fingers intertwined with the loops of Carrie's blue jeans.

Carrie purposely drove slowly at first, but then accelerated the Harley as her rear passenger became more comfortable. She drove to the popular Wollaston Beach and pulled up in front of a hot dog vendor's trailer. They pulled off their helmets and shook out their hair. After getting hot dogs, chips, and cold soda, they sat on a hip high, cement seawall to enjoy their lunch.

Carrie hoped she might glean something helpful from her co-worker as they socialized at the casual lunch. She asked Lan about China and places she would recommend visiting.

"I haven't been to your homeland," she lied again. "I want to take a tour there someday."

Lan told her about some of the popular spots, including museums, art galleries, and parks. The loyal pride she felt for her native motherland came through clearly with a hint of homesickness.

Carrie was initially cautious about getting too personal, about transgressing sensitive boundaries. As Lan appeared to become more relaxed, Carrie cast out her net of leading questions.

After a bite of her hot dog, Carrie said, "I hope to get back to teaching when Project V is completed. I'm looking forward to that. How about you, Lan? Any plans after we finish our mission here?"

"I'll be working for the MSS back in Beijing. General Peng has promised me a high level position in the Ministry upon a successful tour here."

It was the first time Lan had mentioned Peng's name. Carrie's mind went into high gear.

Was she working directly for him? What the hell is Peng's real role in this project?

She decided to test Lan further. "I haven't met General Peng," she said.

"You'll get to meet him. He's got a trip scheduled here soon."

Perfect. I would like very much to meet the silent partner in this project, General Peng.

The lunch trip had been worth it. When they returned to the lab, Lan graciously thanked Carrie for taking her to lunch at the shore on her motorcycle. She gushed about how she enjoyed the outing. It was clear that her insular colleague didn't get out much.

Back at her apartment, Carrie checked her email. There was a new message from Wei Xing.

> Carrie,
> I'm having fun with this genealogy research on Warren Lee. I've made some progress already and have successfully linked him back to the Tang Dynasty. There are only a few more births and deaths with their dates that I need, and I'll send the material to you.
> I will also enclose copies of family histories and news items. They were an interesting and a unique group of people, always interested in the art, music, and poetry. They often went to extremes to teach their children these activities. It was probably their undoing, since they ignored the importance of military defense. They became easy prey for the more militant Hans who forcefully overcame them with little resistance.
> Anyway, I think Warren will enjoy the family tree as his birthday gift. Great idea!
> Call me later this week.
> Love you, Wei Xing

She went back to the lab to check on the tissue tests of agent black in the robotic incubator. She was pleased with what she saw.

Later that night, before slipping into bed, Carrie got a call from Jim.

He told her that the trip to the CDC was well worth it. He garnered some valuable knowledge about developing a super vaccine using Carrie's lock and key model. He also would be bringing back some new software routines to speed up the simulation tests.

"That's great! So when do you think you'll be back in Boston?"

"That was the other reason I called. I got roped into doing some work for the Atlanta chapter of the Chinese American club. Some of my colleagues and friends are active in helping out the club with information about universities, businesses, careers, and anything to help them get over the barricades to advancement in this country. This is the annual conference, and Chinese Americans come in from all around the city and suburbs."

"What does that mean?"

"I'm going to stay a couple of extra days. I'll be a panel speaker one day and act as a life counselor the next. There will be several of us at tables around a ballroom in the Peachtree Plaza Hotel. The attendees, all of them Chinese Americans, can come up to any of us and ask advice about their problems. Many of them don't speak English well and have difficulties in learning how to survive in the American culture. This could be anything from overcoming racial prejudice to getting student loans, housing, and all that."

"If you think that is important, I guess spending another day or two will be all right."

"Carrie, I know this is unusual with all that's going on, but I'm looked upon as a role model within the Chinese American community here in Atlanta. I can catch up on any research time that may have been lost."

"It sounds like a good cause, and it's great to give back. I wish I could be there with you."

"I wish you could be here too. I miss you, but I'll be back late Sunday night."

Carrie then told him about her lunch with Lan and that now she wants to meet General Peng.

"That might be interesting, but you and I are scientists and not spies or Federal agents. Please be careful whatever you do. Neither you nor I know for sure what Lan or General Peng are really up to."

She thought about what he just said, and how he had no clue as to what her primary mission was on Project V.

"There are certainly a few things I like to know about those two."

* * *

The next morning Carrie cut her morning run to two miles. The humid and heavy August morning was too uncomfortable. She retreated up to her apartment, showered, and arrived in the office early. Lan was already busy working at her computer.

"Good morning. How was your night?"

"It was good. Nothing special. I got caught up on my emails and turned in early."

"Before I forget, I made some calls last night and more cameras are being installed at the hospital as we speak. Also, I requested the communications be linked to this room. We should have a viewing monitor in here soon."

The news surprised Carrie. She wouldn't have guessed that installing remote viewing equipment could be done so expeditiously. She was also taken back by Lan making this happen, though it was obvious that she hadn't done it alone. It almost certainly got done because Peng was contacted, but not Jim or Warren.

"Lan, that's great! Thank you for following up on that. I know that Jim will be more comfortable now with the testing."

"Is Jim coming in today or is he still in Atlanta?"

"I'm not sure. He hasn't called in yet," she answered, though of course she knew when Jim was due to return.

Lying must be a big part of the spy business. And I'm getting really good at it.

When it came time for a lunch break, it was Lan who invited Carrie to join her on the patio.

After they filled their trays, they found an empty table. Carrie could sense the others watching the two of them with some surprise. It was rare to see Lan join anyone at lunch.

"I really enjoyed the ride yesterday. I would love to try it again if you're willing. I might get to like motorcycles enough to get one. It would be so useful in China."

"How do you usually get around when you're in Beijing?"

"My bicycle had been my only means of transportation until I started working fulltime for General Peng. He provided a private car and a driver to take me wherever I had to go."

She wanted to ask more questions about that arrangement but hesitated. She didn't want Lan to become suspicious of any obvious interrogation.

"A motorcycle is so liberating. You feel so free as you move by the masses of people, cars, and bicycles. I would be happy to take you for a ride after work some night and give you some lessons."

"Really? That would be so cool. Just let me know when it's a good time for you."

Just then one of the other female research assistants stopped by to join them. The three of them began a different conversation, one of mundane topics and a little shoptalk.

Later that afternoon, Carrie got her report on the Negroid tissue samples. Everything appeared to work successfully in the lab. The liquid sample infected the tissue as planned. The next step was for Jim to make a concentrated batch of the agent black liquid and produce the ice cubes for field testing. She said nothing to Lan, because she wanted to let Jim be the first to know the good news. She also looked forward to telling him about her budding friendship with the ice woman.

Lan prepared to leave for the day by going through her daily ritual of backing up her computer onto a flash drive. She then erased her computer's hard disk of those files. Within minutes, she waved goodbye and was out of the office.

Now left alone, Carrie decided to follow through on an idea she had had since her earlier phone call with Jim. She grabbed the Yellow Pages and found the listing for a professional costume store in Boston. On the phone, she learned that the store carried the items that she wanted. She called Boston's Logan airport and booked a flight to Atlanta.

At six in the evening, Jim phoned. Carrie told him about the installation of the remote viewing monitor and her suspicion that it demonstrated how General Peng was the real power broker in this project and not the Under Secretary of State.

"I feel like Peng is somewhere behind me watching everything I do through Lan Ying's eyes. I haven't even met the bastard, and he already gives me the creeps."

"I think you are doing the right thing cozying up to Lan. It sounds like she might be as loyal to Peng as you suspect, though I bet her immaturity will show that she doesn't know how to keep secrets very well."

"What if she's cozying up to me? What if she wants to get more information out of me? Don't forget, all she wants is the bioagent formula, and she now knows that those files are encrypted. So she might be trying to soften me up to get to those algorithms some other way."

"Please don't react until we know more."

"In any case, she won't get the program files. I'll turn them over to Warren before I ever give them to her."

She was surprised how angry she felt talking about the situation, and took a deep breath. She soon cooled down enough to share her recent success with the initial tissue tests of agent black. The next round of field testing would begin after his return to the lab.

"That's great news! I'm anxious to get back to work again, and I can't wait to see you. I miss you so much."

"I feel the same. When does your plane land in Boston?"

"I should be home Sunday evening."

"Good. I'll be there waiting for you." She tried not to giggle as she thought about the next surprise for her lover.

* * *

The next morning, Carrie noticed that Lan appeared different as she walked into the lab. She was visibly happy with a wide smile on her face. Her hair had been cut to ear length and her face was more vibrant, with pink lip gloss and carefully applied eye makeup. She wore a pink sleeveless V-neck top with snug, white Capri pants instead of her usual blue jeans. The clothes and makeup complemented her tall slender body and attractive facial features.

Lan walked over to Carrie and presented her with a small plate that held two Chinese pastries. The pastries were traditionally eaten on special occasions, particularly the Mid-autumn Festival and Chinese New Year.

"I made these for you last night. They're Moon Cakes and were originally eaten as part of moon worship and autumn harvest celebrations. It is still a Chinese tradition to eat them outdoors under the moon with family members to bring good luck."

"I'm familiar with them from some of my friends. I love them. Thank you. They'll go well with my much needed coffee this morning."

"I also want to take you to lunch today at one of my favorite Cantonese restaurants. That is, if I can ride again on the back of your bike?"

"Lan, you don't have to do that."

"I want to. I haven't had any American friends since I came here. You're my first real friend in the States. Besides, I think you'll like this restaurant, and it's only about five miles from here."

Carrie and Lan had lunch at the Nan Hai restaurant. They ate a light meal because neither wanted to overload their stomachs before returning to work.

"You use chopsticks very well for a westerner."

The hairs on the back of her neck rose. Did she know more about Carrie Bock than she revealed?

"I love Chinese food and have had a lot of experience using them at different restaurants," she replied, though now wondering if she might have made a mistake not using a knife and fork.

They ate in silence for a few minutes while enjoying the various dishes.

"Are you seeing anyone now?" Lan asked.

The surprisingly personal question came out of nowhere as they sipped their cups of oolong tea.

"No. I haven't been seeing anyone for quite some time," she lied again.

"I was just curious if there was a man in your life."

"I'm still single. There's no one."

"If we catch that action movie you recommended, *Force Nine Hundred*, during the late show next week, you could stay over at my place in Cambridge instead of driving home late on your motorcycle. It's quite a distance, and I know riding bikes at night can be dangerous."

"You're right, and I don't like riding in the dark. Thanks. That sounds perfect."

Her mind raced. If she could get inside Lan's apartment, she might get her hands on one of those memory sticks.

"When do you want to go?" Lan asked as she smiled over her teacup.

"I don't care. What night were you thinking about?"

"I was thinking about next Friday. That way we could do something on Saturday. You know, like shopping or bike riding or hanging out."

It was obvious Lan was deeply in need of a friend. But this sudden and new friendship might cost more of Carrie's personal time than she would like. She may have to sacrifice a little to get what she needed.

"That sounds good. Let's see how things go on the project, especially the field testing. I think that Jim will be making batches for agent black soon, and that means you'll be going to Saratoga again."

Lan seemed satisfied. They returned to work and had a quiet, peaceful afternoon.

She watched Lan perform her daily routine, including backing up her data files and erasing the same files. Lan then nonchalantly dropped the stick into her open handbag.

"Thanks for lunch, Lan. I really enjoyed it."

"And I've enjoyed these two days without Jim around," she replied. She walked toward Carrie sitting at her workstation. "I think it was good for you and me to get to know one another without him around."

"I know what you mean," she replied to play along.

"I wanted my hair stylist to give me a haircut like yours, but it didn't quite come out that way."

"I noticed your new haircut. I think it looks nice."

With that Lan moved closer still. Carrie watched as the woman touched her highlighted auburn hair with her long and slender fingers. She could sense Lan's fingertips lightly touching and teasing several stands of her hair. She knew that such behavior wasn't uncommon among Chinese women.

"Your hair is so pretty, Carrie. It's so unique with its color and natural highlights. You're so lucky. We Chinese girls are forever doomed to have only one natural color: ink black." She returned to pick up her bag. "I'm heading out. Enjoy your weekend."

Within seconds, she exited through the secure door.

Carrie left behind her. She was anxious to get to the theatrical costume shop in Boston.

TWENTY SIX

The early afternoon flight to Atlanta was only half full, which gave Carrie more time to plan her coming surprise. She was dressed in jogging pants and a black T-shirt with black, silk, slipper-like shoes.

After landing, a cab took her speedily to the Peachtree Plaza Hotel through the light weekend traffic. She was soon locking the door to her room on the fourteenth floor.

Once inside, she immediately opened her luggage and headed for the bathroom. She plucked her new theatrical makeup kit from inside the cosmetic bag. Slowly and carefully, she applied the pale foundation with a cosmetic sponge to her forehead, face, and neck. The application made her complexion lighter and more even. She carefully padded a dusting of a translucent powder over her skin.

After slipping on a pair of navy blue linen slacks, she buttoned up a bright red cotton top with short sleeves. A colorful silk scarf around her neck complemented the blouse. She then adjusted an ear length, bobbed, black wig after pulling it over her own hair. A makeup pencil colored her eyebrows black with light feathery strokes. Next she opened a small box containing specially designed contact lenses. As she put them in, her eyelids spread out into a single fold, which gave her eyes a slanted effect. The lenses over the pupils and irises were black and covered her own bright blue irises. She primped one last time before leaving her room.

As others approached her in the lobby, she simply smiled and nodded as they did the same. She was convinced that her transformation from a Caucasian woman into a Chinese woman was credible.

The hotel signs for the Atlanta Chapter of the Chinese American Society conference led her into a ballroom located on the lower floor. Inside the festively decorated room, over a hundred Chinese were milling about, talking, and drinking tea or coffee. With her new disguise, Carrie knew that she easily blended in. As she poured herself a cup of tea at the beverage table, she overheard nearby

Chinese discussing the conference activities in Mandarin. Other attendees were at tables picking up literature on learning English as a second language, job postings, legal forms, and student loan information. Much of the literature had been printed in Chinese characters, which she translated in her mind.

At several tables around the perimeter of the room, men and woman were serving as advisors. A makeshift sign indicated the counseling session would end at four o'clock. While pretending to read a brochure, Carrie panned the room until she spotted Jim sitting at a corner table. He appeared to be advising a young couple about something. She peered down at her watch. It was three forty-five.

She ambled towards the corner. Within earshot, she heard Jim speaking fluent Mandarin for the first time. The young couple stood up to leave, shook Jim's hand, and profusely thanked him for his help.

As soon as he was free, Carrie stepped up to his table. She sat down facing him.

Carrie had learned long ago to raise her voice higher than normal when speaking Mandarin. The technique helped her and other Westerner's inflect the correct tones in the multi-tonal language.

Carrie and Jim talked in Mandarin.

"How are you? My name is James Chen. How may I help you?"

"I have several questions and need advice at many levels," Carrie replied.

"Please tell me, what is your top priority?"

"My boyfriend is a very talented professional. He is good to me, but I have deceived him about my background and am feeling bad about that. He thinks that I am working with him, but in reality I was planted in his environment for an entirely different reason."

Carrie knew her disguise was working as planned.

"This is a personal issue, Miss. I am here to provide help for people who have governmental, educational, or financial challenges."

"I understand that, Mr Chen. My problem is governmental. We are both working for the United States government. He is my boss, but he does not know that I was planted in his department to follow the activities of his group and report back to higher government officials."

"I do not understand," Jim said with a frown. "Are you a spy for a different government agency?"

Carrie put her head down and replied.

"Yes, I am a spy of sorts. And now that we…we have become romantically serious, I feel I must tell him. But I was sworn to secrecy about my assigned role on the project."

"The project? What is it that you two are working on?"

"It is a research project. That is not important. I have deceived him. I even know how to speak his native language and I have not told him about that."

"If you speak his native language, was he the government's target of your spying?"

"No, it was another person who now appears to be innocent of earlier speculation."

Jim ran a hand through his black wavy hair. He was still perplexed.

"What is the issue, Miss? Why not tell him you are sorry that you had to deceive him? Tell him you had done so to carry out your official assignment."

"Do you think he will forgive me?"

"I can not speak for him. If he truly loves you, he should understand."

Carrie smiled with a slight giggle. Her fun and well planned ruse had worked exactly as she had hoped.

"Thank you, Mr Chen. You are a very kind man. "

"Is there anything else?" Jim replied, obviously relieved that this particular consulting session was probably over.

Carrie reached into her small handbag and took out a duplicate plastic card key to her hotel room.

She stared at Jim through the colored contact lens and now spoke in English with her natural voice.

"Jim, my room is fourteen forty four. I want you up there in half an hour. We have separate flights back to Boston tomorrow, so we should make the most of tonight!"

She stood up with a smile as she watched Jim's speechless expression. He was frozen in place clutching the room key card as he watched Carrie turn to leave his table. He could only stare at the woman whom he loved as she walked confidently from the ballroom.

Later, they made love twice. The first time Carrie was still in costume with her Chinese disguise and makeup. She felt so good in his arms and telling him in Mandarin how she felt about him.

"*Wǒ ài nǐ*, I love you, Jim," she said over and over in Mandarin and English.

At dinner that evening, Carrie told Jim in detail about her dual role, her personal history with the President, and why there had been suspicions about Warren. She knew that she was compromising her secret assignment, but she had to trust her lover and confide in him.

Jim was stunned, but told her he fully understood.

The next morning, Carrie took a taxi to the Atlanta airport for an early flight back to Boston. As the cab pulled away from the hotel, her purple cellphone rang.

"Carbo, I can't speak long. My family and I are leaving for Sunday services in a couple of minutes. I think your assessment of Warren is right on. I found out more about him from this end. He's very ambitious and has his own personal agenda to run for higher office. That's why he has embraced this new role. He wants to become a national figure—saving the world, so to speak. I think he's benign. But I got some new intelligence reports from the agency last night. There is definitely a mole working for Beijing assigned to the project team. I'm told the operative is well respected but is taking direction directly from the MSS. The mole's purpose is to drive the project but to meet a different agenda. My Intel people tell me that they're pretty certain they know who the operative is. This individual often contacts operatives back in China in very unusual patterns that fit with espionage activity as a way to throw off tracing. They tell me that the China based communications are never on the same phone over there."

"I think I know who it is already, Barbo. I'm one step ahead of you and your Intel sources. It's Dr Lan Ying, right?"

"No. It's not Dr Ying, Carrie."

"What? Then who in hell is the Beijing mole?"
"It's Chen, Dr James Chen."

TWENTY SEVEN

Carrie's heart began to race when she heard Jim's Mustang pull into the garage that evening. After he closed the door behind him and set down his briefcase, she was in his arms. They embraced for a long time, kissed, and whispered into each other's ears.

Holding hands, they walked into the living room. Jim took off his sports jacket and necktie. He looked tired from the flight.

"I'm going to take a quick shower before dinner. Why don't you make us some drinks? I need a few minutes to clean up and to get refreshed."

While he walked into the bedroom, she went to the liquor cabinet and poured a few fingers of scotch into some ice filled tumblers. As she heard the water splashing from the shower, she walked into the bedroom with the two drinks in her hands. After setting down the drinks on the nightstand, she stripped off her clothes.

Completely naked, she padded into the bathroom, opened the shower curtain, and joined him. Taking the washcloth from him, she lathered it up and helped him soap up his body. By the time she was finished and he had rinsed off, they were both fully aroused.

After a pleasant lovemaking session in the bedroom, they both relaxed with only a bed sheet covering them.

"Can you stay the night?"

"I would love to, but I better not. I still don't want to raise any suspicions about us."

Jim rolled over on his side and paused before speaking.

"I got another call from my wife this morning, after you left Atlanta."

Carrie didn't say a word, but turned on her side to read his eyes.

"She told me her father is now comatose. He's not expected to live more than a few more days in the hospital. She asked me to return to China so that I could be at his funeral."

"What did you tell her?"

"I told her I couldn't leave right away, but would as soon as I got a break in my schedule."

"Was she understanding about that?"

"Yes and no. She wants me there and has already had an attorney draw up the divorce agreement."

After a light dinner, they drank coffee in the living room. The conversation shifted to Project V. They talked about how they would create the first batch of the agent black for field testing.

"The best news is what I learned at the CDC. If our assumptions are correct about your plan to fake out the bioagent so that no set of genetic clusters can be found, we'll have a vaccine ready in a short time."

They continued to go over work plans until ten thirty when Carrie reluctantly said good night and left. Soon she was speeding on her Harley back to the Elliot House.

* * *

It was business as usual the next morning. With Jim's return, Lan retreated into her serious, non-social behavior while she sat anchored in front of her workstation.

It took very little time for the communications technicians to install an LCD monitor. It hung from the ceiling near the far wall. The monitor was large and had an accompanying DVD machine to record each session. The transmission signal would be turned on during the afternoon to test the link to the prison hospital.

Later that morning, Jim told Carrie and Lan that the production of the agent black ice cubes would now take place. With that announcement, the three of them filed into the Cold Room.

Both Carrie and Lan watched as the carefully designed procedure was performed in exactly the same manner as that for agent yellow. Jim held the capped beaker of the lethal liquid that he had prepared earlier. After he keyed in his security code, the icemaker door shut and the mixing took place. After mixing, the compound became the potential killer of Black men, women, and children. Within minutes, the familiar noise of ice cubes being made was heard.

Jim nodded to Lan.

"You may take the samples now. Is the container labeled?"

Without saying anything, Lan tilted the stainless steel container so he could see the label. "Agent Black" had been handwritten in Chinese characters in indelible ink. Lan filled the container with the new batch of ice cubes.

For this field test, Carrie and Jim would watch the process take place on the new TV monitor. The anticipation bothered Carrie, but she pushed it out of her mind.

Lan turned away from her two colleagues and walked over to her private freezer chest. She protectively keyed in her access code. The batch of agent black was now her responsibility, and only her responsibility since nobody else could gain access to it.

When they returned to the office, Jim told Lan that he would like her to arrange for the field testing to take place soon. He also politely thanked her for arranging for the installation of the in-hospital cameras and the remote monitor.

Within minutes, he left the office to meet with the other research-ers.

Carrie walked over to the coffee counter and poured a cup of coffee. As she did so, she again saw Lan's reflection on the surface of the chrome coffeepot. Just as before, Lan was staring at her backside. She decided to break the silence.

"Can I get you a cup of tea? I know how you like it."

"Sure. That's so sweet of you."

When Carrie brought the hot tea with lemon over to her col-league, she placed it on her workbench in front of her.

Lan turned toward her and smiled. Somehow the smile seemed different.

"Thanks," she said while looking directly into Carrie's eyes.

Carrie was tempted to glance over Lan's shoulder to look at the text displayed on her computer screen but resisted. She didn't want to raise suspicions. She returned the intent look. Even though Lan was smiling at her, the interaction caused a sudden chill, like an icicle dripping coldly down her spine.

When Jim returned to the office, he appeared very pleased with his brief meeting with the other scientists.

"Lan, when do you think you'll head up to New York for the field test?" Jim asked.

"I'm leaving this afternoon. My assistants already have subjects prepped, and we'll administer the agent tomorrow afternoon. I presume that this is a concentrated volume. I don't want to wait several hours to see the results again."

"Yes. This agent black batch is highly concentrated; the same as our first agent yellow test. If successful, you, or rather all of us, will see results within a short time." His gaze moved towards the overhead monitor.

"Good. I'm going home now to pack," Lan responded. "I'll return to put the agent in the dry ice cooler for transport."

After Lan had left for home, Carrie looked over at Jim. His back was towards her while he focused on his workstation screen.

She said, "I think that if this agent black works, I can have agent white ready in two days."

Jim swiveled in his chair and turned towards her with a grin. "I thought as much. Once you developed the model to identify the racial gene clusters, it's been pretty easy." His grin widened.

"I wouldn't say that it's been easy, but certainly agent yellow was the master model. Each following agent requires some modifications, but they haven't been as complicated to create as the first agent. I also think…"

She was interrupted by the melodic sound of Warren's voice. Another aria echoed in the hallway outside of their office. The Under Secretary opened the door with arms outstretched. He appeared as though he were on a theater stage, and sang the last several bars from his operatic piece. When finished, he took an exaggerated bow while facing both Carrie and Jim.

Jim and Carrie simultaneously applauded his performance.

"You like it? I'm glad. It's from Bellini's famous opera, *Norma*."

"Bravo! Bravo!" Carrie replied still clapping. "You certainly seem to be in a jovial mood today."

The three went into the conference room where Jim provided Warren with a detailed status report.

Warren was elated to hear that the next agent, agent black, would soon undergo field testing.

Later that evening, Carrie stayed alone in her apartment. She called Jim and told him to rest up after his trip to Atlanta. She had something more important to ask her lover, something that had niggled at her since the last call from the President.

"Jim, I have something to ask you."

"Sure, what is it?"

"You've always been truthful with me, haven't you?"

"Of course, I've been truthful with you. What are you talking about?"

"I'm talking about your deal with Warren for the release of your brother from prison. That's planned to take place as soon as the virus agents are all developed, right? And that's the only reason you agreed to come on to Project V. That's all true, isn't it?"

The pause on the other end of the connection seemed too long. Carrie wanted a quick answer, but there was nothing but silence at the other end. The quiet seconds were painfully slow.

"Carrie, what's going on? I've *always* told you the truth. And yes, Warren's deal still holds. When I finish developing the bio-agents, he promised me his Beijing contacts would secure the release of Jiang Ming. He will then come here to live. I intend on getting him a job and helping him to begin a new life in the United States. What the hell is wrong with you? Why aren't you trusting me now?"

Her involuntary swallow in her throat was audible as she reflected on his valid question. It was impossible to ask him any other questions. Since the warning from Barbo, she wondered if his calls back to China, supposedly to his wife or brother, didn't go to PRC officials. She appreciated that he was a private man, though that was perhaps because he was playing a different role on Project V than he had told to her.

Carrie became angry at herself for doubting him. She put away fantasizing on any subversive role Jim might be playing. She re-called how government intelligence is often wrong, or accidentally or intentionally misleading. It happened during George W. Bush's administration and now seemed to be happening with Bowa's administration.

"Jim. I hope…I just hope this freakin' project ends soon. I guess I'm getting a little sick of it and want to return to a normal life. And I'm getting sick of trying to figure out who the bad guys are in this whole thing."

"So am I. I also want to return to a normal life, but only if that normal life includes the two of us being together."

She listened to his words. He spoke them as earnestly and warmly as he always did.

They changed topics to get away from any telephone argument.

Carrie felt better. She found it hard to believe Jim was an operative for China's MSS in any way. His honesty and integrity went totally against the grain of what the President had told her.

TWENTY EIGHT

After notification from Saratoga that the field testing would commence, Carrie and Jim sat in the lab office watching the monitor with anxiety and intensity. They observed Lan's staff administering agent black to a number of volunteer prisoners. Some were Black, some White, and some Asian. There were several mulattos and other racially mixed prisoners. Carrie and Jim watched as each subject was handed a glass of juice with ice cubes. The inmates were instructed to wait a few minutes before drinking the chilled liquid.

Within minutes, the Black subjects showed obvious reactions. Just as with the initial agent yellow test, Black inmates given the agent began to cough and perspire. Telemetry screens showed their temperatures spiking. The onset was quick with the highly concentrated test batch.

Carrie and Jim watched as the Black men and women began to display symptoms of a serious flu virus. They became sweaty. Some began hallucinating, moaning, and coughing, while others simply lay quiet and let the infectious molecules consume them. About fifteen minutes after they ingested the agent, some began to die. After half an hour, all had died. Each of them experienced nasal hemorrhaging with a light trickling of crimson blood from each nostril.

The mixed race subjects and those given placebos had only a few coughing spells and nothing more. The same result was observed for the White and Chinese inmates.

The field test produced the expected results. It was clearly a success.

Carrie watched as Jim stretched up to turn off the TV monitor. She was relieved that the observation period was over. Watching humans die in real time had a deep emotional impact on her. She stood silently with her arms folded and stared at the floor.

Jim approached her and with one finger under her chin lifted her face up to meet his. By then her tears had already begun to meander down her face.

He grabbed her hand and sat her down. "I'll get you some water."

After drying her face with a tissue, she needed to say something about what they had experienced.

"I know that the subjects were volunteers and among the worst of the worst humans from our society. And I know that they were all on death row waiting to be executed. We're still taking human lives. This testing is the coldest, most disheartening thing I've ever seen in my life."

Jim handed her a cup of cold water.

"That's true, but remember these men and women had been fairly judged and were destined for certain death. Yes, we've sacrificed some human beings, as soldiers sometimes inadvertently cause casualties when trying to win a war. But like the soldiers, we're still innocent. We must do this to save legions of humans and provide a safe future for all the human races. We have to win that war. We, you and I, are spearheading a technical project to prevent a heinous mass genocide."

"I know," she replied, though that knowledge did little to lessen her compassion for the subjects or her shame in their deaths.

The phone rang and Jim picked it up.

"Yes, Lan, we watched. We could see everything on the monitor. Yes, the multiple cameras helped tremendously. Congratulations on a successful test. You want to speak to Carrie?"

Carrie's hands waved quietly and she shook her head to indicate that she didn't want to talk to Lan.

"She just stepped out. She's probably gone to the ladies' room. Do you want me to give her a message?"

She smiled at him and gave him a thumbs up for thanks.

"I don't think she'll be around this weekend. She mentioned that she may be traveling to Washington."

He hung up and looked over at Carrie with a grin.

"What?" she asked.

"It seems to me you've got yourself a new, best friend forever."

Carrie let out a long, audible sigh before responding.

"Bullshit! She's certainly not my BFF. I may have created a freakin' monster. Let's go upstairs to my place. I could really use a drink right now."

When Carrie unlocked her apartment door, she noticed she had one phone message. She pointed Jim in the direction of her kitchen cabinet holding the liquor.

"Scotch on the rocks for me," she said.

She hit the play button on her answering machine. Soon Wei Xing's voice filled the room.

"Carrie, it's me. I'm finished with the genealogical research and can send it to you, though I would rather talk to you about it first. Give me a call, after ten thirty your time tonight. Love you, Wei Xing."

"My lady has many boiling pots on her busy stove," Jim said. "How, oh how, do you keep the lids on all of them?" he asked with an affected British accent. He handed her the drink.

She took a substantial gulp in the hope of blotting out the image of the Black subjects being coldly killed with her lethally laced ice cubes.

She explained to Jim the intended birthday gift for Warren, and how her friend had traced his ancestral family tree back to the Tang Dynasty.

"That's a wonderful gift! I admire you for thinking of it. I'm sure Warren will be pleased."

The rest of the evening was spent relaxing, watching TV, and discussing options for the two of them after Project V.

As soon as Jim left her apartment before the 11 o'clock news, Carrie called Wei Xing.

"*Wèi!*" [Hello (on the phone)] Wei Xing answered.

"Wei Xing. It is Carrie." Carrie replied in Mandarin, as usual.

"Girl, I am glad you called! Have I got news for you!" Wei Xing responded in English, as usual.

"Do not tell me. You are pregnant."

"No, you wise-ass. But that would be nice. What I have to tell you has to do with my genealogy research on Mr Warren Lee of the Tang Dynasty."

"Is there a problem?"

"First, let me tell you that I found all of the birth, death, and marriage records with little difficulty. I also found many articles about the Tang people, and as I told you before, they had an affinity for the fine arts. And it does seem that that tradition has been passed down from generation to generation. I did have some difficulty tracking down one ancestor. It was Warren's mother."

"Really? Why is that?"

"At first, I didn't know where or when she was born. Even after I found that information, everything else was still sketchy. It seems that her mother, Warren's grandmother, traveled quite a bit in an effort to study and to learn more about the arts. She traveled to Europe and to North America to gain exposure to worldly artistic trends. She spent a lot of time in Canada, where she met and studied with Luigi Cippiloni from British Columbia."

"Oh, no! I think I know where this is going," Carrie interjected.

"There were many newspaper articles with photos of the two of them together at artsy-fartsy social functions. Some of the dates of these photos were when she became pregnant with Warren's mother. She had not returned to China for several months, so she had to become pregnant while she was traveling the globe. Most likely she got knocked up while in British Columbia."

"What happened?"

"Luigi was already married, as was Warren's grandmother. So she retreated to China with fetus on board, as you doctors would say. Basically, she got pregnant by Luigi."

"My God! Did she get divorced?"

"That I couldn't ascertain. I don't think so. She went off somewhere and had her beautiful baby girl. Later, the baby was welcomed into the family, and she grew up as comfortably as all of the other Tang Dynasty offspring. As an adult, she married and had her own baby, which of course was Warren Lee."

"That is so interesting! I am sure Warren does not know that he has Italian blood in him. By the way, what kind of artist was this Luigi Cippiloni? Was he a sculptor? Or was he one of those European impressionist painters?"

"Luigi was very well known for his love of music and singing. He was one of the most famous opera singers from Italy at the time."

Carrie nearly dropped her phone.

"Opera singer? He sang opera?"

"You bet!"

After a brief pause, Carrie told Wei Xing to forward the genealogy material to her in the regular mail. Based on this skeleton found in Warren's Tang Dynasty closet, she clearly needed to abandon the idea of a Family Tree gift for the man's birthday, though at some later time she may share the ancestry information with him. Now was definitely not the right time.

As she got ready for bed, Carrie reflected on how her own life had changed since she joined Project V. She crawled under the covers thinking about how much happier she will be when her covert assignment is over.

* * *

During the next few weeks, the atmosphere at the research lab was intense and at times uncomfortable. She and Jim worked long hours to develop agent white while also developing a potential vaccine to the lethal bioagents. The vaccine work was done subrosa without Lan or Warren ever aware of Jim's new goal.

"The agent white is more difficult than I anticipated," she told Jim one morning. "I'm going to have to limit the genetic clusters to eye color, melanin, and hair characteristics. I also need to insure that those gene clusters are absent in the Mongoloid and Negroid races."

"That makes sense. The White race is not as pure as the Mongoloid or Negroid. Whatever you have to do, just do it," was Jim's reply.

Lan made more trips to Saratoga to continue additional testing of both agent yellow and agent black with ice cubes of high concentration for immediate results. She then added contagion tests by having similar race prisoners not drink the iced beverage but stay beside the beds of dying victims. Through airborne pathogens produced by the coughing victims, the contagion subjects also became infected and died.

All of the tests were consistent. Jim continued to observe the testing through the remote monitor at the Elliot House. It was unnecessary for Carrie to join him.

One morning, while Lan was again at Saratoga, Warren unexpectedly came into the office.

When Carrie looked up to greet him, she saw that his face had a disturbed and pained expression. He acknowledged her with a slight nod of the head, and asked Jim to step into the conference room.

While the two men met, Carrie tried to keep herself busy, though she couldn't concentrate. She paced around the room for a few minutes and then walked to the dining room patio and paced there as well before returning inside.

It was nearly half an hour before Jim returned to the office. Now it was he who had a distressed expression. Warren left without speaking to Carrie.

She watched as Jim locked up his desk. He looked over at her. "Let's go for a bike ride."

TWENTY NINE

Without speaking, they left the lab and walked briskly to the garage. Within minutes, they were speeding side-by-side down the country roads.

Carrie's heart pounded with anxiety as she followed him up the serpentine roads of the Blue Hills. They stopped at the pinnacle, the same spot where they had come on their first date.

She parked her bike next to his. She had butterflies in her stomach. They both started to walk without speaking. They followed one of the hiking trails that led deeper into the thick pine forest.

"I needed to get away from there," Jim finally said. "I didn't want to tell you about the discussion while we were still inside the lab. This is a better place. Besides, the trip here provided me time to cool down a little."

She remained silent to allow him to choose his words in his own time. She matched his slow pace beside him along the wooded trail.

"As you probably guessed, Warren had some news for me today."

She tried to hide her anxiety, but blurted out, "Obviously something of concern!"

"You were right all along. General Peng does call the shots on Project V. It turns out that he was the negotiator between Warren and the prison officials to get my brother released from prison. Before Project V was put together, Warren had told the General about my professional background. When Warren first tried to recruit me, I turned it down. But Peng learned of my brother's incarceration and designed the deal and asked Warren to broker it. At the time it was a win-win. Warren got me on the project, and Peng controlled the arrangement. I went after the carrot hanging on the stick and agreed to the commitment."

She nodded. "I understood all of that."

"Now that bastard Peng has reneged on his side of the deal. He now wants the vaccine for agent yellow developed before Jiang Ming will be released."

"What about..."

"We were both right about Lan," he interrupted. "She doesn't have the expertise to develop vaccines nor has she made any attempt to do so."

"Was this his plan all along?"

"I'm not sure. In hindsight, I guess that he became nervous when we developed agent yellow first, though that was purely expediency. It apparently wasn't in General Peng's plan. Agent yellow was supposed to be the last virus developed, and in fact I doubt whether it was ever supposed to be created. So now he wants a vaccine for agent yellow developed and for that to be tested immediately. He says we can work on the other vaccines for agent black and agent white later."

"He doesn't know that once you created one vaccine, it'll be for all races. So he still thinks we need three distinctive vaccines to protect people from the three distinct viruses."

"Yes. He's making an erroneous assumption, as is Warren, by the way."

As they walked, Carrie's mind was in high gear.

"How does our charismatic Under Secretary of State feel about all of this shit?"

"He genuinely feels terrible. He admitted to me that he was out maneuvered by Peng. Warren told me everything was facilitated by General Peng and his associates. He was the first PRC official who came to Warren after the project alliance was formed. He offered the Chinese personnel and financial support required for the project. He pays the exorbitant salaries for everyone on the project, including the cash to buy my house."

"Holy shit! Peng really is the only decision maker."

"As you speculated. I now believe that it was Peng's MSS man who initially approached Warren for Project V. And Peng demanded that Lan be put in a lead position with me. You weren't part of the picture yet."

"I now know why she acts the way she does. She is afraid that we'll discover that she is in way over her head."

"But here's the real problem, or at least a problem for me. Warren was clearly ashamed and embarrassed to tell me the latest negotiation with Peng."

"Latest negotiation? What the fuck is being negotiated at this late date?"

"Peng wants the bioagent algorithm turned over to him after final testing along with the coveted vaccine for agent yellow. He has reneged on the original agreement to release my brother immediately after the bioagents are available. With only agent yellow ready, my brother won't be released until we turn over the vaccine to agent yellow. Peng has out maneuvered Warren. And now he's using Jiang Ming and me as pawns to get what he wants."

Wei Xing's voice echoed in her mind: "General Peng has the reputation of being a great tactician."

She grabbed Jim's hand and held it tightly as the two of them walked along the wooded trails. For a while nothing was said as they thought about their predicament.

"What do you want to do?" she asked to break the angry silence.

"I performed some extensive tissue tests for the vaccine the other night. And as planned, the vaccine transmits to the invasive flu virus that it can't identify any racial gene clusters. It defaults to a non-match state. So the virus immediately dies off." He squeezed her hand. "Your brilliance is paying off in big ways."

"I'm happy to hear that."

"The best thing right now is that nobody knows how we're approaching the development of the vaccine. Peng, Warren, and Lan are unaware that we don't need three individual vaccines, that all we need is a single silver bullet."

She stopped and turned to face him. She brought his face down towards her and kissed him gently on the lips. "We'll get your *didi* [younger brother] released from prison. Don't worry. Before long, he'll be living safely here."

* * *

With long hours at the lab, Carrie soon developed agent white and successfully conducted the initial tissue testing a few days later. Jim provided Lan with a test sample of ice cubes to take to Saratoga.

Jim remotely watched the field testing again from the office. Each test was consistent and successful. As usual, each subject who died wore the same dubious badge of honor, a bright red trickle of blood from each nostril.

To stall General Peng and buy more time to develop the vaccine, Jim had Lan conduct more bioagent tests. He mixed the concentration and had a wider variety of subjects selected on the basis of race, gender, and age. There was no shortage of death row subjects of the three major races and varying racial mixtures.

Warren held another meeting with the project leaders. He announced that Jim would take over the role of developing the vaccine with Lan to assist him as required. The change would accelerate the project, he told the group. He delivered the message without his typical flamboyance or confidence.

Carrie soon observed how Lan had become more personable with her and Jim after she was officially relieved of the primary responsibility of developing the vaccine. Despite that, Lan became tired of the marathon of tests that required constant travel between Boston and Saratoga.

Warren visited the lab infrequently. When he did, his demeanor was less buoyant, and he appeared to be spiraling down into depression. He found it difficult to look Jim straight in the eye. Warren obviously felt the wounds of being blindsided by the manipulative weasel, General Peng. He also was now painfully aware that Lan had always been Peng's mole on Project V.

Carrie did her best to maintain a normal life with Jim despite the emotional tension and stress of each day. The pressure to develop the vaccine as soon as possible continued to mount.

One night before going to bed, Carrie got a text message on her purple cellphone from President Bowa:

> Got more Intel today. Don't trust Jim Chen! He's working for PRC, not for US. Very dangerous. Don't blow cover. Above all, be careful.

Carrie deleted the message after reading it again. She put the phone away and slipped under the covers but couldn't fall asleep.

God, has he got that wrong. The intelligence reports are totally fucked up. They think because the Project Leader, Jim, communicates with his brother and his wife in China that he's subversive. I know that's why they think he's a mole. The agency doesn't know the details and have rushed to the wrong conclusion. I've got to get back to Barbo. Doesn't he know that government intelligence can make mistakes? Has he already forgotten how the Bush-Cheney administration sucked us into Iraq? I need to talk with him.

She decided not to let the text message bother her. Soon she fell asleep.

The next morning Carrie learned that the first round testing of the so-called yellow vaccine had failed at Saratoga. The virus still found the targeted genetic clusters and continued to attack healthy cells. The Asian subjects continued to die from the lethal agent.

As the days went by, Carrie grew more and more concerned about Jim. He was working nearly twenty hours a day, sleeping very little, and it showed. He was tired and frustrated. The failures in the lab were taking their toll on his personality. His temperament seemed unpredictable. He was often short with Lan when she asked questions and frequently raised his voice at meetings with the research assistants.

She felt bad for her lover, but despite her initial efforts at algorithm precursors to the vaccine, she was little help now. So she left him alone most of the time. They rarely saw each other outside of work. His emotions dropped to their lowest ebb whenever he received a phone call at work.

She thought how ironic and perhaps telling it was that while Peng applied pressure to develop the agent yellow vaccine no activity by the Pakistani terrorist group, SAN, was reported. The Astola Island incident had faded away with no conclusions.

One morning, Carrie and Jim were alone while working quietly in the office. Lan was traveling back from Saratoga and not expected until afternoon.

When his cellphone rang, he instantly appeared irate with the distraction.

Watching his face during the call, she tried to guess what might be going on. After he disconnected, he walked over and sat down next to her. Before he spoke, he let out a long and deep sigh.

"That was my wife. She has given me an ultimatum. She was disappointed that I didn't make it for her father's funeral, but now she demands that I return to her village immediately to process the divorce papers. She made it clear that she was not willing to negotiate this matter."

Her heart sank as she saw the despair in his face.

"I think you should go. It's something you've wanted for a long, long time. Besides, I want you to distance yourself from Project V for a while. I want you to rest and forget about your work and come back to me as the witty, compassionate man I love."

He looked at her. First surprise, then sadness colored his expression. He hadn't recognized the depth of his dismal unsociable behavior during the past weeks. He nodded in agreement.

"Okay. I'll come back to you as a new and hopefully revitalized man. I'll also come back a single man, though I intend to change that as soon as possible."

She said nothing. She didn't want to be part of the pressure he was feeling on all fronts. Instead, she leaned over and kissed him gently on the lips.

"Before I make arrangements to leave, I want to make up one more batch of viral agents and a new batch of the vaccine. I feel very confident about this next version of the vaccine."

"You'll have to wait until Lan comes in this afternoon."

"That's true for the agents, but not for the vaccine. I want you to store the vaccine ice cubes in your apartment's freezer. There, nobody else can have access to it. Carrie, I think this new solution is a winner. I want to be here and test it myself as soon as I come back."

A little confused at his logic, she nodded and followed him into the Cold Room. Jim had already concocted the ingredients in the lab and created a new beaker of the liquid. He carefully poured the liquid into the machine. Within minutes, ice cubes with the promising vaccine trickled from the ice-making machine. He let them drop into a large zip-lock bag. After carefully sealing the bag, he handed it to her.

"Now hurry upstairs."

She did as he asked.

Later that day, she joined him on the patio for lunch. His face seemed a strange mixture of joy and despair. She offered a smile.

"We can talk every night, can't we? The time will go faster than you think."

He nodded. "If I can, I want to visit my brother at the prison. I really miss him and think of him often. Right now, he's my only family." He looked into her eyes. "But that will change."

"I'm sure it would do your heart good to see him." She watched as Jim's eyes telescoped over her shoulder.

Lan had come onto the patio carrying a tray of food and looking around for Carrie.

Jim hailed her to join them at their table.

She sat down with an obligatory smile.

"I have to go away for several days, Lan," Jim told her, without disclosing his trip's purpose. "I would like to produce more agent samples so you can do more testing while I'm gone. After lunch, let's meet in the Cold Room, and I'll make batches of all three agents."

Lan simply nodded to acknowledge his plan.

Carrie noticed how the attractive Chinese woman had become quiet lately, apparently intimidated by Jim's unpredictably aberrant behavior.

"While I'm gone, we can still move forward. I'm going to give Carrie the access code to the ice-making machine so she can work with you. If you need more bioagents, she can create them. We don't want my trip to cause any delays."

After giving his instructions, Jim excused himself.

"Has his mood improved at all while I was gone?" Lan asked.

"I'm afraid not. He's been a fucking bear. I'm hoping he'll get some rest during his trip and return more like a human being."

Lan fell again into her trap of thinking that the two of them now shared something personal.

"You know something, Carrie? You still owe me a date at the movies."

"That's right. I'm so sorry. I unexpectedly had to go to Washington. I haven't apologized to you about missing that date. There's been so much going on."

Lan smiled in acceptance of her apology.

"There's a new mystery film playing this week at the Harvard Square Cinema. Do you want to go?"

Carrie smiled back at her.

"How about we go tomorrow night, Friday? It'll do us some good to get away from this place and our work for a while. I could use a good movie."

"We'll do it."

After the new batches of liquids were created, Carrie and Lan entered the Cold Room with the glass beakers. Using Jim's access code, Carrie turned on the ice-making machine and poured each liquid agent in turn into the machine. All the agents were in highly concentrated form for a faster onset of morbidity.

As each batch was processed, Lan went through her routine of emptying the ice cubes into labeled cylindrical containers. She keyed in her secret access code to open her freezer and placed them inside. When the freezer lid finally locked, they left the Cold Room.

At the end of the day, Carrie left the office first. Before leaving the Elliot House, she went into the ladies' restroom. While in the stall, she heard the door swing open. Footsteps sounded on the tiled floor. It was the sound of leather boots.

"Is that you in there, Carrie?"

"Yes. Do you need me for something?"

"No. I'm just washing up before heading to my condo."

Carrie stood up from the toilet and peered through the thin door gap near the hinge. She could clearly see Lan standing in front of the sinks and mirrors.

Through the narrow opening, she could see Lan posing in front of one of the mirrors. The mirror reflected everything she did without her knowing that eyes were on her every move.

Ha, ha, you icy witch! Now it's my turn to stare and to spy on you!

Lan turned on the water but didn't use it. It was a decoy to make noise. She opened her handbag and took out the gold tube of lipstick. She opened it and left the cap on the vanity top, but she didn't apply any lipstick because the tube was empty. She then pulled out a memory stick from her front pocket.

Carrie watched her every move.

With the water still running, Lan slid the memory stick into the lipstick tube. She closed the tube and dropped it back into her handbag.

"Carrie, I'm leaving now. See you tomorrow!"

That's how she gets the flash drive by the security scanner and the Homeland Security guards. The drive is hidden in the lipstick tube everyday when she leaves the Elliot House. It's probably lined with a layer of lead to foil the scanner.

* * *

Carrie drove her Harley to Jim's house. While waiting for him to arrive, she went into the bedroom and began packing his suitcase for him.

When he finally came through the door, she greeted him with a tight hug and kisses. She tugged on his hand to encourage him to walk with her to the bedroom.

"Thanks for packing for me," he said, as he nodded at his suitcase. "Now I have time to show my appreciation." He took her face in his hands and gently kissed her mouth.

They made love slowly. It had been so long since the last time that she was glad he didn't want to rush. She wanted to remember each tantalizing moment of his hands gently touching her and the pleasurable feeling of him inside of her.

Afterwards in bed, she looked over at him. He seemed more relaxed after their intimacy. She could see that he was fighting the urge to fall off to sleep because he had a nine o'clock flight from Boston to Beijing.

He rolled over to look at her. "I would still like to know more about Lan and her role in this whole project. Is she a full-fledged operative of Peng's or merely a mole who reports all that goes on?"

Carrie could see the concern in his face. She told him what she had witnessed in the ladies' restroom earlier in the day. Now they both knew Lan was compromising security by sneaking top-secret data off US government property.

"I would guess that she puts all of her work on that memory stick, except that the 256 GB capacity is overkill to say the least. We don't work with high-resolution graphic files, and even if she managed to copy all of your files and mine, it would still be overkill by a hundred gigs or more."

"It's still a mystery to me too."

"I wonder if there's a way we can get to her?" Jim asked rhetorically.

Carrie rolled onto her back, became pensive for a moment, and stared up at the ceiling. She mused how she needed to do whatever it took to get close to Lan. The information on those memory sticks could be critical, not only for the project, but also for national security.

She whispered, "I think I know how to learn more about her and what is on those memory sticks."

She put a finger to his lips as he was about to ask her how.

He understood. He nodded, gave her a kiss, and slipped out of bed to take a shower.

They didn't talk at all until they were fully dressed.

"I want to give you something," Jim said.

"Gee, Jim, I thought you did that a little while ago," Carrie replied in an effort to create some levity before he left.

"Let me go get it," he said.

A chilling sensation shot down her spine when she saw Jim return with a gun in his hand. The vision of Barbo's text message flashed across her mind. Her heart palpitated forcefully in her chest, and the air seemed to blow out of her lungs.

Got more Intel. Don't trust Jim Chen! He's working for PRC, not for US. Very dangerous. Don't blow cover. Above all, be careful.

Was it really possible that he was the spy that the President and his intelligence service believed him to be? And more, an assassin because she was getting to close to the truth about the Chinese mission in the project? For the moment, Carrie didn't know what to think. It had to be the stress of work. It *had* to be.

"Jim, what…what the fuck are you doing with a gun?"

"It's for you. I've had this thirty eight for years for protection but haven't used it. With me away and you getting involved with Lan, I think you should have it."

"Oh." The air came rushing back into her lungs.

"We still don't know who that scar-faced stalker is, or who the hell hired him. In any case, I'll feel better knowing you have some protection when not at the lab. You'll have to leave it with the guards when you enter, of course."

Carrie's heart finally kicked in and began beating normally again. "Jim, I don't like guns, and I don't think that I really need one."

"I insist. You never know what might happen while I'm in China. Here, the safety is on, and I'm going to put it in your handbag. It's small and light and fully loaded. Please keep it with you when you leave Elliot House."

As she watched him put the gun into her handbag, she felt both a great relief and a great shame. What kind of spy was she if she couldn't even trust the man she deeply loved and by every sign, every look, and every caress loved her just as deeply. It was the most difficult and painful job she had ever had—by far.

Before walking outside in the chilly air with Jim, she grabbed his black leather jacket off the back of a chair and slipped it on.

"You look good in that jacket, even if it's too big for you. Keep it so you can wear it when I return."

She gave him a wink. "And what would you like me to wear underneath?"

"Hmmm," he responded.

"Keep that thought while you're away," she teasingly told him.

He gave her the grin that made her knees weak. It was the smile that she would miss while he was in China.

They held each other for a long time before separating. Without saying a word, he threw his luggage into the trunk, got into his Mustang, and drove off.

THIRTY

When she awoke the next morning, Carrie's first thought was her movie commitment that evening with Lan. She sensed that Lan's interest in her was almost too friendly, but perhaps she could use it to her advantage. If Lan still wanted her to sleep over at her apartment as originally planned, it would provide the perfect opportunity to find out more about the mystery woman.

After her morning run and shower, she looked at herself in the mirror. Today she took extra care to apply a smooth layer of foundation and some eye shadow to bring out the color of her eyes. She curled her hair and fluffed it lightly with her fingers. She checked herself out in the full length mirror before going downstairs.

Am I prepared to do what it takes to see what is on Lan's memory sticks? The risk is incredibly high. If I get caught, General Peng will know immediately. The repercussions for me, for Jim, and his imprisoned brother could be devastating.

When she arrived at the lab, Lan gave her a warm greeting.

"You look so nice today," Lan told her.

"Thanks. I guess I needed a change."

Later in the morning, Carrie took a break and jogged upstairs to pack her overnight bag. When she was alone in her apartment, she dialed Jim's cellphone. When he answered on the first ring, she was glad he was still awake.

They chatted for a while.

"I've given it some thought about the vaccine test. There's no need to wait for me to return before testing that last batch. I thought maybe you could fabricate a story. Why not tell Lan you made the vaccine on your own during late hours? You can tell her that you temporarily had to store the cubes in your apartment freezer until she arrived at work."

Carrie paused to digest what he had just told her.

"Are you sure, Jim?"

He sounded sincere and confident. It was obvious that he was anxious to get his younger brother freed from incarceration and to get him out of harm's way. That wouldn't happen until the vaccine was tested successfully.

"Okay. First let me see how things go tonight," she responded. She then explained her movie date with Lan.

Carrie finished packing cosmetics, a T-shirt, underwear, and an outfit for the next day into a small backpack. Before leaving her apartment, she slipped on a favorite mint-green cardigan with deep front pockets in anticipation of a chilly weekend.

Carrie and Lan worked quietly as usual but took lunch together.

"Carrie, what if we leave early today and walk around Harvard Square? The students who hang out there are so interesting. I love to people-watch."

"Sounds perfect."

Lan was visibly excited about their social evening together.

The afternoon was spent in and out of the office to speak with research personnel or to collect tissue samples from the Cold Room.

During the late afternoon, when she returned to the lab, Lan was out of the office. Carrie spotted the mystery woman's large handbag still under her workbench loosely opened as usual. The thought crossed her mind about picking up the bag. She could grab the memory stick but considered the risk of getting caught too great. Instead, she walked over to the supply cabinet. Inside was the box of memory sticks with the label: "Lan's flash drives, DO NOT TAKE!" She opened the box and pulled out one of the devices. As she dropped the new memory stick into her green sweater pocket, Lan came through the doorway.

"Carrie, let's start our weekend now. I think it's time you and I got the hell out of here. What do you say?"

"I'm ready." And she was.

* * *

Carrie sat rigidly in the passenger seat while Lan sped along the streets of Boston in her Honda Accord through the busy traffic along Massachusetts Avenue and over the Charles River into Cambridge.

They arrived at Harvard Square near the Massachusetts Bay Transportation Authority station and began by checking out the college campus shops. They poked around in almost every boutique for nearly two hours before becoming hungry and entering a small pub to get a sandwich and beer.

They later scurried across the street for the eight-thirty film showing at a popular theater. The film turned out to be a sensual mystery thriller, a whodunnit drama featuring unknown actors. It was the kind of off-mainstream movie typically presented at the Harvard Square theater. Carrie and Lan shared a box of popcorn while they sat riveted to the movie.

After the film ended, they jogged to the car in the night's chilly air. Lan drove more slowly to her nearby condo.

Carrie was impressed with the interior lobby's shiny marble floors and walls. The building was an upscale, modern structure that couldn't have been more than a couple of years old.

I'm sure the rent for this place comes out of General Peng's pocket. He treats his lackeys well, at least this lackey.

They took the elevator up to the tenth floor. As soon as Carrie walked into the condo, she knew that she would like it. A full glass wall at the far end of the living room overlooked the Charles River and beyond to downtown Boston.

"This is beautiful! You must love living here."

"It's great. The view, the layout, everything is so comfortable."

The living room was large but sparsely decorated, so characteristic of Asian tastes in décor.

Lan grabbed Carrie's hand. "Here, let me show you the rest of my place." She led the way into a small dining area and showed her the kitchen and a small den.

"This room has a sofa with a pull-out bed that can serve as a guest room."

Lan next led her down a short hallway into a large master bedroom. The huge room held a king-sized bed, modern bureaus, and two sitting chairs. A large LCD TV hung on the far wall.

The room also contained a desk with new computer, extra large monitor, and business grade, multipurpose printer. Carrie's eyes locked onto the extraordinary home office.

"Now, my friend, let me show you the *pièce de résistance.*"

Still holding Carrie's hand and giving it a gentle squeeze, Lan led her through a door off of the bedroom. It opened up into an expansive marble tiled bathroom. The tile was a mixture of light salmon and sea foam colors. It was a sensuous room that fostered a feeling of peace and tranquility. The all glass, round shower was four times normal size. Inside were various shower attachments at different heights and angles. It was definitely a shower built for two. Beyond the toilet and bidet, three tiled steps led up to a large Roman-styled hot tub. Behind the tub, a wide horizontal window provided a view over the Charles River that was similar to the view from the living room.

"It's just gorgeous. I love it," Carrie told her.

Lan squeezed her hand again before releasing it. Taking a few steps forward, she leaned over the hot tub and turned on the faucets. After the tub filled a few inches, she pressed a button and bubbling currents began to swirl in the warm water. A light scent of perfume wafted through the air.

"This is where I spend a lot of time. I take a hot tub every night before retiring to bed. It relaxes me, and lets me fall off to sleep so peacefully."

They walked back into the master bedroom.

Carrie watched Lan as she placed her handbag on the computer desk.

Lan pulled opened the black leather tie string, reached inside, and grabbed her coveted tube of lipstick. She dropped it back into the bag as she became aware of her absent-minded action.

She must automatically take the flash drive out each night and leave it near her home computer. But today she remembered that she had a guest. Jim was right. She might be good at some things, but she's immature at many, and certainly not an experienced subversive.

Carrie resisted the urge to stare at the elusive prize, the leather handbag that was a few feet away. Her focus had to remain on Lan.

"What kind of wine would you like? We have to have some wine while we relax in the tub."

"Some chilled Chardonnay would be fine. But I didn't bring a bathing suit."

"Carrie. You're now in the home of a Chinese woman. I'm sure you've read somewhere that Asian women always bathe together in the nude. There's a dressing room right over there." She pointed to a door adjacent to the bathroom door. "You can get undressed and grab a towel from one of the shelves. I'll get the wine and join you in a moment."

When Lan left the bedroom and stepped into the kitchen, Carrie waited to hear the refrigerator door open and the sound of a glass bottle being removed.

Would there be enough time to switch the memory stick with the one I brought before she comes back?

Carrie's heart pounded rapidly as she made the attempt. She walked towards the computer desk while keeping her eyes on the bedroom door and her ears tuned to sounds coming from the kitchen. She just touched the leather tie to the handbag when the sound of wineglasses clinking together and coming closer made her jumped.

Oh shit! Too late.

Spinning around, she hurriedly stepped into the dressing room and within seconds her clothes were off.

She was well aware of the centuries old Chinese practice of public bathing. Although Wei Xing and she had bathed in public bathhouses many times, this was different. This time she would be sharing that experience with someone to whom she wasn't close, someone who was not only a mystery but also potentially an enemy. Too much was at stake for her to balk now. She needed to do everything possible to keep Lan relaxed and happy...and away from the memory stick with whatever secrets it contained. This might be her only chance.

With a large white towel wrapped around her and another draped over her arm, she stepped out of the dressing room as Lan entered the bedroom.

"That looks good," Carrie said, as she nodded at the tray with a bottle of chilled wine and two wineglasses.

Her plan was to keep her hostess relaxed and preoccupied so she wouldn't suspect any hidden agenda.

"Look," Carrie said, as she held out the extra towel, "I got a towel for you."

Trying to show enthusiasm, she led the way into the sybaritic bathroom. Lan followed.

Stepping up to the bubbling hot tub, she dropped her wrapped towel and slowly eased her naked body into the sparkling water. The water felt good. The digital display showed ninety nine degrees, which was hot enough to soften her tense muscles.

Lan smiled at her and set the tray next to the tub. Without any inhibition, she stripped off her clothes to reveal her slender but smoothly rounded body.

Carrie politely avoided staring at her companion's taut physique. She moved her gaze up to Lan's eyes as the Asian beauty slowly immersed her body into the tub.

They giggled softly as each submerged their bodies even deeper into the effervescent water. Soon both were seated in the tub with the water line at their necks.

"I can see why you do this every evening. It's so relaxing," Carrie said.

And it was. She let the jets of warm water pulsate and sooth her tense muscles. She soon began to feel mentally as well as physically relaxed.

Lan filled the glasses and handed one to Carrie. She slid closer to her guest and lifted her glass in a gesture to make a toast.

"Here's to a lovely day with my new friend. I am so happy we're together."

"As I am," Carrie replied, as she clinked her glass against Lan's.

"In China, we toast with the words, *Gānbēi*! It implies good luck, but literally translates to 'empty your glass!'."

Thanks for the lesson, but I have toasted in Mandarin many times.
Carrie took a long drink with the hope that some liquid courage would help her continue. The wine first warmed her throat and then her stomach.

Lan stared at her guest. She took in Carrie's innocent smile, and kept close, though without physical contact. The wine was within reach, and she diligently kept their glasses full. They chatted about the movie they had seen, with each making witty or funny comments about the plot and acting performances.

Soon Carrie could feel the effects of the alcohol and thought Lan was feeling it too. The Chinese woman's eyes appeared dreamy as she grinned through wispy clouds of steam.

Lan suggested that they raise the water temperature a bit. She slid very close. Her thigh rubbed against Carrie's as she leaned forward and turned the thermostat to the maximum of one-hundred and four degrees.

"That's nice," Carrie commented.

"Not too hot?" Lan asked.

"No, it's perfect."

She watched as Lan maintained her smile. She was also aware her new "best friend," as Jim had called her, didn't move back.

Carrie soon felt the difference in the increased temperature. The room became steamier, which made her feel even more relaxed.

The condensation blurred the view of the Boston skyline on that chilly fall evening. As they both gazed out at the twinkling city lights, Lan topped off their wineglasses.

When their glasses were empty, Lan placed them on the adjacent tiled surface.

Now feeling the combined effect of the hot water and the wine, Carrie let her head lay back on the soft neck rest bordering the tub. She closed her eyes and feigned submission to the moment, though she reminded herself to stay focused on her reason for being there.

Lan's fingers began touching her hair.

Without opening her eyes, she spoke to Lan in a slow dreamlike tone. "You like my hair, don't you?"

"Yes. It is quite beautiful. I love the color. It is so different, so unique."

"I'm glad you like it." Carrie smiled. Her eyes were still closed as she felt Lan's hand move through her hair. She then felt Lan's fingertips trace the outline of her face with a light touch that traveled delicately along her jaw, chin, and lips.

"But it's not only your hair that I like. I like your bright blue eyes that sparkle like the ocean. And your lovely smile...always so sincere...such a beautiful smile, my Carrie has."

As she heard Lan speak, a tingling sensation come over her. Her body reacted to the gentle touch, the heat, and the wine. She had never felt like this before, anxious yet excited.

She reached for a rational thought about what was happening. She had come here to complete a mission, to get the computer files. Now she was engaging in an adventure she hadn't planned. It was something she hadn't done before. Tonight was only a means to an end, she told herself.

Carrie had guessed that Lan was a lesbian. Now she had proof. The Asian woman's sexual preference fit her behavior in the lab.

Lan's fingers continued to gently caress Carrie's face and then slid down to her shoulder, stroked her soft skin, and continued their journey downward until they found Carrie's left breast and expanding nipple. Lan gently rubbed and squeezed the flesh around the nipple and massaged it until it became fully erect.

Carrie reacted to the gentle touch with a tingling sensation between her thighs. Still with her eyes closed, she focused on Lan's touch and the new sensations. She sensed Lan coming closer to her until she felt Lan's full soft lips cover hers lightly and then back away. Within seconds, the moist touch returned, now a little more forceful.

Carrie opened her lips to invite Lan's probing wine-flavored tongue to sensually explore her warm mouth. Without thinking, her own tongue returned the gentle invasion to taste the inside of Lan's mouth and feel her passion.

Lan's hands moved lower and began to caress Carrie's thighs under the steamy, churning water. She whispered soft moans of anticipation into Carrie's ear with feathery kisses on her neck.

Lan moved away. When Carrie opened her eyes, Lan was standing up, her tall, smooth body glistening with water. After receiving such intimate touching, Carrie felt comfortable staring at the sensual body in front of her. She looked up at her companion's smiling face, dropped her gaze down to Lan's flat hard stomach, and then glanced at her pubic area with its wisps of fine dark hair. Lan's shapely hips accentuated her narrow waist. Her breasts were full, like soft pale globes. Carrie drank in the sight of the seemingly perfect body in front of her.

"Come with me," Lan said softly.

Holding hands, they helped each other out of the tub.

Lan began drying off her American friend's body with an over-sized towel. She began around the neck and slowly and gently moved down to Carrie's breasts, torso, buttocks, and legs.

Carrie in turn began slowly drying Lan, with a sense of excitement of doing something she hadn't experienced before. She also realized that she was now in too deep to pull back.

Lan took her hand again and led her into the dimly lit bedroom. Remaining naked, they fell into the oversized bed. Lan first pressed her lips onto Carrie's lips and then next to Carrie's ear.

"I have been dreaming about this since the first day we met," she whispered.

Feeling awkward, Carrie didn't know what to say.

"I've never done this before, I….," she whispered in return.

"Shhh…," Lan interrupted, as she placed a finger across Carrie's lips. Again she moved her lips to Carrie's ear.

"Don't worry. I'll show you. There is only one thing I want you to do," she whispered.

Carrie felt a shock of anticipation.

"What?" Carrie whispered and then took a deep and nervous breath.

"I want you to call me Orchid. Just call me Orchid while we're in bed together."

Carrie had recognized the upward rising tone in Lan's name when Lan introduced herself and immediately guessed that *Lán* was short for *Lánhuā*, which is "orchid" in English.

What Carrie didn't know was why the translation to English was so important to her.

* * *

The next morning, as the sunlight came through the bedroom windows, Carrie opened her eyes with a sense that someone was staring at her. She turned to her side and saw Lan propped up on one elbow and smiling at her. She was topless with the bed sheet hiding only the lower part of her breasts.

"I've been watching you sleep. I didn't want to wake you since you looked so peaceful. I made you some hot tea and poured a glass of orange juice. They're on the night stand."

Carrie sat up. Her head instantly began to spin from the wine and the memories of last night. She gulped down the chilled juice.

Lan moved closer to her, raised her upper body, and exposed her full bosom. She softly kissed Carrie's forehead. As she moved closer, Carrie noticed a small dark blue tattoo underneath Lan's left breast.

When Lan saw her looking at the markings, she said, "That was my assigned number as a child. See?" She raised her breast to expose the underside with the numbers 121844 tattooed clearly in dark blue ink.

"Your assigned number?"

"Yes. I was an orphan from the day I was born. I was saved by a Christian Missionary organization in Shen Yang. When you're sent to an orphanage in China, you are assigned a registered number. Since the organization was Western, the ID number was tattooed in digits rather than Chinese characters. The girls were tattooed a few inches under the left nipple and the boys under their right armpit. We learned our personal numbers early. It was also stamped on all of our clothing, books, toys, whatever we might come to own."

"I didn't know that..."

"Hey, I was lucky!" Lan interrupted. "Most baby girls were killed soon after birth. I was lucky to be put into an orphanage. I personally picked my own name later after I learned to speak. I chose the name *Lánhuā* because everyone said I looked like a delicate flower, like an orchid."

"Lan, I'm sorry if I brought up sad memories for you."

"It's okay. It was the best and the worst of times for me, I guess."

Carrie sensed that there was more that might be gained from this subject. Since Lan seemed so relaxed and content, this might be the best time to pry a little. She nonchalantly reached for the cup of tea and asked, "How long were you at the orphanage?"

"I was there until I was thirteen. That's when Mr Peng, General Peng at that time, came and got me out."

"He adopted you?"

"No, but he took a liking to me and found a family home for me. It would be like what you Americans refer to as a foster home. I did get moved around a bit, but fortunately Mr Peng always looked after my well-being. He arranged to get me into good technical schools and eventually into the university. I'm very much indebted to him."

Pieces of the puzzle are now falling into place. She became a piece of Peng's property that he invested in while she was a kid. This way he was guaranteed loyalty for whatever he wanted her to do.

Lan leaned in as if to kiss Carrie but was interrupted with the sound of a musical ringtone. Lan jumped out of bed to grab her cellphone.

Carrie now remembered where she had heard that ringtone before. It brought back memories of when she had lived in Beijing. It was the national anthem of the People's Republic of China.

Lan began speaking loudly into the phone. She had no idea that Carrie was fluent in *Pǔtōnghuà,* standard Mandarin.

In bed, Carrie turned away to feign indifference while listening carefully to the conversation.

"*Wèi! Wèi!*" [Hello! Hello!]

"*Peng Xiānsheng.*" [Mr Peng.]

"*Shì.*" [Yes.]

Carrie couldn't hear his voice but guessed that Peng was either giving her directions or asking her questions.

"*Méi yŏu. Méi wèntí.* [No. No problem.]

Lan nodded while listening to her mentor and not interrupting.

"*Xièxie nín.*" [Thank you.]

Carrie didn't learn much from the conversation. She noticed that Lan used the respectful form of "you" when she said "thank you," even though Peng must have been like a father to her; and that she appeared disturbed by the call.

"Please excuse me for a while," Lan told her. "I'm going to take a shower."

As soon as Carrie heard the sound of the shower, she scrambled out of the bed and headed towards the closet. She retrieved the blank memory stick from her cardigan pocket; and with her heart pounding and her eyes repeatedly glancing at the bathroom door, she glided over to the desk and removed Lan's lipstick tube from the handbag. From the tube's weight, she guessed (as she had earlier) that it was lined with lead to avoid detection by the Elliot House scanners. She swapped Lan's flash drive with the blank one, and then placed the lipstick tube back into the handbag. After dropping the stolen drive into her sweater pocket, she scrambled back into the bed. She forced a calm expression on her face, though her heart continued beating loudly.

Lan stepped out of the bathroom with a pouting expression on her face.

"Carrie, honey, I'm sorry to tell you this, but I must leave. It was unexpected."

"No problem," Carrie replied, as she walked over to the dressing room to retrieve her clothes. She dressed as Lan slipped on a clean pair of panties and bra and then a light tangerine colored dress and high heels of a deeper orange. The dress fit her well. The high neck in the front swooped down in the back to end just above her bra strap.

It was the first time Carrie had seen her colleague in anything but slacks or blue jeans. It was obvious Lan was going to meet someone important and was dressing appropriately.

"Carrie, that phone call was Mr Peng."

Evidently Peng expected her to be dressed to the nines whenever the two of them met.

"Oh?"

"He wants to meet with me as soon as possible at the Elliot House dining room. He's meeting with Warren today at noon. So I must leave right away. Would you like to stay here? I should be back in the early afternoon."

"No, thanks. I really have lots to do."

* * *

Half an hour later, Lan was driving along the Cambridge streets with Carrie. She explained how Peng was upset there was no progress on the vaccine for agent yellow. He now wanted to know if Warren needed more resources to accelerate the project.

Carrie immediately knew what she must do. After all, she already had Jim's approval.

"There's something I wanted to tell you last night before…"

"Before we made love?" Lan interjected, with a wide smile on her face.

The previous night was almost a blur for Carrie. Between the wine, hot tub, and their encounter, it was like a hazy surreal dream.

"Yes. What I want to tell you could impact your meeting today."

"Like what?" Lan asked.

"The other night I made up a new batch of test vaccine. I've been looking over Jim's shoulder since we all want to find the vaccines as soon as possible. It was during the wee hours when I made up a batch of yellow vaccine. Since you weren't around at the time, I put the ice cubes in my apartment freezer."

"You what?" Lan asked in a loud, angry voice.

"The vaccine is only for agent yellow, as Jim had been directed," she lied.

Lan turned to her with a serious look that turned into a frown. She then turned her head away to focus on her driving.

"I have no idea whether it'll work, but it's worth a try. Why don't you tell Peng that we now have our first test batch of vaccine for agent yellow?"

Lan said nothing but kept the deep frown on her face. She accelerated the car while navigating the Boston streets.

"Carrie, you shouldn't have done that." Her voice was stern. "I know that Jim gave you his code to operate the ice cube machine, but that was only if we needed more bioagents in his absence. You shouldn't have made the vaccine without letting me know. I should have been there to transfer it directly into my freezer. You know the procedures."

Carrie had to soften the situation. She didn't want to have an angry Lan Ying at this critical time. Without a word, she stretched out her left arm around Lan's shoulders. In the silence, she let her fingers gently massage the back of Lan's neck in an intimate and affectionate manner. She continued for a few minutes while Lan stayed focused on driving.

"Lan, you're absolutely right. I shouldn't have made the vaccine without you. I wasn't thinking. I'm sorry. I was so excited with the results from the tissue tests that I couldn't go to sleep."

There was a long silence.

I thought that this would be a problem, but I had no choice. I had to tell her now. It might buy some time before Peng sends more of his henchmen over here. She's really pissed off. I better make nice to her or there'll be a larger battle on my hands with Warren and Peng.

Carrie's fingers continued to lightly massage Lan's neck. She leaned in closer to Lan's ear and asked in a soft, pleading voice, "Please, please forgive me?"

There was no answer while Lan continued her driving. An angry expression still colored her face.

Carrie put her right hand on Lan's thigh. Her fingers brushed back and forth along Lan's leg in an intimate manner. Slowly she slid her hand down to Lan's knee and glided it upwards under the dress. Her fingers gently caressed the soft inner thigh as they inched upwards. Soon her fingertips brushed Lan's panties between her legs. She leaned even closer to Lan's right ear, her tongue tracing the outer ear.

"Can you please forgive me, Orchid?" Carrie whispered.

The contrite request, and using the name "Orchid," along with the gentle finger stroking created the reaction she wanted.

Lan smiled again. She understood Carrie's attentions to mean that last night's sexual encounter meant something special to her American friend. She burst out laughing. Taking her right hand off the steering wheel, she held Carrie's hand at her silky crotch.

"You're going to make us have an accident. I forgive you! I forgive you!"

She squeezed Carrie's hand tightly and pulled it out from under her dress. Lifting it up to her lips, she softly kissed Carrie's fingertips.

After arriving at the Elliot House, she and Lan headed in different directions. While Lan walked down the main corridor to the dining room, Carrie skipped up the staircase to her apartment.

As soon as she unlocked the door, she re-locked it behind her. Her heart was in her throat as she reached into the pocket of her cardigan sweater. She pulled out Lan's memory stick. She had no time now to investigate the contents, but did have enough time to copy the files onto her own computer.

It took several minutes to transfer the files. Now she had to plan how to replace the drive back into Lan's handbag while retrieving the blank one.

She stripped off her clothing and took a long, hot shower. While massaging shampoo into her hair, she thought about Jim to displace last night's sexual experience. In her heart, she knew he was the only one who could make her feel good and feel like a real woman in bed. She decided not to let him know about last night's encounter unless it became absolutely necessary.

As she dried her hair, her thoughts reflected on General Peng and his plan. The last thing they needed was more Beijing scientists working on Project V to develop the vaccine. If Lan tells him that they now had a vaccine to test, she'll be on her way to Saratoga very soon.

Carrie desperately hoped that Jim's latest batch of vaccine would be successful in the field test. That would put an end to all the political pressure and deceitful power games.

Pulling on a sweatshirt and blue jeans, she shoved the flash drive into her front pocket and jogged downstairs to the office.

Just after she logged onto the network, she got a text message on her purple cellphone.

> Carbo,
> Just learned our new target, Jim Chen, is now in China. You should be aware of this. I'll await reports on who he meets. Stay alert upon his return.
> Good Luck,
> Barbo

She ignored the message and deleted it.

It was nearly noon when Lan came into the office after her meeting with Peng. It had been enough time for Carrie to make a plan for swapping the memory sticks.

THIRTY ONE

"It worked, my sweet Carrie!" Lan announced. "Mr Peng is happy now that we have our first batch of agent yellow vaccine to test. I'm so glad you told me you had it. The only bad news is that I have to leave today for Saratoga. He wants to know the results by tomorrow, if possible. I already called ahead to my Saratoga staff with a test scheduled for midnight."

She walked over to Carrie and gently placed both hands on her shoulders.

"I so wanted to be with you again tonight."

"There'll be time when you get back," she replied, to continue her act.

A smile lit up Lan's face. In high heels, she had to bend slightly before brushing her lips against Carrie's. Her breath was sweet with the scent of peppermint candy.

"God, we had better be careful," Carrie said, as she stepped back. "Warren could come in at any time."

Lan nodded, walked to her workstation, and dropped her handbag onto the workbench. She unlocked her desk drawer.

"I'm not even going to download my backup files. I won't be working here today."

"You'll be on your way to Saratoga soon?"

"Right now, I really have to go to the ladies' room. You can meet me later in the Cold Room after you get the vaccine from upstairs. Please bring all of the ice cubes here."

As soon as Lan left the room, Carrie stepped over to Lan's handbag. She removed the empty drive, slipped it into her jeans, and replaced Lan's original drive back into the lipstick tube. After a long sigh of relief, she left the office and ran upstairs to retrieve the zip-locked bag of test vaccine.

When Carrie entered the Cold Room with the bag, Lan already had her storage freezer opened. She handed the bag to Lan.

Lan carefully poured the contents into a cylindrical container and labeled it "Agent Yellow VACCINE." She transferred the container to her dry ice cooler.

"Are you going to bring the other agents to perform additional tests?" Carrie asked.

"No, since the vaccine only works in Asian subjects. All I need are agent yellow and the vaccine. I'll give all the subjects agent yellow, but only half of them the vaccine. The good news is I can use Peng's private helicopter to fly up to Saratoga today. He doesn't need it, and I'll be there in an hour."

Carrie smiled and held up crossed fingers for Lan to see.

"Let's hope it works," Lan said with a wistful tone. "If so, we can immunize all Asian people as soon as possible."

That says everything, doesn't it. I doubt that General Peng would be happy hearing her say that to a Westerner.

"I'll be observing the test on the office monitor," Carrie commented.

Without another word, Lan turned, picked up her cooler, and left with a brief wave of her hand.

The ensuing quiet that filled the office gave Carrie time to think about what would happen if the new vaccine failed. The thought caused acid to percolate up from her stomach.

Not wanting to work, she cleaned up her desk and was about to leave when Warren came storming through the doorway.

"Carrie. I need to talk with you."

"Good, Warren, because I was about to call you. I wanted to let you know that I sent Lan off to Saratoga to test our first batch of vaccine."

"So I talked with General Peng. I had a quick lunch with him. I understand you only have the vaccine for agent yellow. Is that correct?"

There would be time later to inform Warren of the details, so she decided to keep quiet.

"We don't know exactly what we have right now. This test is critical. If you like, you can watch it with me on the monitor. Lan expects to have the subjects screened today. Her testing will begin around midnight."

He nodded.

"How's everything else going?" Carrie asked.

Maybe this was her chance to dig for a little more information out of him.

"Not bad. I got a call from Peng last night to meet him here today. He was angry that progress was so slow on the vaccine development. I'm glad you had some vaccine to test with today."

"Let me ask you something."

"Shoot."

"How well do you know General Peng? I mean, did you know him long before you were involved with Project V?"

"I only knew that he was one of the most powerful men in Beijing and the head of the MSS. Before Project V was assembled, he asked to meet with me."

"Do you know anything about him personally? Is he married, divorced, does he have any kids?"

"In Chinese culture, men don't ask those personal questions, as men do here. If a man wants to speak about his wife or kids or whatever, he'll raise the topic. To answer your question, I don't know."

"I thought that since you two worked so closely..."

"We haven't worked that closely. I've only been in Peng's company a half-dozen times. At those meetings, we've only discussed the project at a high level, its funding, its resources, things like that. He always sent his staff to meet with me to work out the details."

"I see."

"I've got to make some phone calls. I'll meet you down here before midnight so we can watch the field testing."

Within seconds, he was out of the office.

As she prepared a second time to leave, her cellphone rang.

It was Jim.

"Carrie, I couldn't wait until tonight to tell you the good news. I am now a single man. The divorce proceedings are over."

"I'm happy for you."

"And I'm happy for us."

"Jim, I've got lots to tell you."

She brought him up to speed about the vaccine test scheduled for later that evening. She also described how General Peng was clearly more influential than they had first thought. Her revelation about a threat to bring on more Chinese scientists was followed by several swear words from Jim, the first that Carrie had heard him speak. He then said, "I hope there's good news with tonight's test. Will you call me as soon as you know something?"

"Sure. Warren wants to watch as well. He'll be here with me."

"I wish I was there with you."

A wave of guilt flooded her mind. While she had been in bed with Lan, he had most likely been thinking of her. She had to get over that. She had had no choice; she had used the one night stand to accomplish a vital mission. She shoved the memory away.

"Jim, I can't wait to see you." Her voice told him she meant it.

"I'm trying to get a flight back tomorrow. If so, I'll be in Boston the next morning. I still haven't seen Jiang Ming, and I did want to before I left."

"Go and see your brother. Everything is under control here, and one more day won't matter. In fact," she teased, "it will only make me want you more."

Back in her apartment, Carrie sat down at her computer to look at Lan's mysterious files. She was amazed to find hundreds of photo images, images that didn't make sense to her. None of them had to do with viruses or vaccines. There were no scientific formulae or notes. Each of the photo images was tagged with a five digit index number. The images were of public water sources, including reservoirs, lakes, and rivers. Some had municipal water tanks with the town name painted on them

She left the computer and lay down on her bed. She decided to leave the computer data for another time and let herself have the luxury of a nap. Within minutes, she was in a sound sleep.

When her cellphone woke her in the evening, the bedroom clock displayed nine fifty five. She thought that it might be Jim.

"Hi Carrie, it's me, Orchid."

"Hello. How are you doing at Saratoga?"

"Great, but that's not why I called. I wanted to tell you that I miss you already. I hope you can come to my condo again soon. Carrie, you are so sweet. I can't tell you how happy I am."

She had to put a stop to this. Lan's romantic cooing was making her uncomfortable.

"I'm sorry I can't talk right now," she replied. "Warren is waiting for me in the next room. I must go. Is the testing still on for midnight?"

"Yes. I'll let you go."

"Before you do, I want to know which subjects will be given the vaccine. How will I identify them on the monitor?"

"I have already thought of that. They'll each have a black armband on their left arms. I've already given them the vaccine masked in apple juice to give the serum time to travel throughout their bodies. The next glass they drink will have the agent yellow in it."

"Good Luck!" Carrie said, though the statement was really meant for her and Jim, not for Lan and Peng.

When she arrived at the office, Warren was already sitting at her workbench sipping hot green tea. She made herself a cup of black tea, and they chatted until the televised images of the prison hospital came up on the monitor. She explained to him about the black armbands.

At precisely midnight, a young white woman dressed in colored hospital scrubs and a white surgical mask came into the ward. She pushed a cart holding glasses of apple juice and a closed container of ice cubes. The subjects were instructed to take a drink after the ice cubes were in the glass for a few minutes.

Since the sample of agent yellow was highly concentrated, those who hadn't taken the vaccine would expire quickly.

Warren's eyes were riveted to the monitor. He didn't say a word as the convicts soon began coughing and showing flu-like symptoms. Several subjects cried out as they became more feverish and uncomfortable.

He stood up and nervously paced without watching the monitor. He was obviously uncomfortable seeing such manipulated murder take place. After walking away, he filled a paper cup with water from the office cooler.

After what seemed an interminably long wait, Warren spoke with an excited voice. "Look, Carrie! The subjects with the black armbands are no longer coughing or feeling discomfort. They appear to be okay. Only those who didn't take the vaccine are dying."

Carrie looked up at the monitor, emotionally relieved by the successful test, which among other things underscored Jim's expertise.

"Warren, the ball is now in your court," she said as she looked directly at him.

"What? What do you mean?"

"I know all about Peng's arrangement regarding the release of Jim's brother from prison. Now Peng has his fucking agent yellow vaccine. Wasn't that the deal? Now you have to pick up the phone and call him. Jim is in China right now. He's probably at the prison visiting Jiang Ming this very minute."

Warren's mouth gaped open as he stared back at her. He pulled out his cellphone from his inside jacket pocket.

She could hear the phone conversation in Mandarin, though she decided to still keep Warren in the dark about her knowledge of the language.

Her heart fell as she listened to Peng respond to the Under Secretary of State. He told him he wouldn't release the prisoner until he heard the test results from Lan.

After ending the call, Warren said, "This man is a total prick. How am I going to get Lan to call Peng right now, right this minute, and give him the vaccine test results?"

"I'll take care of that."

She called Lan and told her Peng was waiting for her to tell him the successful results of the vaccine test. Lan promised to make the call immediately.

She and Warren looked up again at the monitor. The Asian subjects without armbands had died within thirty minutes of ingesting agent yellow. They all had light trickles of blood oozing from their nostrils.

"I guess we're done here," Warren said. "I'm glad all this shit is coming to an end. Will you join me for breakfast later this morning? You can be the first to wish me a happy birthday."

"I would be happy to."

She thought about the genealogical material still in the sealed envelope that she had received from Wei Xing. She would give it to him later when it was the right time, if there ever was a right time.

Still energized from her earlier nap and the results of the vaccine test, she knew she wouldn't be able to fall asleep. She retreated to her apartment to sit in front of her computer again in an effort to make some sense of Lan's image files.

After scanning over many digital photos, she identified a correlation between the text data and indexed images. There were notations in the relational database that still puzzled her. Each image had a location of the water source identified with longitude and latitude coordinates. The only other information accompanying each photo was the mercury levels in the water. The measurements were listed in parts per million.

Why in hell were mercury levels so important? There had to be hundreds of other contaminants in the reservoirs. Why was that chemical element singled out? And why was it so important to know how much of the element was in each body of water?

Despite the mercury puzzle, Carrie's conclusion about the reason for the images was frightening. Without looking at any more screen shots, she began printing off files until her printer cartridge ran out of ink.

She tried calling Jim's cellphone but got no answer. She guessed that he had to turn it off inside of the Chinese prison. The good news about the vaccine would have to wait. She hadn't yet decided to tell him the bad news as well.

THIRTY TWO

"Here's the birthday guy. Good morning." Carrie walked over to the Under Secretary who was sitting at a dining table and gave him a congratulatory peck on the cheek.

His trademark smile lit up his face. "Thanks, Carrie. And a good morning to you."

They both drank coffee and talked about the prior evening's activities. Warren was pleased with the results of the vaccine test, but something appeared to still be bothering him.

"I wanted to tell you I talked with Peng again early this morning. He assured me that he has given the detention house orders to release Jiang Ming. Jim should be bringing him back here soon."

The news washed a feeling of relief over her. She couldn't detect any happiness from Warren.

"That's such good news. But something else is bothering you."

"It's General Peng. Although he agreed on Jiang Ming's release, he also asked a favor of me."

"More negotiating?" Her sense of relief had diminished.

"No more deals. He asked that I let him use the Elliot House lecture hall for a private session. He wants to use it tomorrow, in fact. He plans to call in a number of the visiting Environment Exchange engineers who came here to share ideas and technology on controlling pollution."

"Why?" she asked.

"Since they'll soon be returning home to their own cities and villages in China, he wanted to applaud them and congratulate them with a nice luncheon and meeting. Peng expects about fifty to come here."

"It sounds like the proper thing to do. Why does that bother you?"

"The purpose is fine. However, he specifically asked that no Americans be invited. That includes me, even though I work for the State Department and could represent Secretary Hinton. He was adamant that none of us be present while they lock themselves up in our lecture hall for a few hours."

Carrie couldn't hide her confusion, and her face wrinkled into a deep frown.

"It's strange to me that he wouldn't at least have you say a few words to the group and then you could leave them their meeting. After all, it was you and the State Department who pulled the program together."

"I agree."

"Warren, you need to know that Peng isn't a man who does nice things."

"I think you're right about that," Warren commented with his heading nodding slowly.

They quietly finished their breakfasts without much conversation.

As soon as Warren left the dining room, she dialed Jim's cell number.

He immediately answered. "*Wèi! Wèi!*"

"Jim, it's me."

"Carrie, I'm sorry, I didn't look at the caller ID. I thought it might be Jiang Ming or one of the authorities at the detention facility."

"Jim, I wanted to get to you before you went to bed. The vaccine test worked! The testing at Saratoga went fine. Warren watched it with me, and Peng has been notified. He'll make arrangements for your brother to be released. So keep in contact with the prison officials. Warren was convinced you could bring him home with you."

"My God, Carrie! That's great news. I didn't want to stay here any longer than I had to, but I'll do what it takes to get my brother released. I still miss you so much."

"I miss you too."

"Now I can bring Jiang Ming back to the States with me."

"I've got to tell you something else. I got my hands on Lan's computer files. I switched memory sticks and copied her files onto my machine. I have looked at some of them, and what I found scares the hell out me."

"What? What did you find?"

"Profiles and photos of water supplies throughout the United States. The profiles contain the type of supply, level of security around each, and how many gallons are contained in the resource. The profiles are linked to photographs of the water resources."

"Why would she want that information?"

"And for all of fifty states."

"What are your thoughts?"

"I think I know what's going on, though I hope to God I'm wrong. I think that Peng and Lan never had any intention of developing a bioagent vaccine."

"What?"

"As I said before, I'm convinced that Peng only wanted to get his hands on the white and black bioagents, or at least the software algorithms so they could create them back home in Beijing. They want the power, the potential, to commit mass genocide of all White and Black people living on any continent. Remember that the original requirement was for the agents to be insoluble in water, not so that they would be safe to handle in ice cubes but so the virus would survive in a water resource. That requirement came directly from Peng. That way the agents could easily be delivered by dropping them into water resources throughout the United States or any other country."

"But Peng was upset that the vaccine wasn't developed yet. Why would he want to pull in more scientists to get it done?"

"He only wanted the Mongoloid vaccine to protect Chinese people as insurance. Don't forget that he and Lan think that we developed a vaccine to protect only the Mongoloid race from agent yellow. That's all he needs. In retrospect, Peng must have been wild when Warren told him that we developed the bioagent targeted for Mongoloids first. That derailed his original plan. He really only wanted the white and black bioagents developed and tested. After that, he couldn't give a damn about any vaccines being developed. He would have walked away from Project V long before that."

"I do remember that meeting. His orders from Peng were clear. We were to develop the bioweapon virus in a specific sequence: first white, then black, and finally yellow. I…"

Carrie interrupted him. "We would have never developed agent yellow, Jim. Don't you see? Peng would have the world by the balls once he had the white and black bioagents. That's all he ever really wanted. We fucked up his strategy when we developed agent yellow out of sequence. That forced him to change his original plans."

"This is incredible. You and I are in the thick of some high level, clandestine espionage."

"Remember that your vaccine can be used for all races. So we have completed our jobs. We only need to keep Peng and China's MSS from getting their hands on the software algorithms."

"Carrie, I hate this. You and I got into this biomedical field to protect people, not to kill people."

"And Peng's purpose is just the opposite. He wants a super weapon. He's played Warren like a puppet, and he used your brother as the carrot to get you on board with Project V. Soon he'll have the power to launch selective genocide on any continent he chooses. Now that he has the water supplies of America carefully profiled, he's that much closer to obliterating the White and Black populations of this country."

"Don't hand over the software formulas to anyone until I get back. Maybe I can come up with something before I return."

"What can we do? If we give him bogus information, he'll know it almost immediately. That's when it gets dangerous for you and for me. Lan has the test agents stored in her freezer right now. With some effort they could duplicate agents without even knowing the formula."

"I know," Jim replied. "Damn, with hindsight, I should have insisted on access to Lan's freezer when I became Project Leader. I made a mistake with those procedural security checks and balances in the Cold Room. Do you think you should alert the President?"

"Not right now," Carrie replied. "He's traveling to Europe and Africa this week. I'll also try to think of something, but there's going to be a lot of pressure on me, on us, to turn over everything to Lan soon. And get this, Peng has asked to have his own special meeting with the environmental engineers who are here on the Environmental Exchange Alliance. He told Warren that he wants to thank them formally before they return home. And listen to this bullshit! He specifically asked that Warren and me not attend."

"I don't like any of this. Is there any way we can get a tape recorder into that meeting?"

"I doubt it. He's undoubtedly going to have his own staff to control entrance to the meeting."

"I wish there was a way either you or Warren could gain access to that session. I don't like the sound of Peng holding court, especially in our own territory. He must have something important and secretive to say to those people if he's excluding you two."

"I'll see what I can do."

"Carrie, please be careful."

* * *

At nine in the morning, Lan strutted into the office with a bright smile on her face. After closing the door, she darted over to Carrie and stood by her desk. She opened her arms wide to invite Carrie to stand and receive her embrace. Still playing her role as Lan's lover, Carrie stood and received Lan's hug and her kisses on the cheeks.

"You did it! We now have a successful vaccine. I'm so happy and so proud of you."

Carrie broke away from her embrace. "It was Jim who really did it. But we're all happy the vaccine seems to be working. Remember, however," Carrie said in her best lecturing voice, "it's only a vaccine to protect the Mongoloid race." She lied with conviction. "Now we need to develop vaccines for White and Black people. And we need to do more tests on this vaccine before we break out the champagne."

Lan's face had a sheepish expression.

"Yeah. More tests will be coming soon." She promptly changed the topic. "How was viewing on the monitor?"

"Warren and I could see everything clearly."

"Was Warren happy with the results?"

"Sure. Would you have expected otherwise?" The response came out sharper than it was meant to be.

Lan shrugged her shoulders without a word and turned her sulking face towards her computer.

Heavy silence hung in the office for the remainder of the morning. At noon, Warren called and asked Carrie to join him for lunch.

When she met Warren in the dining room, he skipped any greetings and immediately continued their previous conversation about General Peng. "I had another brief talk with Peng this morning. He's still adamant about not having any Americans in his meeting, even after I requested to say a few words to the audience. He told me it was something *he* had to do and it was important that no outside influence be at the session."

"That bastard's up to something."

"I really don't know this man. I worked mostly through his staff people. He did tell me he's hosting a coffee and tea hour in the lobby before the meeting. It's an opportunity for the attendees to meet one another. You and I are welcome to join them for that informal gathering."

"Do you think there's any way we can eavesdrop on the meeting? You know, bug the room?"

Warren looked at her with a shocked look on his face.

"Carrie, for God's sake, we're not spies. We can't let our imaginations lead us into something that we will regret later. It's much too dangerous to even think about spying on Chinese officials."

"What the hell do you think they're doing to us?"

"What are you talking about?"

Carrie told him what she had told Jim earlier, that is, her conjecture about why the agent yellow vaccine was so important to Peng. His eyebrows arched when he heard about the photos and information on US water resources. The bronze color of his face drained and then turned crimson as she explained the details of Peng's strategy.

"What you're telling me is that I've been duped all along. This top-secret project was set up to have me recruit the best talent, Jim and later you, to do all the work developing a racial bioagent. He never intended it to be a defensive device but an offensive weapon."

"I suspect that the whole project has been orchestrated by Peng and his gang, including Lan. I doubt that President Hu and the Politburo are aware of his clandestine activities. I've learned that Peng has a reputation of acting on his own."

"If your speculation—no, it's obviously more than that—is true, that son-of-a bitch used me. He used all of us."

"That's not the problem. We have to stop them, without creating a global panic." Carrie had to focus Warren's anger.

"Even though I believe that everything you say is very likely to be true, I can't confront him yet. We have no concrete evidence yet that what we've discovered is a malicious plan. He could easily tell me that his surveys of our drinking water resources were part of the Environmental Exchange program. And your copying Lan's files was unlawful or at least unethical. He not only still has enough wiggle room to escape justice but also enough to make us look bad, permanently bad."

Of course our careers are on the line, and it's no secret how fanatical you are about yours, Warren. But what are they compared to being right about Peng? Nothing.

"Let's meet later tonight," he said. "Maybe we'll come up with something by then. I've got some serious thinking to do."

* * *

After Warren left the dining room, she remained seated. She certainly didn't feel like going back to work. She wanted to avoid confronting Lan again, now that she knew Lan was more than just a pawn in Peng's strategy.

Dr Lan Ying knows exactly what she's doing.

Carrie walked slowly upstairs to her apartment. After locking her door, she decided to peruse the stolen files again. As she looked at the images and data, the extraordinary severity of the situation clouded her mind: she had to do something but couldn't think clearly, analytically as she was use to.

A bike ride often cleared her head. The early fall weather had begun, and she reached into her closet for a windbreaker or sweater. When she saw Jim's jacket, she touched it as though she could feel him through the garment. Her fingers gently caressed the sleeve. She pulled the jacket out and slipped it on. Although it was large for her, when zipped up it fit better. She grabbed her handbag. After stopping at the gate to pick up Jim's handgun, she drove her Harley out of the retreat grounds.

THIRTY THREE

The bike ride cleared her head. The chilled air made her crouch down on the seat, but she still enjoyed the freedom of riding along country roads with little traffic. As the sun went down, she started cruising back to the Elliot House.

During the return trip, she spotted the tavern where Jim had taken her on their first date and pulled into the parking lot.

When she walked inside, she found the bar busy with commuters stopping on the trip home. She sat on a barstool and ordered a beer and a small pizza. She appreciated that the bartender was non-communicative. Within a short period, she ate the pizza, drank her beer, and left the tavern.

As she hopped onto her bike, she noticed the silhouette of a man sitting in a car near her Harley. At first, she ignored the car and the driver with the thought that he was waiting to meet someone. Then she remembered seeing a black Mercedes before. It was identical to the car that had followed her and Jim after lunch some weeks ago. She recalled how the scar-faced stalker had tailed them from the restaurant, and he was the same creep that followed them after the Red Sox game.

She started up her bike and drove slowly around the front of the building to the opposite side. She continued slowly to the back of the tavern. After shutting off her bike, she manually rolled it behind a large dumpster that butted against some wooded property.

As she expected, the Mercedes followed behind at a very slow speed. The driver couldn't see her or her bike behind the dumpster. From the security light on top of the restaurant, she could see everything clearly from around the dumpster. The scar-faced man slowed the car to a stop. He stepped out of the car and looked for the motorcycle and rider.

Carrie hadn't planned on a confrontation. She only wanted to see the car's license plate and later follow up on the mystery stalker. When she remembered the handgun, she reached into her handbag and pulled out the snubnosed thirty eight. She quietly waited for the stalker to come closer. When he came within a dozen feet of the dumpster, she jumped out while aiming the gun directly at his head.

"Stop right there, asshole! Hands up right now or I'm shooting."

"Wait! Wait! This isn't what you think, Professor Bock."

The surprised man was the same one who Jim and she had seen tailing them after lunch weeks ago and the same one Jim had spotted in the restaurant after the ball game.

With the security light dimly lighting the area, she could still make out the thin scar that stood out on an otherwise unblemished, dark-toned face. He was dressed in a suit and dress shirt but without a tie. He raised his hands.

I guessed that this bastard knew my name. I wonder what else he knows about me and about Jim.

"Just keep your hands up. Who the fuck are you?"

"My name is Gianni. I'm Gianni Gregorio."

"Okay, Gianni Gregorio, why the fuck have you been stalking me?" Her rattled nerves evoked a loud anger.

"It's my job. I was hired to follow you."

"Hired? Hired by whom?"

"That I can't reveal, Professor. It's classified information."

Classified information? Is this guy an FBI agent? Who the hell is he?

"Take off your jacket now and slowly drop it to the ground. One wrong move and you'll be a fucking dead stalker with classified information, Gianni Gregorio."

She had to act tough or she could easily end up a corpse inside of a trash dumpster. This guy looked like he could handle himself quite well. She watched nervously as the man slowly took off his suit jacket and dropped it on the hardened dirt surface. He had a leather gun holster strapped around his chest. The butt handle of a handgun poked out from under his left armpit.

"Unbuckle that holster slowly and drop it on the ground."

"Listen, Professor, Carrie. This isn't necessary. I just...."

Carrie impulsively pulled the trigger. Although she had consciously aimed the gun at the ground near the man's feet, she startled herself with the act. The loud bang of the shot was accompanied by an explosion of gravel and dirt near his expensive looking loafers.

Gregorio jumped.

"Jesus, Carrie, be careful! No-one needs to die over this. I'm only on a surveillance assignment. That's all, I swear."

"Drop the gun now!"

Gregorio slowly unfastened the holster buckle. He dropped his hands as it fell to the ground with the gun still inside.

"Get your hands back up in the air. Now tell me who the hell you're working for."

"I told you it's classified. It's, you know, federal government stuff. My assignment came from Washington. And who hired me is top-secret information."

"Mr Gregorio, I'm putting a bullet through your fucking head in about ten seconds. If you want to die a loyal government hero, so be it. I'm still protecting myself from being killed by you. Self defense is still the best defense, government agent or no government agent."

"No! Wait, I'm not an agent. I'm no G-man. I'm a private investigator, a fucking PI for God's sake. I was hired by someone in President Bowa's administration to follow you. I report on where you go, who you're with, and shit like that. That's all my assignment was. I'm supposed to keep an eye on you. There wasn't any violence associated with this gig."

"Why, Mr Gregorio? Why would anyone in the government want to keep an eye on what the hell I do and who I do it with?"

Carrie felt personally violated after she said the words out loud.

This son-of-a-bitch has been tailing me for a long time. He knows about my relationship with Jim Chen, and everything we've done. He knows about my father in the Alzheimer's home and every time I visit him. He must have been the mystery biker I couldn't identify. And he's the one who followed me to the shopping mall that afternoon. He probably tailed me to Lan's condo in Cambridge the other night.

"I'm not supposed to divulge anything about this assignment. My contact told me to be tight lipped if I ever got caught."

"How the hell did you know when I left the compound? Did you sneak onto the grounds?"

"No. I couldn't get beyond the gates and guards, nor was I supposed to. I followed you whenever you left the Elliot House."

"How the hell did you know when I left?"

"There's a GPS tracker under the seat to your bike. I attached one to your bike and also to Dr Chen's bike the first night you came to this restaurant. There's one in Dr Chen's Mustang as well. That's how I could find out where either of you were."

"Jim was followed too?"

"Yeah. When I reported how you two were seeing one another, I was told to follow him and report everything he was up to."

"Walk slowly over to my bike and take off the fucking GPS device. Throw it down on the ground near the holster."

Gregorio did as she asked while she kept the gun aimed at him.

"I don't know anything about you, Carrie. I was…"

"Shut up and get that GPS device."

"Yeah. I was told to follow you and to send a report to some unknown email address every other day. I got a nice freakin' paycheck to do it, so it was a sweet assignment. I don't usually do shit like this. I'm usually hired to track down some cheating husband or wife, for God's sake. You can check with the Boston Police Department. They know who I am. I've got a solid reputation as one of the best PI's in town. They'll tell you that."

"You told me you're working for someone in the administration. I know it's not the President, so who the hell is it?"

Gregorio continued to hold his hands up in the air. He offered no response.

"Okay, Mr Gregorio, your family and friends will notice your tight lips while you lay dead in your fuckin' casket. I personally don't give a shit if I kill you right now. And only I will be around to give the details of this encounter."

She took a half step closer while still aiming the gun at the man's head. Cocking the hammer to the small handgun made a loud, clicking sound.

253

"It's Zachary Hinton! Jesus, don't shoot! Hinton hired me. Now, put the damn gun down. Please."

"Hinton? Why the hell would the Secretary of State hire you to follow me?"

"Hell, Professor, I don't know," the private investigator answered while keeping his eyes riveted on Carrie's gun. "For Christ's sake, be careful."

Carrie slowly reset the trigger and dropped the handgun down to her side.

"Let me tell you something, Gianni Gregorio. Your top-secret assignment is finished. I'll let the Secretary of State know you did a great fucking job. Now listen and listen well. The last place you want to be is anywhere near me or Jim Chen from now on. Do you understand? Stalking is a crime in this state, a dangerous crime."

"Yeah, I want out of this weird gig anyway," he responded while dropping his arms to his side.

"Now piss off. I'll keep your gun, holster, and GPS tracker. The FBI may return them after you've been cleared."

Gregorio took little time jumping into his car and pulling out of the parking lot—but not without Carrie memorizing the car's license number.

After he sped away, Carrie took out her purple cellphone and texted the President.

> Barbo,
> We need to talk.
> Carbo

THIRTY FOUR

The next morning Carrie got up early to jog her usual four miles. As she was finishing, she noticed limousines parading through the wrought iron gate. Several Chinese men and a few women stepped from each vehicle. The men were dressed in suits and Western-styled neckties. The women wore conservative dresses or business suits with slacks or a skirt.

After showering and dressing, she made her way downstairs to the lobby. There were tables with coffee, tea, fresh juices, an array of bagels, donuts, and other pastries. She guessed that there were more than fifty people already milling around, all speaking Mandarin.

She made her way to a table for a cup of coffee while trying to catch bits of the loud and animated conversations.

A light tapping on her shoulder surprised her. When she turned she came face to face with Lan Ying.

Lan wore a tight fitting, light green dress of silk with pale blue embroidered flowers across the bodice.

"Carrie, there's someone here I would like you to meet. General Peng, this is Dr Carrie Bock, a personal friend of President Bowa and a member of our project team."

She had to peer down at the diminutive man who stood barely five feet tall. She could have easily picked him out of the crowd based on Wei Xing's description. He had a square, short frame. His receding hairline met a closely cropped haircut. Peng's eyeglasses struck her the most. They were a black, horn-rimmed retro style from the last century. The lenses were so thick that they appeared to be made of glass instead of modern plastics. His dark American-styled navy blue suit and white dress shirt contrasted with a bright red silk tie.

"I am so happy to finally meet you, Dr Bock. Lan has told me so much about you. You are an esteemed scientist and a great asset to the project," he said as he shook her hand.

Carrie was amazed at how small his hand felt inside of her own. It seemed as if she were shaking the hand of a prepubescent boy. As she stared icily into the little man's gimlet eyes, she cordially responded, "It is a pleasure to meet you as well."

They chatted briefly until a tall, thin Chinese man came by to usher Peng and Lan away. He wanted them to meet someone who had just come into the gathering.

Moments later she spotted Warren entering the lobby. It wasn't a happy looking Warren. It was a tired and stressed looking Under Secretary of State.

She got a cup of coffee and a pastry and walked around the growing crowd. Most people acknowledged her presence by nodding with a smile. She didn't know anyone there, so speaking to any of them was not socially expected. They all spoke Mandarin, so she easily understood the conversations she could hear. What surprised her most was that apparently few of the attendees had met before this meeting. She thought how that made sense since they had come from different parts of China and were assigned to different locations throughout the United States.

As she milled about, she noticed that none of the attendees wore name tags, a feature typical of American events such as this one. As she kept an eye on Lan and Peng working the crowd, she realized that they too had little or no personal acquaintance with most of the attendees.

As she prepared to leave, an idea struck her with a force so strong that her legs almost buckled. Reacting immediately, she hurriedly passed through the crowd and headed for her apartment.

After slamming her apartment door shut, she ran into her bedroom. She pulled out a navy blue skirt with a matching jacket from her closet, and shrugged out of her slacks. She grabbed the wig, special contact lenses, and makeup that she had used in her surprise trip to Atlanta.

This disguise worked for me before, and it sure as shit better work again! I can mingle with this crowd downstairs and find out exactly what the hell Peng is up to.

Using the makeup kit, Carrie transformed her complexion. After adding the black wig, she popped in the special contact lenses to widen the shape of her eyes and change her blue irises to black. She twirled around in front of the full length mirror to check how she had again morphed into an attractive Chinese woman. Last she slipped her feet into navy blue pumps that matched the business suit.

When she returned to the lobby, she was surprised to find it empty. Only the house staff cleaning up from the social hour were present. When she looked towards the entrance of the Lecture Hall, she saw a Chinese man about to close the door.

Without thinking, she yelled out, "*Děng! Qǐng, děng yíxia* [Wait! Please, wait a moment]."

The doorman looked at her running towards him and smiled.

"*Duìbuqǐ, duìbuqǐ* [Sorry, sorry]," she called out in an apologetic tone.

"*Hao. Bié zháo jí* [Okay. Don't rush]," he replied as he waved one hand and kept the door opened with the other.

"*Xièxie* [Thanks]."

After allowing her to enter, the doorman closed the doors and remained outside.

With her heart pounding, she peered around the massive lecture hall. The hall was an amphitheater with a large, elevated stage that held only a lectern. Some of the attendees were still milling about before the program began.

She sucked in a deep breath and exhaled as she walked nonchalantly down the aisle. She took an empty seat at the end of a row next to an older woman who politely nodded as she sat down. Without saying a word, she caught a quick glimpse of the woman. The woman's salt and pepper colored hair looked familiar. When Carrie saw that the woman's right arm had been amputated and had no prosthesis, she recalled a television news segment of the Secretary of State Hinton launching the Environmental Exchange program. It was that same woman who stood in the front line of the visiting group.

After everyone settled in, General Peng marched onto the stage. He ignored the lectern, undoubtedly because he would appear even smaller to the audience next to it. A wireless microphone enabled him to walk around the stage as he spoke.

Carrie focused on every word. She was thankful Peng spoke Mandarin clearly and slowly. Her Chinese vocabulary was still good enough that she could get the gist of what he said, even if she missed a technical word here and there.

At first, his talk was filled with gracious appreciation for the work that the engineers had done the past few months. He also underscored the sacrifices that they had made.

Then the substance and tone of his talk took a dramatic change. He next thanked the audience for their tenacious effort to collect data on America's water resources. He joked about the quality of some of the photographs, but reassured them that the information, including the security profile of each site, was invaluable.

He publicly acknowledged his associate, Dr Ying Lan. He told them how she had gathered the data from all over the United States sent to her by the attendees, and had created a comprehensive database of America's consumable water resources.

Carrie squirmed angrily in her seat and peered around at the audience. They seemed pleased that their efforts were dutifully acknowledged by General Peng, the powerful Minister of State Security.

Looking at the members in the audience, Carrie was struck by one chubby man dressed in a dark gray suit. He had another familiar face, one with a wine stain birthmark on his cheek. He was also in the TV news segment with the Secretary of State.

These people aren't environmental engineers who came here to learn new techniques and technologies to protect the earth. They're agents of the MSS and General Peng. Their mission was to locate water sources into which bioagents could be unleashed to infect and wipe out the White and Black people of America. I'm now sitting inside a fucking room filled with Chinese spies!

A cold shiver went down her spine as the reality of the situation set in.

Peng next told the audience he had an exciting announcement. He described the objective of Project V to the agents, and then proudly acknowledged the leadership and brilliant work that Dr Ying Lan had done.

"We now have a racially targeted bioweapon that can be distributed efficiently through drinking water sources anywhere in the world," Peng announced. "Ying Lan, my lead scientist, will now describe this new potential weapon to you."

There was a brief silence as Lan confidently walked up onto stage and up to the podium. Using a computer presentation, she described the development of the bioagents during the past several months and her extensive field testing at a prison hospital. A number of screen shots showed subjects who had died from the manufactured agents, including several close ups of subjects with blood below each nostril.

Lan didn't mention Warren Lee, Carrie Bock, or Jim Chen, but did mention "limited American scientific support" on the project.

Lan stepped away after finishing, and Peng again took center stage.

"You have heard what we have been striving to produce for years. Most scientists, including geneticists, never believed such a lethal viral compound could be developed. But we have done it!"

Members of the audience reacted differently. Most were elated with the news. Carrie could tell from the shaking heads and facial expressions that some of the attendees were uncomfortable with the news and some appeared skeptical that the bioagents worked.

Peng spoke again. "In a matter of hours, we will have control of the programs for developing these weapons. I have asked Dr Ying Lan to return to China next week and head up her own laboratory to produce and refine these bioweapons. They will become the most powerful defensive weapons in the PRC's arsenal. If China ever finds itself in a confrontational situation with a foreign power, we can use them without sacrificing our Chinese countrymen in battle. The use of conventional warfare with ground soldiers will soon be obsolete, as will nuclear warfare. This biological weaponry is more effective than costly and unpredictable nuclear warheads. The bioweapon will destroy aggressive and irresponsible peoples of any country who defy our philosophy and position.

"In addition, we will mass produce the newly developed vaccine to protect against any country having access to agent yellow or some facsimile."

While Carrie listened, she was ready to jump out of her skin. She hoped that her anger didn't manifest into a reddish glow that showed through the pale makeup. As she had speculated, Peng only wanted to get his hands on the agent white and agent black algorithms. Once Lan got her hands on them, she could manufacture the viral compounds in her own facility in Beijing.

Peng then did something that Carrie hadn't seen before in any Chinese forum. He opened up the discussion to questions from the audience.

The questions ran the gamut from water solubility to contagious qualities of the virus. Other members of the audience were interested in the shelf life of the bioagents and the time of onset of the lethal disease. Lan told them about the ability to store the compound in an inert state in the form of ice blocks or ice cubes for long-term storage.

Lan answered all questions confidently and with ease.

Carrie could only inaudibly sigh at the whole performance.

Jim and I trained the bitch well.

Carrie stirred in her seat as she formulated her own question. She repeatedly memorized the question in her head using proper Chinese grammar. The question was much different than the others. Although she already knew the answer, her question had a different and specific purpose. She only needed the courage to ask it. Carrie nervously raised her hand.

Lan pointed at her.

Carrie stood and loudly articulated her question, all the while silently praying that Lan wouldn't recognize her voice or see through her disguise. Her Mandarin words flowed naturally.

"Dr Ying, most of us here are concerned about the vaccine to prevent us from exposure to agent yellow should the United States or another country decide to use it against us. You mentioned that the vaccine had recently been developed and tested only once. How can we, and our countrymen, be assured, and I mean unequivocally assured, that the vaccine will protects us against any biological weapon?"

She quickly sat down after speaking, with her hands trembling so badly that she was forced her to clasp them together. Although sitting back in her seat made her appear more relaxed, she felt nervous beads of sweat forming on her forehead.

The audience reaction was surprisingly good. There was a lot of loud chatting, and a few attendees openly applauded her courageous and valid question.

Peng stepped near the podium to restore decorum and to field the question himself. Her question had touched a collective nerve. It was now up to him to convince them that the vaccine was effective enough to protect the Chinese population.

"First, let me say I fully understand the concern for agent yellow and its prevention. I have had a long discussion with Dr Ying about the new vaccine, and she has assured me that it is totally effective."

If Lan had a real understanding of medical research, she would know that a single test is never conclusive. A vaccine test was no exception.

Peng went on. "Having said this, I have an idea about how we can quell your concerns. We intend to conduct more tests tomorrow up at the prison hospital."

Tests for tomorrow? What the hell is he talking about? I control the generation of more bioagents and vaccine. Where does he get off telling these spies that he can conduct more tests whenever he likes?

"Here is my proposal," Peng continued. "For those of you who can return here, we will have a large monitor set up on this stage. We have recently installed a camera system so that we can get video and audio signal directly from the hospital. You can observe the field test as it takes place from here. We will schedule the testing for ten o'clock tomorrow morning.

"Now, I will address the validity of the testing. With Dr Ying's confidence and my confidence in her, both of us will become subjects for this vaccine test!"

The audience gasped.

The General continued. "We will take a dose of the agent yellow vaccine, and a short time later we will ingest the agent yellow virus along with the other test subjects. You will see that only subjects given the vaccine, including Dr Ying and I, will remain unaffected. I think that your anxieties will then be put to rest."

The audience stood up and thunderously applauded the unusual and bizarre proposal in response to Carrie's question.

After a few closing remarks, the meeting ended.

Carrie moved out of the lecture hall with her head down to avoid any conversation. Once outside, she darted through a side door to get to her apartment as swiftly as possible. There she removed her disguise.

Her mind worked frantically as she hopped into the shower. Her entire body still trembled after her earlier heroics among the Chinese MSS agents. She had bought a little time, but now needed to come up with a way to stop Peng and Lan from taking the formulas back to China.

After drying herself, she went into the bedroom and peeked out the window. The Chinese agents were getting into their limousines and leaving.

Her cellphone rang. She thought it might be Warren looking for her. They hadn't had a chance to talk during the morning coffee hour.

"Carrie, it's me."

"Jim! How's everything going?"

"Not well. I'm at the detention facility and I'm being told they have not received any word from General Peng to release my brother. I don't know if they're stalling or what the hell's going on. Is there any way you or Warren can contact Peng?"

"Of course. I won't go into detail now, but you should know that I managed to get into Peng's meeting today. It's worse than we had imagined. Peng now needs me to make up more batches of the agents along with the vaccine. But I won't lift a finger until Jiang Ming and you are on your way here."

"That's amazing! I want to hear all about the meeting, but for now I want my brother free. I bought two tickets on a flight that leaves Beijing at six in the morning. I couldn't risk booking an earlier one with this new delay. There isn't much time if we're going to make that flight."

"I'll get on it."

Just after she hung up, her cellphone rang again. She thought that Jim had forgotten to tell her something.

"Carrie, it's me, Lan. General Peng wants to meet with you and me immediately."

"For what?" Carrie asked with a caustic tone in her voice.

"He wants you to make more testing agents. And we'll need more vaccine for agent yellow. He has committed me to do another field test for tomorrow morning."

She closed her eyes to think. There was no need to alienate Lan, but she still needed to come up with a plan. There had to be a way to thwart the slimy General Peng and his protégé.

"What does Peng have in mind?"

Lan paused before answering.

"He would like to meet in the Cold Room now. He wants to observe the process for making the agents. He's joining me at Saratoga tomorrow morning for further tests of both the agent and vaccine.

"Tell him I can't do it."

As soon as she said the words, she felt the sudden surge of confidence running throughout her entire body.

"What? You can't do it?" Lan shouted.

"No. I have to fly to China right away. I'm expecting a call from Jim at any moment. He's having some difficulty with the prison authorities releasing his brother. If he and his brother aren't on a plane soon, I'll be heading to Beijing. Tell Peng I'll be happy to produce the agents and vaccine on my return. I gotta go."

She ended the cell connection.

Carrie knew that she had Peng by the balls. And he would know as well soon.

She took her time changing into blue jeans and a maroon T-shirt with a denim shirt over it. She sat down and flicked on the TV. She wanted to stall for time before heading downstairs.

CNN news showed a brief clip taken last evening with the Secretary of State meeting with a small group of Chinese engineers. He stood behind a podium with dozens of media microphones. He was in his element, and it showed in his brief speech.

> And so we bring to a close this successful cultural exchange program with our Chinese allies. The new commitment of the

Beijing government is to retool and redesign their environmental programs to prevent pollution from destroying the planet. And this program, which I initiated not long ago, is only the beginning of a new positive relationship between our countries to solve other issues in our global community.

Zachary Hinton, took a step back to stand with the Chinese visitors. They all smiled for the cameras.

What an asshole! If he only knew what he has done.

Carrie turned off the TV and lay on top of her bed. She had too much to think about to sleep. Her ringing cellphone interrupted her efforts to grasp the whole complicated and potentially catastrophic situation.

"Carrie, it's me, Clancy."

Her mind filled with an image of her beloved colleague, recently retired Professor of Microbiology, Clancy Roche.

"Clancy, I've missed you. You're a hard man to find."

"Yes, but I'm back in the States now and wanted to let you know. How are you?"

"I'm good, but very busy. We have to get together soon, before you take off again."

"I'm home for a few months. That is why I called. When you're ready, give me a call and we'll get together."

"Clancy, I have a biochemistry question for you before we hang up. What's so important about mercury levels in water resources?"

"The obvious, as you know, is that mercury is a neurotoxin. And too much in drinking water can cause morbidity."

"I know that. But what if the levels aren't anywhere near that toxicity level? If they're at safe levels, what harm can mercury do?"

"Nothing by itself, but what most people don't know is that mercury at low levels is an excellent transporter?"

"A transporter?"

"Mercury is a great bonding agent. If there are germs, viral cells or other contaminants, in the water, they'll bond with the mercury and be carried around without weakening or dissolving. Some scientists believe mercury is the transporter of many cells, such as carcinogens, viruses, bacteria, and other toxins in drinking water."

So that's why the Chinese agents identified the mercury levels in our drinking supplies. The bioagents would bond with the mercury and be able to last for long periods inside the water supply. Peng and his henchmen had to know whether there was sufficient mercury to keep the bioagents viable long enough to do their dirty work.

Carrie's cellphone indicated another call coming in.

"Clancy, thanks for reminding me of mercury's dirty little secret. I've got another call. I'll call in a few days, and we'll get together."

It was Jim.

"Carrie, you're a miracle worker. Jiang Ming and I are in a government limo heading for the airport. The flight takes off soon."

"I won't begin mixing any agents until I know that you're on the plane and taking off. Please call me again when you're airborne. I don't trust Peng. He may pull a fast one at the last minute."

After the call ended, Carrie headed downstairs.

Peng was seated next to Lan when she entered the office. It was obvious they were both eager to get things going.

Her confidence surged once more. It was nice to have some leverage for a change.

"I'm waiting for another call from Jim, and then we can begin. I want to be sure there is no more *red tape* holding up his return to the States with his brother." She enjoyed putting emphasis on the phony excuse.

Peng's tiny jaws clenched and made a vein raise in his temple. He managed a false smile. He then excused himself from the room, ostensibly to go to the restroom, though it was obvious to her that he had to make another long distance call.

I was right to be extra cautious with this bastard. He must have given orders to his henchmen to stop Jim and Jiang Ming from boarding the plane.

Barely able to control her anger, Carrie began the initial preparations for producing the bioagent and vaccine.

Lan clearly couldn't hide her nervousness over the tension between Peng and Carrie. She paced the floor and then abruptly stopped and sat at her workstation without a word.

"I meant to ask you, Lan, how did the big meeting go this morning?" Carrie asked.

"It went well," she answered without enthusiasm.

"The attendees won't be here after today, right?"

She was testing whether Lan might reveal any information. After a long pause, Lan answered. "That's not really true."

"Not really true? I thought the arrangement with Warren was that they would be here for only one day. When will they return?"

"Tomorrow morning some of them will return to the lecture hall."

"If you and Peng are going to be in Saratoga, why would they be coming back? I'm going to be real nervous with all these environmentalists milling about with our highly classified laboratory right beneath them. What the hell is going on, Lan?"

Checkmate. Damn, there is at least some short-term satisfaction in this espionage business.

If Lan told her that they were going to watch the field testing on a monitor in the amphitheater, the entire top-secret project would be blatantly compromised.

Lan was noticeably shaken by the question. She got up from her workbench and stepped over to the supply cabinet. She picked out another memory stick.

"Look, Carrie, I don't have the answers. This is Peng's project, and he calls all of the shots. I just do what I'm told."

She stared at her Asian colleague long and hard.

Lan lowered her face with embarrassment that Carrie had stripped away the thin veil of her persona.

Within ten minutes, Carrie's cellphone rang again.

"Jiang Ming and I have just taken off on American Airlines Flight 144. You were right again, Carrie. We were stopped and detained inside the airport terminal and weren't permitted to board the plane until a military guard got a phone call. I've gotta hang up now. I'll call you when I get home."

The low temperatures of the Cold Room cooled the tension a bit, though the atmosphere remained serious.

Lan explained the process to Peng beginning with Carrie using her recently acquired access code from Dr Chen.

After accessing the mixing hopper, Carrie made a batch of agent yellow. After the compound was mixed and processed in the ice-making machine, Lan collected the ice cubes.

Lan carefully placed the deadly ice cubes into her personal freezer. She demonstrated to Peng how entering her access code automatically opened the lid to the freezer. As she spoke, she emphasized how she was the only person who could open the freezer.

Carrie prepared the vaccine and repeated the process.

Lan proudly explained how after the bioagents and vaccine were in her freezer, she was in total control of the outcome of the project.

Peng seemed pleased to hear this.

"When are you leaving for Saratoga?" Carrie asked.

Peng answered her question.

"It's too late today. We'll leave on the helicopter about seven in the morning. I want the test to begin precisely at ten o'clock."

"That means we should be here to collect the agents and vaccine about six thirty. We can jump in the helicopter and take off soon afterwards," Lan said. Then she turned to her American friend. "You can watch the results on the monitor."

Carrie only nodded.

"We're finished here. We're leaving now to get a good night's rest before a busy day tomorrow."

Lan looked physically and emotionally drained from the intensity of the day.

"You should do the same, Dr Bock," added Peng, his piercing eyes staring directly at her.

"You know something, Mr Peng? I think I will get some sleep. I also have a busy day tomorrow," she commented without looking back at him.

* * *

As Carrie walked upstairs to her apartment, a depressed mood overtook her. She thought about what she had learned today.

That Machiavellian prick, Peng, will soon be armed with the most vile bioweapon every produced by mankind, and I am the scientist who developed it. The vaccine that is already in Lan's freezer will insure that Peng's show is a success.

She had to find a way to prevent Peng from getting control of the algorithms. She had successfully set Peng and Lan up with her bold question about vaccine validation at the conference. She still had no way to make the test fail and was running out of time. On their return to the lab, Peng would ask for the software to take back to China with him and Lan.

When she got to her bedroom, she had a tension headache and needed some sleep.

She took off her denim shirt, and fell onto her bed fully clothed in jeans and T-shirt. It didn't take long before she dropped off into a deep sleep.

Sometime later, she woke up with a start and sat up with her entire body shaking. Her head was feverishly hot. She was perspiring and her heart pounding as if she had run a few miles. The bedroom clock showed three minutes after midnight.

She pivoted on top of the bedspread and hung her legs over the side of the bed. It took her a moment to figure out that she had had a nightmare.

She went into the kitchen, took a bottle of cold water from the refrigerator, and splashed some of the water on her face. As she walked back into her bedroom, her mind reconstructed the nightmare that had woken her. The fragmented images restored themselves in her mind. In a blurry scene, Lan was laying naked in bed with her. She was looking down at Carrie and staring at her with a seductive and demonic smile. It was as if Carrie were reliving that one night with Lan in her condo, with Lan pointing at the faded blue tattoo under her breast.

What had Lan said that night in her apartment about the tattoo? It's a number she had to "carry with me for the rest of my life." 121844. Six numbers. Six numbers that were with her from the orphanage. Blue colored numbers tattooed under the globe of her left breast. Numbers nobody else could see or knew about.

Carrie almost choked on a sip of water. She jumped from the bed and bolted for her apartment door leaving it wide opened as she headed downstairs. Racing down the empty dark hallway, she looked up at the security camera leading to the office and the Cold Room.

Once inside the Cold Room, her heart pumped with anxiety. She stepped up to Lan's storage freezer. She paused to catch her breath and then methodically keyed in those same six digits tattooed on Lan's body, 121844. When she finished pressing the tiny keypad, she stepped back. Her heart stopped beating in hopeful anticipation. Her eyes opened wide as the lid lifted automatically.

She had guessed correctly.

Grabbing the container labeled agent yellow VACCINE, she emptied all of the vaccine ice cubes into a freezer bag. After closing Lan's freezer, she ran upstairs to her apartment. Within minutes she had stored the bag inside her kitchen freezer and returned downstairs to the Cold Room.

She soon prepared a batch of yellow agent for the ice machine's mixing hopper. Soon the machine produced a batch of the highly concentrated agent yellow ice cubes. After opening up Lan's freezer again, she placed the new batch of agent yellow cubes inside the vaccine container. She closed the freezer for the last time.

Carrie had made the deadly decision almost without thinking. She was confident Peng would live up to his promise because of his boast that the vaccine would protect him and any living Chinese person. Even if he tried to dupe the audience by not taking the yellow virus ice cubes, he would take the vaccine in the belief that there was no risk. Now there would be no vaccine.

Carrie shuddered at what she had done. There was no other option, and she would have to hold onto that idea.

After returning to her apartment and locking the door, she stripped off her clothes and was preparing for bed when her cell-phone rang. Tired, she grabbed the phone without looking at the caller identification. When she heard the voice on the other end speak her name, it was the last person that she had expected to call her.

THIRTY FIVE

"Dr Bock, this is the charge nurse at Holly Home. I hate to call you at this time, but it's an emergency," the nurse said in a monotonic voice.

"What's wrong with my father?" Carrie asked nervously.

"He has had a cardiac arrest. We had him transferred to Quincy City Hospital. I don't have a detailed report now, but I knew that you would want to know. He's stable now but is in the Cardiac Intensive Care Unit."

Within minutes, Carrie was speeding towards the city hospital.

When she arrived at the CICU, she talked briefly with the head nurse, who told her that her father was stable but the next twelve hours were critical. She advised Carrie to go into the waiting room and get some rest. She would call her if her father's condition changed.

In the waiting room, Carrie paced around for over an hour to burn off nervous energy. At seven in the morning, her cellphone rang. She hoped that it wasn't Lan or Peng. The caller ID showed it was Jim.

"Carrie, it's me. I'm driving to the lab now. I dropped Jiang Ming at my house and will be at the lab within five minutes. Where are you?"

She told him about her father's sudden heart attack.

"My God! Let me get over there right away."

"No. There's no need. After I tell you what I did earlier this morning, you will see why I need you at the lab."

Without details, she told him that she had cracked the access code to Lan's storage freezer and had swapped the vaccine ice cubes for the virus ice cubes. Backfilling her story, she told him about Peng's promise to demonstrate to the MSS agents, by remote monitor in the lecture hall, his confidence in the newly developed Mongoloid vaccine.

"Peng made that commitment to his staff? That stupid son-of-a-bitch! So Peng, and perhaps Lan, will be drinking agent yellow in the belief that they're ingesting the vaccine?"

"That's right."

Neither spoke for awhile. Carrie still couldn't believe that she had forged ahead with this premeditated murder. Homicide wasn't something either one had ever thought about doing. In this case, it was mandated. There was no other way of preventing the most dangerous genocidal weapon ever created from getting into the hands of a man capable of using it.

"How the hell did you get Lan's security code?"

"I need you to trust me on this. Can you do that for me?"

"I will," he replied with conviction.

"I need you to do something. I want you to watch what goes on at Saratoga through the monitor in our office, and record it on a DVD so I can see it later if necessary."

"Okay."

"Peng's agents are going to see the same thing you're watching. I don't know how many will show up to watch the show today, but there'll be a strong reaction coming from the first floor lecture hall. I want you to tell our own team to return home as soon as they come in this morning. Then order the Homeland Security guards to secure the entire lab."

"Why?"

"Because I think that everything associated with this project should be destroyed as soon as possible. Warren will agree when he learns what took place."

"As do I."

"Please call me as soon as the Saratoga test is done."

"Will do."

After disconnecting, she yawned and wiped her tired eyes. With the waiting lounge still empty, she stretched out on a large sofa with Jim's leather jacket as a pillow. Within seconds, she was in a deep sleep.

When Carrie woke, she didn't know where she was for a brief moment. A young couple was sitting across from her. As everything came into focus, she panicked. Her watch showed five minutes past noon. Jim hadn't yet called. Or had he? She looked at her cellphone. She had missed one call, from Jim's cellphone. He had called at ten thirty in the morning.

She tapped in his number and was relieved to hear his voice.

"I slept through your call. Tell me, how did it go?" she asked, her heart pounding rapidly and her breathing suspended.

"Just as you planned. I watched everything on the office monitor. It happened quickly. They both died within a half an hour after taking the concentrated agent. Peng announced to the viewing audience while looking directly into the camera lens that he and Lan would ingest the vaccine to protect them and all Mongoloids from any racially designed virus. He referred to it as Step One. Then they would drink the juice with the lethal bioagent. He referred to that as Step Two. As the two of them ingested what they thought was a prophylactic drink, they soon showed flu symptoms and died within half an hour. Step Two never began."

She closed her eyes and listened to what he had said with the realization that she had intentionally killed two human beings. She also realized that there wasn't an ounce of remorse within her soul. Who knew how many future lives around the world she had saved by stopping General Peng and Lan?

"Jim, do you believe I did the right thing?"

"Of course you did. Now we have to wait for the PRC's reaction. With Peng's agents witnessing the event, I'm certain word got to Beijing within seconds."

"And the agents knew the demonstration was Peng's idea. Lan emphatically told them that it was technically *her project*. In fact, most of them don't even know who you and I are. The MSS agents will believe that there was a horrible error made."

"Is there some way we could let Washington know that Peng led the march to their own deaths?" Jim asked.

"Let me work on that. Did all of the attendees leave soon after?"

"Yes. The cameras were shut off at Saratoga immediately after the deaths. About ten minutes later, several limousines collected the thirty or more agents who came this morning."

"I need to check on my father; but after that, there is something that I need to do."

"Good Luck!"

She disconnected and hurried back into the CICU unit where she met the head nurse.

"Your father is stable, Professor Bock. The cardiologist thinks that there is only minor damage to his heart. He's going to be fine and wants to see you."

"With his advanced Alzheimer's, I don't think he knows who I am."

"I wouldn't believe that. He called out 'Carrie, Carrie,' several times."

"He did?"

"He did. The other nurses heard him as well."

Carrie hurried into the unit and sat by her father's bedside.

He was quiet, but smiled to let her know that he recognized her. She gently held his hand until he fell asleep.

While sitting there, she decided to text her boss, the President of the United States.

> Barbo.
> We have to talk ASAP.
> Carbo

She left the hospital with her father in a restful sleep. Outside, she hopped onto her Harley and headed back to the Elliot House.

As she walked up the stairs to her apartment, a text came through on the purple cellphone.

> I'll call at 7 tonight.

* * *

At exactly seven that evening, President Bowa called. It took her only about five minutes to tell him what had happened at the lab and at the test site. She also told him about Hinton's hired investigator, Gianni Gregorio.

The President took it in without interrupting her.

"I'll get to Hinton right away, Carbo. I want you to come to the White House as soon as you can. We can go over all of this with the CIA and the FBI. I'll do whatever is necessary to help bring this to closure. That may include insuring that the President of China and his countrymen will not lose face because of General Peng's maverick tactics—assuming that my intelligence analysts are convinced that Peng had been acting on his own. If not...well, I hate to think of the world reaction."

For the next several minutes, Carrie brought him up to speed on Warren, Jim, and Jim's brother, as well as the status of her recovering father.

"Carbo, I'll never know how to thank you. I had no idea so much was going on in and around this project."

"No problem, Barbo. I got a lot out of this too," she said with a broad, happy smile.

* * *

Warren came to Carrie's apartment with a loud rapping on her door.

"Carrie, Carrie, what the hell happened? Lan and Peng are dead!" His voice was rattled and loud as he entered her living room.

"I'm not really sure, since Jim and I weren't a part of the field tests," she lied. "Warren, I want you to do something. It's very important."

"What's that?"

"First let me tell you something. I managed to disguise myself as a Chinese woman and sat in on Peng's private meeting at our lecture hall yesterday. There I identified two people who I had seen earlier in a TV news report. They are both easily recognizable. One has a distinctive port wine birthmark on his chubby face, and the other is a tall, older woman with salt and pepper hair. She also has an amputated forearm."

"What about them?"

"They're spies. They came over here with the environmental exchange program."

"What?"

"All or most of those environmental engineers in the lecture hall were working for Peng. That's why we weren't invited to attend. I can explain it all later, but you need to have these two agents picked up and questioned. I know they'll tell you about the meeting and Peng's plans. Don't let the FBI release them until they have been fully interrogated them."

"Hell, Carrie, I can't have the FBI pick up these two."

"Yes, you can. If the FBI brings in these two spies, they can get them to tell their full story before they're released. These are only two of many operatives who were embedded in the Environmental Exchange program. They were asked to come here by Peng to gather data on our water resources and not for any pollution control studies."

"Is this all true? You mean, my boss, the Secretary of State, Zachary Hinton was misled with his program to build a new cultural exchange program? These environmental engineers were actually brought here to plan our destruction?"

"Yes! Hinton unwittingly almost did our country in. You were originally contacted and duped into this project to assemble Project V. Peng played you well, but he also followed through with his secret MSS agenda by exploiting Hinton's well known hubris."

"President Hu Jintao and the Politburo will be desperate to prove that they knew nothing about Peng's scheme. Whether the President and other world leaders believe them, I can't say. I had better make some calls," Warren replied, his voice shaken and weak.

THIRTY SIX

Carrie spent the morning visiting her father at the Quincy Hospital. She was pleased with her father's recovery and prognosis for his discharge to the nursing home.

In the afternoon, Carrie returned to the Elliot House and was surprised to find Warren in his first floor office. Sitting on the carpeted floor, he was surrounded by empty cardboard cartons and stacks of materials on chairs, on his desk, and on the floor. Black plastic trash bags were filled with items to be discarded or shred. She knocked on the open door.

"Hello, Carrie. Please, please come in. I'm putting the final nails in the coffin of Project V."

She could see that he wasn't the same Warren. The energetic, charismatic persona was gone. Instead, she saw a tired looking, washed out man who had lost the lifeline to his soul, at least temporarily. Rather than dressed in his typically dapper suits and tie, he wore a gray sweatshirt and blue jeans.

She shut the door behind her.

"I'm packing up some of my personal things. After I fill these cartons, I'll ship them to my home back in Maryland."

"Will you be coming back?"

"Me? Hell, no! There is nothing more to do. Besides, this place raises too many bad thoughts."

She found an empty chair and sat down while Warren thumbed through some file folders.

"Warren, what happened could have happened to anyone. You were misled. Peng and his henchmen snared you into a trap that you couldn't see."

"For God's sake, Carrie. I should have known what the hell was going on. I didn't stay close to the details, and in fact I let General Peng run the show. I almost turned the safety of our country and of our people over to China's Ministry of State Security. They could have obliterated us within months or at least used their new found power for tremendous leverage."

"That won't happen now. Tell me what happened with the FBI interrogation?"

"Your strategy was right on. The two operatives you identified turned out to be cooperative. They had no qualms about verifying to the FBI what Peng had been up to. They knew that they could no longer continue the deception, and they hoped for some leniency by claiming that they were only doing what they were told by Peng. But not all of the attendees at the demonstration were agents. Many were legitimate engineers who were hearing about the bioagents for the first time. Peng deceived his own people to get what he wanted."

"That doesn't surprise me."

Warren stopped what he was doing and stared across his desk at her. His eyes were riveted on her own.

"I keep thinking about something. Carrie, wasn't it awfully convenient how Peng died at Saratoga before getting his hands on the bioagent software algorithms and the vaccine?"

She stared directly back at him with her head held high and steady. She had already made peace with herself and guessed that in time Warren too would move on.

"Yes, it was convenient. One might call it serendipitous."

They both held their unwavering stares.

"I do feel bad that Lan died along with him," Warren added.

She kept her focus straight into his eyes like a laser beam.

"I wouldn't, Warren. Lan was joined at the hip with Peng. Here, let me help you with your packing. Do you want all of these books on the bookshelves packed?"

He tipped his head, nodded, and let out a loud sigh.

"That would be great. Are you moving back into your condo?"

"No. I'm moving in with my fiancé, Jim."

Warren dropped a manila folder from his hands that sent papers flying.

"You and Jim? I had no idea."

She laughed, which released some of the tension.

"We hope to have the wedding in a month or so. You must come."

Warren walked over to a dark mahogany credenza and opened one of the lower doors displaying bottles of liquor.

"This calls for a celebratory toast. My God, Carrie Bock is marrying my old college roommate, Jim Chen. I can't believe it. Scotch is your drink, isn't it?"

"Thanks."

They both sat down to sip their drinks.

"I'm sorry I have no ice," he said, "but if you have any of those agent yellow ice cubes left downstairs, I might have you drop one or two into my drink."

"Things aren't that bad," she chuckled. She knew it was now time to tell him. It wasn't the perfect time, but nonetheless, he should know.

"I don't know about that."

"Agent yellow wouldn't work on you."

"Why wouldn't it work on me? Am I not Chinese?"

She told the Under Secretary about the genealogical research her friend had performed for her in China.

"I wanted to surprise you with a Family Tree gift. My friend Wei Xing discovered that your grandmother had an affair while in British Columbia. She fell in love with an Italian while she was touring. It was he who became the biological father of your beloved mother."

"What? Are you sure?" he asked incredulously.

"I have the documentation upstairs. I know that this maybe isn't the best time to tell you, but you are not a pure Tang ancestor. You have Italian blood in you. You see, my agent yellow ice cubes wouldn't affect you."

Warren looked at her with his mouth open.

"I'm part Italian?"

She smiled at his quizzical expression.

"Yes. Haven't you wondered about your height, your hairy arms, and your double-fold eyelids like those of a Westerner?"

"But I was told…"

"Yes. But the Tang people didn't have any of those physical characteristics. And besides your Italian biological grandfather was a performer, much like you!"

"Performer?"

"Yes. He was a famous opera singer. Evidently, he had a great operatic voice!"

Warren set down his drink. He dropped his head into both hands and slowly lowered his head down.

When he slowly brought his hands and head up, he opened up his hands showing his face to Carrie. His mouth had a small curl that soon broadened with a loud laugh. He kept laughing and laughing. He didn't stop for several minutes.

"So, I'm not a Chinese thoroughbred after all. I'm a mixed breed, a hybrid," he said with good humor.

She joined his contagious laughter. "Like many of us hybrids inhabiting this earth."

Warren stood up and walked around the desk. He reached out and embraced her tightly with sincere warmth.

The surprising news seemed to help Warren deal with his inner demons and lift him from a depressed state. Before he took leave of the Elliot House, he thanked her for all she did for him and for the country.

* * *

When Carrie returned that evening to Jim's house, he had knotted a colorful silk tie around his shirt collar. He slipped on a navy blue blazer.

"I want to take you out for a nice dinner tonight. You and I deserve a special night out on the town." he said. His fingers inconspicuously felt the velvet ring box inside his jacket pocket. "Besides, we have to plan our future together."

"We're going out to a nice dinner tonight? Like where?"

"How about we go into Boston to, say, Great Bay or Olive's or perhaps, Le Mansion on Beacon Street?"

She smiled at his thoughtful suggestions.

"I agree we need to do something special tonight. But those places are a bit too much for me."

"Okay, you pick it. Where would you like to eat tonight?"

She chuckled as she thought about her suggestion.

"It's a Thursday night, and I'm in the mood for some tasty homemade chili with an ice cold beer. I would like to go to a place I truly enjoy. It's in South Boston, called the Shamrock Tavern.

His face became a quizzical grin. "The Shamrock Tavern?"

"Trust me, you're gonna love it."

"While you finish dressing, can I make you a scotch on the rocks?"

Carrie grinned from ear to ear. "Sure, but not on the rocks. I'm staying away from ice cubes."

About the Author

Gordon Mathieson has been writing fiction and non-fiction for the past ten years. He published many articles for high tech journals and periodicals during his tenure at Yale University. In addition to his own work, he has ghostwritten books for others.

His writing traces some of his own life experiences and places where he has lived. Before his career in academia, he was a Mandarin Chinese translator for the National Security Agency. This role became the genesis for his latest novel, *The Color of Ice*, where he brings the reader to the brink of a suspenseful, top-secret project that has mixed messages exchanged from Beijing to Boston.

Gordon resides on Cape Cod with his wife where they both lead busy lives with a variety of hobbies and interests.

More about Gordon and his other books are available on www.gordonmathieson.com.

CPSIA information can be obtained at www.ICGtesting.com
Printed in the USA
BVOW06s0723040716

454345BV00048B/1141/P

9 780976 925965